THE STAR NOVELS

by Edgar Award–Winning Dana Stabenow

Second Star

Star Svensdotter's exciting debut! It's a dirty job, but someone has to clean up Earth's first space colony . . .

"An impressive first outing that shows promising talent."
—*Locus*

"An exciting and thought-provoking story . . . complete with intriguing characters and a plot with many twists!"
—A. C. Crispin, bestselling author of *Sarek*

"This story is action-packed and the settings visualized with almost cinematic vividness . . . Recommended."
—Roland Green, *Booklist*

A Handful of Stars

Star heads out to the asteroid belt, mankind's last wild frontier, to make her fortune. Or lose her life . . .

"A great story . . . exciting, fun, spellbinding . . . for the SF fan, this is a must-read!" —*Voice of Youth Advocates*

And Don't Miss Her Edgar Award–Winning
Kate Shugak Mysteries . . .

"Compelling, brutal, and true." —*Boston Sunday Globe*

A COLD DAY FOR MURDER
A FATAL THAW
DEAD IN THE WATER
A COLD-BLOODED BUSINESS

Ace Books by Dana Stabenow

SECOND STAR
A HANDFUL OF STARS
RED PLANET RUN

RED PLANET RUN

DANA STABENOW

ACE BOOKS, NEW YORK

This book is an Ace original edition,
and has never been previously published.

RED PLANET RUN

An Ace Book / published by arrangement with
the author

PRINTING HISTORY
Ace edition / January 1995

ISBN: 0-441-00135-1

ACE®
Ace Books are published by The Berkley Publishing Group,
200 Madison Avenue, New York, New York 10016.
ACE and the "A" design are trademarks
belonging to Charter Communications, Inc.

PRINTED IN THE UNITED STATES OF AMERICA

10 9 8 7 6 5 4 3 2 1

For
Sean Stewman, David Carlson,
and Eddie Parish
Up, up, and away, boys

—1—

Worlds Enough

> Many have imagined republics and principalities which have never been seen or known to exist in reality; for how we live is so far removed from how we ought to live . . .
>
> —**Niccolò Machiavelli**

"You want to move the river *again*?"

Roberta McInerny's square face settled into stubborn lines. If Outpost could find a way to bottle it, we could sell Roberta McInerny Mule Tonic to cure hull composites for spaceships.

"Roberta," I said, amazed at and proud of the patience I heard in my voice, "the contract requires that this World be built in a substantial and workmanlike manner. It does not require us to redesign it every five minutes."

"They changed my original design," Roberta stated.

Architects have this obdurate and universal determination to inflict order and proportion upon a highly disproportionate and disorderly world. *Their* order and *their* proportion. I think it's genetic. I know it's a pain. "It's their

World," I pointed out, for approximately the 756th time, but who's counting? "They're paying for it. If they want to repaint the interior in Black Watch plaid, that is their misguided privilege. We're only the builders. They're going to be living in it, and it's our job to give them what they want. These particular owners happen to want a plain, simple river, a meter and a half deep, no falls, no white water. Just a shallow, humdrum, mundane, pedestrian, commonplace"— I ran out of synonyms—"boring little stream that circumnavigates the equator and provides a reliable, no-frills aeration process for the recycling system. Now then, can we do that?"

"It isn't a question of 'can,' " Roberta said. "It's a question of 'should.' "

"Interesting demonstration of an immovable object intersecting an irresistible force," Archy observed.

"Shut up, Archy," I said, without any real hope of being obeyed. I abandoned the appeal to common sense for the streak of avarice inherent in any Belter worthy of the name. "Look, Roberta, I'd like for us to get paid sometime soon, like within this century, and those engineers are not about to turn over the balance due before we finish the job."

Roberta drew her stocky self up to her not very considerable height, managing nevertheless to radiate a towering disdain. "Money is not the issue here."

"The hell it isn't," I snapped. "We're not Thoreau, this isn't Walden, and this shack's going to cost us a tad more than twenty-eight dollars and twelve and a half cents. We're eating a lot of the start-up costs as it is for promotional purposes, not to mention which there's a clause in the contract that calls for a penalty for every day we run over the scheduled completion date. Terranova's already screaming about the profit margin. Be reasonable. If we're going to get paid on time, if we're going to show a reasonable profit for the Terranovan gnomes, and if we're going to have enough money in the bank to start work on World Two, we've got to deliver the product when we said we would." I leaned forward, weight on the knuckles of my clenched fists, and said, "And we can't do that if you keep putting waterfalls in the goddam river."

Fortunately, you can't slam doors on Outpost, but even the hiss of it sliding closed behind her sounded malevolent. I dropped my head in my hands and rubbed my eyes. I wanted to feel sorry for myself, but anyone who starts a business hollowing out asteroids for customers with more money than brains deserves everything they get. Especially when they hire a construction crew with more brains than the customer.

The door hissed open. My tall, sixteen-year-old son, Sean, sidled inside, his twin sister, Paddy, right behind him. I was immediately wary. "Hi, kids. Why aren't you in class?"

"Crip's jumping for 6789Cribbage today. Can we go, too?"

"What's today, Wednesday?" They nodded. "Hydroponics, right?" They nodded again. "You got your weekly assignments in to Ari?" Silence, and I said, "You know the rules. No work, no play."

Mad, they looked even more alike than usual, flushed skin the color of coffee with cream, dark blue eyes darker with anger, jet-black hair winding into tight, irritated little curls. "Oh, Mom, come on," Sean said hotly. "We haven't been off-station in a month and we haven't seen Mom and Pop since the new baby was born."

"Yeah," Paddy said. "Who do you think you are, William Bligh?"

At least they weren't finishing each other's sentences anymore. Not out loud, anyway. "That's Captain Bligh to you," I said. "Now get on to the lab and finish your projects."

They stamped out, spines stiff with outrage. I waited until the door was closed. "Archy? Where's Crip?"

Archy, Outpost's computer, conscience, and chief cook and bottle washer, sounded doubtful. "I think he's still in bed. He got in late last night and told me not to set the alarm."

"Beep him anyway."

A moment later a voice growled, "Whaddya want?"

"Good morning to you, too. This is Star. Paddy and Sean tell me you're making a trip out to 6789Cribbage today; is that right?"

"Where?" There was a murmur in the background. "Your lovely daughter; who else calls at the crack of dawn?" Into the pickup he said, "I didn't get in until five this morning, Star, and if I'm going to make deadline on the new charts, I'm not going anywhere I've been before any time soon."

There was a sinking feeling in the pit of my stomach I did my best to ignore. "Okay, Crip. Sorry to bother you. Go back to sleep."

"Esther dear, is there something wrong?"

"Good morning, Mother. Sorry to wake you."

"We weren't sleeping, dear, but your timing leaves a great deal to be desired." Mother actually sounded tart, which told me that my timing in fact did leave a great deal to be desired. "Are you sure nothing's wrong? Your voice sounds odd."

"I'm sure. I've got to get to work or I'll be late for court. See you tonight."

I spent another hour cleaning up all the little chores that accumulate in keeping a space station successfully in orbit in the Asteroid Belt, all the while with the sense that I was turning my back on a ticking bomb. St. Joseph alone knew what the twins were up to this time.

Oh nine hundred hours saw me suited up, boarding a solar sled. The eye on the end of the hawser slipped easily from the hook attached to Outpost's hull. I shoved off with one hand, letting the sled drift for a bit.

Outpost was made of the two spaceships, the *Hokuwa'a* and the *Voortrekker*, that had brought us out to the Belt sixteen years before. They had been moored parallel to each other, bow to stern and bow to stern, and connected with corridors to form a sort of square-sided circle. We put on spin and, *voilà*, a rotating habitat that didn't make more than ten percent of the crew seasick at any one time, and most of them Charlie cured with an inner-ear monitor she invented that I kept telling her she should patent. But when did my sister ever listen to me? She just nodded her head like the little doggy in the window and went off to invent some other life-saving and/or life-enhancing gadget to give away. The woman had absolutely no sense of business. Fortunately, her husband, Simon, more than made up for her lack.

Outpost was orbiting Ceres at 60 degrees west Ceres' prime; at 60 degrees east was World One, or what I devoutly hoped would be at some point in my lifetime: an asteroid, once a played-out mining claim, and now in the process of being planeformed into a self-contained habitat for a group of Terran engineers and their families who'd had about enough of Terran smog and politics.

The urge to check on the progress on World One was almost overpowering. I resisted temptation and fired the jets, letting the rotating wheel of the space station and the gray sphere of World One recede in my rearview as the bulk of Ceres loomed ahead.

1Ceres was a large, 750-plus kilometers in diameter, more-or-less round rock, orbiting Sol from some 450 million klicks out. Charcoal-gray in color and pitted and pocked worse than the far side of Luna, it was the first asteroid to be discovered from Terra, the biggest of the bunch, and the first stop on the Hallelujah Trail for every dreamer in the Solar System with a one-way ticket in one hand and a pickaxe in the other.

The hangar, a shallow cavern that served as a parking lot for Piazzi City, was packed bumper to bumper, and it took iron nerves, great skill, and daredevil maneuvering to slip the sled into a Lilliputian space between a puke-yellow Norton Runabout with more klicks on her than Voyager II and a brand new, bright red Mercedes XL. I noticed with mean pleasure that the Norton had managed to leave a yellow crease down the spacetruck's brand new port side.

There wasn't a mooring buoy free within a hundred meters, so I left the sled unhitched and rotated through the airlock, shedding my pressure suit inside and stacking it next to a thousand others, standing in formation like an uninhabited army. I reminded myself to talk to Mayor Takemotu about more suit storage at the main lock. A p-suit is a perambulating collection of finely tuned, delicately balanced instrumentation; it doesn't do to leave it in a heap on the deck for any length of time.

The subsurface cavern that was Piazzi City seemed to double in size every time I revisited it, what with the constant influx of wannabe Belters and the equally constant drilling of new tunnels to accommodate them. The halogen lights of my first visit fourteen years before had been replaced by an indirect solar panel array, which brought a bright, steady, and altogether merciless light to bear on the chaotic and incredibly filthy scene stretched out in front of me. There was a town square of sorts, with a few rudimentary blades of grass struggling to grow next to a square-sided column invisible beneath a blizzard of want ads touting everything from beds for rent to scooters for sale to wives for hire. Surrounding the square on more sides than I cared to count were numerous rooms carved out of the sheer face of the rock wall, from saloons to outfitters, and—will wonders never cease—now even a Hilton Hotel. I wondered if they rented the rooms by the day or by the hour. Either way, they were going to retire rich.

The place was teeming like an anthill and buzzing like a beehive. Everyone was constantly in motion and incessantly in speech, and I caught bits of half a dozen different conversations as I dodged through the crowd.

"Strasser says the League's talking strike."

"Not again? We're already making more money than God."

"What's your price?"

"Four AD's a kay."

"Four bucks! You gotta be kidding! I wouldn't pay four bucks a kay for my own mother! One and a half."

"—so he told them the moral of the story is, don't ask if you don't want to know the answer."

"Did you believe it?"

"Of course I believe it. I believe any story French Joe tells a bunch of Terran rubberneckers. It's easier, and it goes without saying that it is one whole hell of a lot safer. Hey, Star, how you doing?"

"Fine, George, good to see you."

"Court in session?"

"Almost."

A tall man with a long white beard flowing down the front of a longer, whiter robe strode toward me, parting the crowd like the original Moses parted the Red Sea. "Star Svensdotter." He raised a massive hand and made the sign of the cross in front of my face.

I hate uninvited blessings; whatever soul I have I prefer to tend to myself. Still, it never hurt to be civil, or so I had been raised by the woman who was presently rectifying her youngest daughter's sense of timing back on Outpost. "Brother Moses. How are you?"

"I am with God, sister," he said, sorrowful that he could not say the same for me.

I also hate being called someone's sister when I'm not. But dignity, always dignity. "Good to see you, Moses," I lied. "Sorry I can't stay to chat but I'm late for court."

"Ah," he said, a wide, wise, and wholly patronizing smile spreading across his face, "one should leave matters of judgment to God."

"One would," I couldn't help retorting, "if She'd show up in the next five minutes to take my place on the bench."

He raised his hand and I cringed, but instead of a condemnation of my blasphemy, he turned with a sweep of his white robe and issued forth a proclamation. "I hereby declare this demonstration of the Save the Rocks League, before God and the Ceres office of A World of Your Own, Inc., to be blessed by our Father, the one true God and Protector of all living things."

Taking dead rocks and making them into live habitats didn't sound like exploitation to me, but every nut has its own magnetic field, and behind him I saw a dozen protesters assemble, carrying hand-lettered signs sporting various epigrams such as "Save the rocks!" and "Preserve a planetesimal! Shoot a miner!"

Sounded like a plan to me, starting with Brother Moses, who had made his pile out of an iron mine on 16Psyche before turning to God and asteroidal conservation. He was speaking again. "We must preserve the precious relics of our Promethean forefathers against the exploitation and ravishment of the forces of corporate greed." One force of corporate greed could feel her neck getting hot. We took every precaution in scouting possible future Worlds for anything that might smack of being man-made. Because we hadn't found anything after the discovery, twelve years before, of what *might* have been a man-made petroleum reservoir, Brother Moses assumed we had and were destroying them so as not to interfere with the World of Your Own production schedule, at the same time destroying evidence of the Prophets of Prometheus, or Those Who Had Gone Before. I'd taped our scouting teams in action, I'd invited Brother Moses to inspect our procedures in person—hell, I'd even told him we'd train one of his own to run the thump truck. He had graciously declined, of course. Seeing is believing, and God forbid—you should pardon the expression—Brother Moses should see something that might change his belief in a stand that was bringing cash donations in from every crackpot in the System from Boise, Idaho to Copernicus Base, Luna. There's no business like the evangelical business for turning a profit.

I should have made Charlie join up; Brother Moses would be just the man to teach her the art of the deal.

As if he'd read my mind, Brother Moses said, "God forgive you and keep you, Sister Star." He gave a regal bow and paraded off stage left.

I watched his retreating back, thinking how nice it would be to see an eight-inch knife protruding from between his shoulder blades. I had an active fantasy life.

And then I saw something that truly terrified me: I saw the twins in the procession, both of them parading signs through Piazzi City when they should have been studying the speed at which asparagus sprouted on Outpost. Paddy's sign read "Honk if you love asteroids"; Sean's "Clap if you believe in kobolds." Both pairs of dark blue eyes were narrowed and fixed in concentration on Brother Moses' back. Neither of them looked the least bit devout.

They must have grabbed a ride on the mail scooter that broke orbit before I left Outpost. I waved. They either didn't see me or didn't want to. I started forward, only to be swallowed up in the same crowd that had swallowed them.

"Paddy!" I tried to yell over the increasing roar of the crowd.
"Sean!"

They either didn't hear me or didn't want to, and disappeared from my view.

"Hey, Star, is court in session?" a miner greeted me.

"Almost," I said, and with a last, despairing glance I
abandoned Brother Moses to his fate. After all, according
to him, God was on his side.

The crowd was there partly because it was market day, as
the temporary booths around the Hitching Post ten-deep in
customers demonstrated. It was also partly Miners' Court,
convened once a month to address all Belt grievances, real
and imagined, civil and criminal, presided over by a rotating
bench of three magistrates selected once a year by a popular
vote of the League of St. Joseph. The only reason I was
here was because I'd been unable to con or bribe Simon
into taking my place. It was really Perry Austin's month
but she was conveniently downarm, settling yet another
dispute between 7683Gypsy and 8102Rom. I only hoped
the Gypsies took her for the fillings in her teeth.

I pushed and shoved my way to the O.K. Corral, one of
the bigger saloons holding most of the early drinkers. The
bartender and owner, a diminutive, plump-breasted, bright-
eyed man, waved me over to the bar. "Good morning, Ms.
Svensdotter," he yelled.

"Morning, Birdie," I yelled back. "Court's in session."

"One moment, please." He disappeared for a second, to
reappear with an air horn. The single blaring jolt of sound
stunned the crowd into momentary silence, broken by someone yelling, "Here come de judge!" but they dispersed ami-
ably enough. Birdie closed the door behind them, hanging
a sign on it which read "Court in session. The Honorable
Star Svensdotter presiding. The bar is closed until further
notice."

The two of us working together pushed the stools against
one wall. Birdie produced a table and a chair more his
size than mine, and stood on the chair to help me into a
black robe, a ceremonial garment only recently introduced
into the proceedings. The collar was too tight, the hem

barely covered my knees, and the sleeves fell a good ten
centimeters over my hands. I sat down, wedged my legs
beneath the table (the judge used to stand behind the bar, and
personally I preferred it but it offended Birdie's rigid sense
of our dignity), and took the gavel Birdie handed me with
a ceremonious bow. "Okay, Birdie, call the first case."

Birdie's red-cheeked countenance stiffened into what he
considered to be a properly bailiffed expression, his usual
bobbing gait lengthened into an authoritarian stride, and he
stalked to the doors and flung them open. "Hear ye, hear ye!
This Miners' Court is now in session! The Honorable Star
Svensdotter presiding!" He consulted a clipboard hanging
next to the door. "First case, Kandinsky versus Townsend,
assault."

Two figures pushed through the crowd, to be overtaken
by an enormous third clad in the dazzling white jumpsuit
and red badge of the Star Guard. "Sorry, Star," he puffed.

"It's okay, Joseph, we're just starting. Birdie, enter Joseph
Smith as today's sergeant-at-arms."

"It's James, Star."

"Oh. Sorry, James." The trouble with triplets. Identical
triplets, all three of whom were members of the Star Guard
of exactly the same rank and so wore exactly the same
uniform.

"No problem." James grinned, displaying two adorable
dimples in an otherwise perfectly blue-eyed, clear-skinned,
square-jawed face, and perched on a stool next to the door.

The two smaller figures behind him now came forward.
"Beth." I rose, with difficulty, and extended a hand from
which I had to peel back the sleeve of the robe.

Beth Townsend took it in a warm grip. "How are you,
Star?" She was slim and wiry, as so many Belters were. We
consumed vast amounts of calories and expended equally
vast amounts keeping warm in vacuum, and the result was
a lot of muscle and bone and very little fat. She shaved her
head, something many do for convenience but a style few
look good in afterwards. Beth Townsend had the cheekbones for it; she looked like Bathsheba when David fell
for her.

This morning Beth was looking uncharacteristically subdued. "I just want you to know this wasn't my idea."

"No? Whose idea was it?"

"Mine. Joel Kandinsky." I disliked him on sight, a freckle-faced, sandy-haired man with a permanent scowl who exuded self-importance the way a British peer did superiority.

"You're bringing charges against Beth?" He nodded, and I said, "What for?"

"She assaulted me for no reason, an entirely unprovoked attack that resulted in injuries to my person and caused me extreme mental anguish!" He looked down his nose at me as if he expected me to pass sentence on the spot.

I looked at Beth, who looked resigned. "He stole my p-suit."

Kandinsky erupted. "I didn't steal it; I just borrowed it for a while, I—"

"He what?" I stared at Beth, who nodded. I looked back at Kandinsky. "You took her pressure suit?" He nodded. Even more incredulously, I said, "And you admit it?"

"Yes, I took it. I had to get to 2Pallas; I had a deal pending there that—"

I looked back at Beth. "He ask your permission?" She shook her head. "He hurt it?"

She hesitated. "Not much."

"Not much?" She remained silent, and I said to Kandinsky, "And you have the gall to sue *her* for assault?"

Kandinsky's face turned the color of old liver and he huffed out an impatient breath. "As I tried to explain—"

I cut across his words. "Mr. Kandinsky, there is no explanation adequate to your offense. You're on an asteroid, orbiting in space one point eight astronomical units from Terra. There are a hundred thousand other rocks in more or less the same orbit, half of them uncharted, and each and every one with its own eccentric orbit. Every Belter lives with the daily prospect of collision with another asteroid. Our only hope for survival in the event of a decompression event lies with everyone's pressure suit being exactly and precisely where they left it, and in working order. Archy, when's the next Volksrocket scheduled to depart?"

"Tomorrow morning at eight."

"Good; he gets only three free meals off us." I nodded at James, and he rose from his stool to stand behind Kandinsky. "Kandinsky, you are convicted of pressure suit theft. You are fined whatever valuables are on your person, to go toward any necessary repairs to the suit you stole, with any remainder to go into the judicial fund of the League of St. Joseph. I also sentence you to serve—how much do I sentence him to, Arch?"

"Twenty-one hours, thirty-six minutes, boss."

"I sentence you to twenty-one hours, thirty-six minutes in Piazzi City Jail, or until such time as the next Volksrocket departs 1Ceres. Upon your release, you will be issued a blue ticket for HEO Base and escorted to the departure terminal." I leaned forward. "Mr. Kandinsky, a piece of friendly advice? Don't miss that rocket."

"Now wait just a minute! This is no kind of court of law! I demand an attorney! I have my rights! I—"

Again I interrupted him. "Mr. Kandinsky, count yourself lucky that it was Beth's p-suit you stole. Another Belter would have stuffed you out the nearest airlock, and I would presently be ruling on a case of justifiable homicide." James hauled Kandinsky out, yelling for his lawyer all the way.

"Thanks, Star."

We shook hands again. "No problem, Beth. It's a shame we can't declare stupidity a capital crime. Next case, Birdie."

Birdie crossed off Townsend versus Kandinsky and called out the next two names on the sign-up sheet. A partnership in a claim on 9204Hell had suffered what we called a vacuum fracture, the result of too much time alone on a rock too far from home, and the two miners were fighting over who got what. It hadn't been the richest claim, doubtless one of the problems, and the chief bone of contention appeared to be the speeder. I suggested they sell it and split the proceeds. They demurred. They demurred so loudly and for so long that I suited up, located the speeder in question in the parking lot, punched the starter, and sent it off Ceres on a heading for Alpha Centauri. Back inside I inquired, "You have any other assets requiring judicial disposition?" They decided they hadn't. "Good. Your partnership is dissolved. Archy, spit out a writ to that effect, four copies, one to the League, one to the Star Guard so they can update their patrol schedule, one for each of the partners."

"It's done, boss."

"Gentlemen, your dissolutions are available in the mayor's office. I fine each of you one thousand Alliance dollars or its equivalent weight in ore, first for wasting my time, second for making me crawl in and out of my p-suit for the second time in an hour. Birdie, collect the fines and call the next case."

I was at it the rest of the morning and most of the afternoon, finishing up with a wedding at which the groom recited one poem, the bride another, and I was required to recite a third. Left to myself and knowing the two parties involved, I would have quoted, "Now's the day and now's the hour, see the front of battle lour," but no, they'd written a whole brand-new poem in honor of the sacred occasion. It went like this:

> **Him:** Two A.U.'s from hearth and home
> Here on Ceres, far from Nome.
> No more to Maggie's will I roam
> Now that Erma is my owme.
>
> **Her:** I swear by my shaker table
> I'll be as good a wife as I am able.
> Though Wally ain't exactly stable,
> In the good stuff he's cape-able.
>
> **Me:** Wally, take her for your wife.
> Erma, take him for your life.
> Live with love and never strife
> And hide all the kitchen knifes.

I felt silly as hell, especially when I looked up and saw Helen Ricadonna watching from the front of the crowd.

"With the authority vested in me by the League of St. Joseph, I now pronounce you husband and wife, with all the rights and responsibilities granted to members of the League and signatories of the Charter. There is no law but the law of the League."

"There is no law but the law of the League," the crowd repeated.

I closed the handbook. "Congratulations, Wally and Erma. Don't forget to rerecord your claims with the Star Guard."

A cheer went up, Birdie crossed the last item off the sign-up sheet, reopened the bar, and a thirsty crowd swarmed inside to drink the health of the newlyweds. I fought my way out of that damn robe while Helen bought us a pitcher of beer, and we retired to a dark corner. I poured carefully in deference to the low gee, and took a long, long drink that required an immediate refill. Birdie's beer was better than most found on Ceres, an asteroid notorious for its lack of hops fields, and it was cold. Life could hold no more.

"Well, that was romantic," Helen said, jerking her head toward the happy couple now heading for the door.

"That's one word for it. Most of the marriages I perform nowadays are more a matter of establishing joint rites of survivorship than promoting romance."

She studied her glass. "Remind you of anything?"

"No," I lied.

Ignoring me, she said, "It reminded me of your wedding to Caleb. Kate's Place, remember? The whole bunch of us half in the bag, except you, because you were pregnant and Charlie wouldn't let you anywhere near a shot glass. Uhura and Natasha attended on the tri-vee. We stopped the party in mid-swing, and Frank witnessed your vows like he was conducting the band on the *Titanic*. He was afraid a husband and babies would slow you down on your way out here."

I studied my glass, admiring the light refracting around the spout. "How is Frank? And speaking of marriage, what would you call yours and Frank's? Business or romance? Or maybe just a pooling of data?"

"Stop snarling at me," she said, mildly enough.

"What are you doing here, Helen? You're supposed to be chiseling money out of the First Bank of Terranova to finance the next World. And where is Frank?"

"I left him holding the fort at O'Neill."

"So, what, you just came out for a friendly visit?" I drained my glass.

Helen watched me refill it a third time. "You're pouring that stuff down like it tastes good. Take it easy."

"Judging is dry work."

"So it seems, but I'd prefer you sober to hear what I came here to say."

"And what's that?"

"I want you to go to Mars."

Helen Ricadonna had always been a past master of the non sequitur but this was going a bit far, even for her. "You want me to go to Mars."

"Yes."

There was a pause while I listened to the babble around me and looked at Helen, her hair, completely white now, standing up as usual in a corona all around her head. I wondered, not for the first time, if she cultivated the likeness to Einstein. Her ego was certainly up to the task. I drained my glass and signaled Birdie for another pitcher. "You may not want me drunk, but I've got the feeling I'm going to have to be to listen to what comes next." The pitcher arrived and I poured. "You want me to go to Mars," I repeated.

"Yes, for a year, a Martian year. The ship has already been built; in fact, it's en route to Outpost as we speak. ETA is two weeks. It's an interesting design; I think you'll like it. It's an airship."

I stared at her. "An airship? What, like a dirigible? What did they call them—zeppelins?"

"No, this one's soft-sided."

My glass paused in midair. "You mean a *balloon*?"

"Well, yes. Two actually, one inside the other. The cabin's a toroid." Her ephemeral smile came and went. "I know how much you like toroids."

A balloon. "I see." I drank. "Mind telling me why you want me to go to Mars in the first place?"

She had a one-word answer ready and waiting. "Cydonia."

"Cydonia."

"Yes, Cydonia. You do know where and what Cydonia is, don't you?"

"Yes," I said, aping her tone of sweet reason. "I know where and what Cydonia is; it's a bunch of ruins in the northern hemisphere of Mars, first sighted in the next-to-last decade of the last century, confirmed by Eurospace's Endeavor IV probe three years ago, best guess is E.T. built it five hundred thousand years ago, plus or minus a century, function unknown, builders unknown, so what?"

"So what?" Helen looked as scandalized as an impenetrable shield of dignity and equally unshakable sense of decorum would allow. "Aren't you interested in finding out exactly what is there?"

I shrugged, mostly to annoy her.

"Star, a lot of the hard data and most of the educated guesses about Cydonia were destroyed when World War Three took out JPL and Houston. But now there is Prometheus."

I groaned, and wished for the millionth time we'd never found evidence that the Asteroid Belt used to be a planet. "Oh God, not you, too. You and Brother Moses, God help me. I can't handle another half-baked theory-cum-revelation about the advance guard of heavenly host sent to Terra by the One True God from the One True Planet."

She went on as if I hadn't spoken. "If there is anything at Cydonia, it may predate what happened on Prometheus. There may be records—"

"Always supposing we could read them."

"—equipment—"

"Always supposing we could run it."

"—and evidence that whoever built Cydonia may have destroyed Prometheus."

I couldn't help it, I laughed. "Helen," I said when I could, "that ranks right up there with the Big Lie." The Big Lie was just that, a fabricated message from the "Beetlejuicers" that Frank and Helen arranged to be intercepted by the Odysseus II deep-space probe back in the eighties when space exploration and colonization were dead in the water, or at the very least becalmed. Frank and Helen decided to send the space program back to sea with a handmade gale that developed into an entirely unexpected hurricane when the real aliens we called Librarians showed up on Terranova.

All experience is an archway wherethrough, the poet said, and yet . . . for the first time I questioned the consequences of the Big Lie. If we hadn't gone full-throttle into space, we wouldn't have built Terranova. If we hadn't built Terranova, Simon wouldn't have built Archy to run it. If Simon hadn't built Archy, the Librarians would not have been intrigued enough to introduce themselves. If the Librarians had not introduced themselves, my niece Elizabeth would still have been with us instead of light-years across the galaxy, enrolled at Cosmos U., separated by space and time from home and family, perhaps never to return.

That untraveled world gleamed less brightly for me after her departure. And to the rest of humankind, space became less a mystery and more a resource. Back before the discovery of a planet predating the Belt, back before the Librarians came to top off the tank on Sol and returned home with Elizabeth, anything went in imagining what was out there. Bug-eyed monsters chased little green men in flying saucers equipped with light-speed and ray guns. After the Big Lie, after Frank and Helen "proved" there really was life in them thar stars, the scales tilted toward resource, and exploitation shifted into high gear. The Librarians' appearance gave the Big Lie credence; and, more recently, the discovery of evidence supporting the hypothetical existence of a planet orbiting where the Belt was now only confirmed the fact that we were not alone, may in fact have been the sole residents of our own Solar System for less than three thousand years. Much of the mystery was gone, and most of the romance, and I was only just beginning to realize our lives were the poorer for it.

"The Big Lie jumpstarted us back into space, didn't it?" Helen retorted, but her fleeting smile came and went. Serious again, she said, "Star, there is evidence that Cydonia and

Prometheus are connected. We've had a team of archaeologists at Cydonia for the last six months, did you know?" I shook my head, and she said, "They've been studying the ruins and transmitting their findings to Maria Mitchell Observatory. They've found what they think was an observatory."

"So?"

"So, the instrumentation's not pointing out; it's pointing in, toward the inner planets."

"Toward Prometheus?"

"Tori Agoot thinks so, and he's not exactly a virgin in the good-seeing business." She fiddled with her glass, still half full of her first beer. "Three months ago they sent us a message that they think they've found what might be a projector of some kind."

My voice was unintentionally sharp. "A weapon?"

She nodded. "Could be. And they think it's pointed in the same general direction as the observatory."

Along with a mesmerizing, often paralyzing gray stare, Helen had a voice with the seductive qualities of all the Lorelei put together. I'd seen Alliance senators tremble, Patrolmen quail, and career bureaucrats throw open the doors to the treasury under the influence of that voice. In the thirty-two years I'd known Helen, since we'd been roommates at Stanford, overseer and slave on Luna, and tyrant and worker bee on Terranova, that voice had lured me onto the rocks more times than I cared to remember, certainly more times than I would ever admit.

I studied her over the rim of my glass. She could have been lying through her teeth, propounding another outrageous hoax to spur exploration ever onward and outward. On the other hand, she could have been telling the absolute, unvarnished truth. With Helen you never knew. I didn't really care one way or the other.

"I don't want to go poking around a bunch of dusty old ruins, Helen, always supposing there actually is anything there to connect Cydonia with Prometheus, which I seriously doubt. Let somebody else do it, somebody who knows what to look for—an anthropologist, more archaeologists,

somebody like that. Mother would jump at the chance—
ask her."

Helen focused on the one point in my diatribe she could
legitimately attack. "What's wrong with ruins?"

"What's wrong with ruins?" For a moment I was stumped,
but only for a moment. "Well, for one thing, they're *old*."
She would have said more. I shook my head. "Don't. Just
don't."

Her eyes narrowed on me. "Is this about Caleb?"

It was unlike Helen to be blunt, and it took me a moment
to recover. "No. Of course not. How could it be? It's been
almost twelve years."

She nodded. "And for twelve years you've just been going
through the motions, just living till you die."

"Go to hell." Even my anger lacked force.

She dropped her voice an octave. Her technique was flawless, her tone hushed, each word dropping like a stone into a
still pond. "Caleb's dead, Star. He's been dead for twelve
years. You going to mourn him the rest of your life? You
going to sit and feel sorry for yourself forever? Do you
believe for a moment it's what he'd want?"

"You start talking like Mother," I said through my teeth,
"and I'll take you outside and see how high you can
bounce."

"In vacuum, I'd say pretty high," she said, bristling. "Take
your best shot."

We glared at each other. My communit beeped.

The feminine voice was hurried but composed. "Star?"

"Perry?" I said, startled. "What are you doing in range?
I thought you were downarm."

"Just got back, and just in time. Somebody's in the process of hijacking an ore carrier on Ceres. Six dead, a bunch
bloody. They've taken hostages and are fighting their way
onto the landing field. I'm on my way down. Charlie's with
me."

"I'm on Ceres; I'll meet you at the hangar. Birdie!" At
my shout the little man looked up. "Your laser pistol!" I
barked. "Now!"

Birdie had an arm on him like a mass launcher. Pistol and holster sailed over the heads of the crowd and I caught it and checked the magazine on the run. I was across the square, down the tunnel, and at the airlock before I knew Helen was still with me. "You're not coming with me, Ricadonna." I grabbed for my pressure suit and began jamming myself into it.

"I sure as hell am not," she agreed, helping me tug the torso and shoulders up. "I'm a lover, not a fighter." She pulled the helmet over my head and locked it down. I smacked the speaker. "Green board?"

She ran one finger across my chest readout, held up an OK sign, and buckled on Birdie's holster. Her palm thumped my helmet and I was in the lock and out the other side. A pressure suit bounced up, and I recognized Kevin Takemotu's grim visage just before the solar sled touched down. His voice over my headset was curt. "Perry, Star, glad you're here. Charlie, we've set up a first-aid station in the square. Mother Mathilda's in charge."

"Good." Charlie's voice was breathless over the headset, and I relieved her of the suit sealer she was carrying. "Thanks, Star. I'll let Mother Mathilda handle things inside. I'm going with you."

"What can you tell us, Kevin?" Perry asked.

"About an hour ago a freighter inbound from 19301Buena Suerte landed at Dock Four. The crew was disembarking when they were attacked by a gang with laser pistols." He looked at Charlie, his face taut behind its visor, his anger a tangible presence on the commset. "Most of the wounds are clean; I'll say that much. Hands and feet sliced off like baloney. Glad you brought the suit sealer."

He turned to Perry. "They've got at least two of the freighter's crew members as hostages. Sandy O'Connor and James Smith have them pinned down outside the ship. That Sandy is some kind of sharpshooter; every time they make a try for the hatch she pops off at them with that laser pistol of hers. She's nailed three of them so far."

"Let's go give her some help," Perry said. "Weapons check?"

We drew pistols and slapped ammopaks into the pistol butts. "Loading."

"Lock 'em down."

"Locking."

"Let's go."

We followed Perry across the hangar and up a set of rudimentary rungs carved straight up the face of the rock. Ceres, as the saying went, had enough gravity to keep your feet and your food down provided they started out that way; still, in p-suits and carrying weapons and first-aid equipment, most of us were out of breath when we emerged on the planetesimal's surface.

The landing site was one of many spaced evenly about the leveled plateau. The berth itself was functional, not fancy, defined by a series of concentric rings and tie-downs at intervals around the outermost circle. In the half-dawn, half-dusk of Sol's distant light, I could see six or seven other ships.

I had time to make out the bulky, utilitarian lines of a SeaLandSpace freighter berthed at Dock Four before Perry swore and ran forward. Beyond her moving figure I could see other, smaller figures climbing the hull of the ship. One of them stopped to look back, a rifle rising in his hands.

The trouble with landing sites is they've been leveled and flattened within an inch of their lives, which is good for setting down a spaceship safely but not so good for finding cover when someone is shooting at you. A thin beam of red light sliced through the rock in front of me. I ran after Perry, bouncing with every step, hoping my next one wouldn't hit with enough force to send me into orbit.

A figure in a black pressure suit materialized out of the ground and tripped me as I went by. I went down hard, bounced twice, and hadn't even stopped moving before I found myself rolled to my back with a knee on my chest. The knee shifted and his helmet bent forward as he looked down.

A click sounded in my ears, followed by a voice I didn't recognize. When the words registered, I looked up into eyes with no iris, pupils dilated and black, and so cold I shivered inside my p-suit.

"Well, well, well," the voice purred. "Star Svensdotter in person; what an unexpected bonus."

I heaved beneath him. A gauntleted hand smashed into my visor. Miraculously, it held, but my ears were ringing and my vision was blurred. "Now, now, now, mustn't try any of your shenanigans, darling Star; you'll make me angry." He chuckled beneath his breath, a sound so horrible and so seductive that I couldn't move.

"How shall I kill you, hmmm?" His voice came clearly over the ringing in my ears. "Shall I rip out your oh-two connector?" I felt the pressure of a hand behind my shoulder. "Or I could unlock the ring on your helmet." Something fiddled with my neck ring. The chuckle again. "But no, I think I prefer the direct approach."

My vision cleared enough to see the fisted gauntlet rise, and I heaved again, trying to get my legs up to where I could snag his head, my arms immobilized between the weight of his boots and the bulk of my suit. The fist smashed into my visor. My ears rang with the sound of the blow, and the faceplate misted over as the waste system began leaking, but the visor held.

"Kwan! Are you on this channel! Kwan, answer up!"

The gauntlet, raised to strike again, paused. "Kwan, we are leaving! Move your ass, dammit!"

I felt the vibration of a drive powering up beneath my back. The gauntlet descended again, and I came alive enough to twist one arm free and block the blow. "Another time, darling Star." He was laughing, face split wide in a feral, manic grin as he leapt to his feet and bounded off; graceful, bouncing strides that carried him quickly to the ship. He hurdled the rapidly reddening circle surrounding the stern and caught the sill of the hatch with his fingers. Rough hands pulled him in the rest of the way. Those same hands shoved out two other figures, and they fell helplessly into the ship's exhaust.

"No!" I stumbled to my feet, only to be thrown back by the blast of the exhaust as the ship lifted up and out and away. On my back, I stared up as the ship arced above Ceres, into the vast blackness of deep space, until it faded into a cold light to match the distant stars burning their icy brands into the universe's hide, until it faded from sight altogether.

I was afraid to move, afraid that either I was broken or my suit was. "Star? Star!" My sister's voice came thinly over the headset. "Star, where are you?"

"Charlie?"

"Star! Where are you?"

"Over here." I looked around and found a marker. "By the Dock Three marker. Are you okay?"

"I'm okay, how are you?"

"I'm all right, I think." I moved a hand, an arm, a leg. My fists still clenched, I still felt my toes; the telltales inside my helmet were green all the way across, although I didn't see how they could be. Even the mist was clearing from my visor, or maybe it had been my vision that had fogged up.

I pushed myself up to my feet. I saw a pressure suit approaching and took a step in its direction. Something tripped me and I almost fell. I looked down to see a human hand, extracted somehow from its p-suit gauntlet, lying palm up on the surface of Ceres. Its blood had boiled away in the vacuum, and all that was left was crumpled skin and bones, a withered claw frozen forever in a futile clutch at something it would never grasp, now.

I heard another voice over my headset. Perry. "What was the cargo? What was that freighter carrying?"

Kevin answered her. "Oh-two, nitro, and the big H."

A silence, then Perry's voice again. "Everything they need to make water and air. And sell it."

"Oh yes." Kevin, grim. "They knew what they were after, all right. Buena Suerte makes this run once a month to Piazzi City Utilities." He paused. "At least, they did. I don't know if there's anybody left back on Buena Suerte to continue the practice."

Perry sounded tired. "Sandy, this is Perry. Which Guard has the Buena Suerte beat?"

"Kamehameha's already on his way."

"Alone?"

"Dila's meeting him there."

The pressure suit moving toward me got close enough for me to see Charlie's face behind the visor. She followed my gaze to the hand at my feet, and immediately began looking for the rest of the person. She found him, twenty meters away. He wouldn't be needing the hand.

On her way back, Charlie found the suit sealer where I had dropped it. "We won't be needing this."

I looked across the field at the two charred lumps, all that remained of the two crew members tossed into the exhaust. "I guess not." My stomach turned, but my p-suit had taken enough abuse for one day. I managed not to puke until I was back on Outpost.

I cleaned up and joined Perry in her office, where I found her assigning patrols with darts thrown at the Guard roster. I ducked out of the way just in time. Neither of us laughed.

She sighted in on a last dart and let fly. "Good, Klell takes the Sutter cluster. That should do it, Archy. Post the assignments."

"It's done, Perry."

"Thanks, Arch. Austin out."

Perry wasn't as calm as she pretended; I saw her hands shake as she collected the darts and put them away. I stood where I was and we stared at each other in bleak silence.

Into it she said, "I'm resigning my post with the Star Guard, Star. I've already talked it over with Ursula. She's ready to take over, and she'll do a good job."

It wasn't what I'd expected, and I was caught off balance, not knowing what to say. "Perry, I—is it what happened today?"

"No."

"Is it the pay? I can—"

She gave a brief smile. "You know it isn't. What with the bonuses you keep throwing at us, I've got more banked on Terranova than I can ever spend." She grinned unexpectedly, a mischievous grin I'd never seen before on that terrierlike face. "But I'm going to try."

Some people you can buy with more money or authority; some you can sell on the importance of the job itself; some you can flatter with inflated estimates of their ability. Perry Austin wasn't for sale and was beyond flattery, and if she thought the job important, it was a matter of little more than holding the door and getting out of the way. Once the job was finished, it was again a matter of holding the door and getting out of the way. Perry had been a pilot with STS and with the Department of Space, and had pioneered the return of the Big Dumb Rocket. Crip, my chief pilot, had lured her to the Belt because she'd never been there before, and she convinced herself to stay when she and Ursula Lodge and Caleb Mbele O'Hara had conceived the notion of a Star Guard, an asteroidal answer to the Royal Canadian Mounted Police, 1.8 A.U.'s out from the Klondike.

Perry was one hell of a starter, but not much of a finisher. It was a wonder she'd sat still for as long as she had. If you could call patrolling millions of klicks of Asteroid Belt sitting still. I don't waste time fighting battles I've already lost. I sat down, more heavily than the half-gee of Outpost required. "Where are you going?"

"Back to Luna, for starters. I've been on the net to Deke at SSI. We've already started preliminary design on a ship."

"And when you get it built?"

She shrugged and grinned again. "I was at JPL when the Odysseus II pictures started coming in. Ever since, I've wanted to see one of those Ionian lava volcanoes up close enough to singe my eyebrows by. I talked it over with Tori Agoot at Maria Mitchell Observatory; he thinks he can get funding to underwrite part of the trip as long as I promise him pictures and data."

"They going with you?"

"Who?"

"The Smith triplets."

Perry looked surprised. "Of course."

Of course. When Crip had signed Perry on I'd thought they'd be company for each other. Instead, the day after Crip moved in with Mother, the Smith triplets, John, Joseph and, yes, James—three very large brothers from Orem, Utah— moved in with Perry, a conclusive demonstration of why I have no future in matchmaking.

So there went four of the Star Guard's most experienced veterans at one whack, one of them a founding member, three of them in the first draft of trainees. "Wonderful," I said. Perry looked a little flattened, and I said, infusing my voice with as much enthusiasm as I could muster, "Wonderful, Perry. Of course I'm sorry to lose you—all four of you," I added a trifle grimly, "but your own ship? Your own itinerary?" *Your own harem?* I thought, but didn't say. "There's no way you can pass this up. Hell, I envy you. Have fun."

"I intend to." She gave me an appraising look. "You should try it yourself one day."

Her words were such a strong echo of the conversation in the O.K. Corral that I was immediately suspicious. "Has Helen been talking to you?"

She looked startled. "Is Helen here?"

"Yeah, she—forget it; it doesn't matter."

Perry put a hand out. "I'll miss you, Star. Working for you has been an education in how to get things done. I've learned a lot, and I feel like I've made a good friend. Thanks."

I took the hand and tried to smile. "That means something, coming from you. Thanks."

We shook on it. "Now, about this mess."

"Who were they?" I sat down across from her. "Do we know?"

"I've got an idea." She nodded at the dart board. "It's why I've got Klell out in the Sutter cluster. There's been a bunch causing trouble out there for the last year."

"I know. But not like this."

"No," she echoed. "Not like this." She looked at me, transmitting a sheer, scorching, all-encompassing rage all the more impressive for its dead-calm certainty. "We'll catch them. I swear to you, Star, my last official act as head of the Star Guard will be to bring you their heads on a fucking platter."

I summoned up a smile, a weak one. "I know."

Perry knew me pretty well. "What is it?"

I was silent for a moment. "One of them had me down. He was just about to punch my faceplate out when I heard someone call his name."

She sat up. "You were on the same frequency?"

I licked my lips. "He read mine on my chest readout and switched over. He recognized me, Perry."

"And?" she prompted.

"And I don't think he liked me much. He had a good time discussing various ways to shuffle off my mortal coil, until somebody on the ship got the right channel and told him they were taking off."

"Did you get his name?"

"The other guy called him Kwan. Mean anything to you?"

Perry put her feet up on the desk, clasped her hands behind her head, and stared at the ceiling, a frown on her face. After a moment she said, "Archy?"

"Yes, Perry?"

"Access Holmes for me. Scan for William Kwan."

"You got it. Kwan, William, born Beijing, Terra, 1976, entered Patrol Academy, 1994, sworn in 1998, posted to Orientale Base, G.C. Lodge, commanding, also 1998."

I jerked upright. "What?"

"I'm not finished, boss. He made PFC half a dozen times and was busted back down to private every time, for everything from fighting in ranks to insubordination. This guy wasn't exactly Sergeant York." Archy paused. "This is the best part. Kwan was one of the Patrolmen on liberty on Terranova that day at Kate's."

A chill feathered up my spine. The memory, seventeen years old, was still painful, and still painfully clear. "You mean Kwan was one of the soldiers who raped that girl?"

"Yes."

"Wait a minute, Archy," I said sharply. "Those Patrolmen, with the exception of the sergeant who was executed a week later, were sentenced to life at hard labor in Luna Maximum. It was the last right thing Grayson Cabot Lodge the Fourth did in his life."

"Kwan escaped. Ten years ago, with a dozen others. A Volksrocket disappeared off its launch pad that night. They must have come out here."

"Bingo," Perry said, frown clearing.

"Son of a bitch!" I rose and paced, furious. "So that's how he knew who I was!"

"Yup. You remember him?"

I paused, and shook my head. "Uniforms is all I remember. They all looked so neat and so sharp for having gang-raped and then beaten someone senseless. Talk to me about Kwan out here."

"I didn't know it was Kwan until today, and most of the rest is rumor. Over the past seven years there have been a series of attacks on some of the more isolated Belter claims. The claims are stripped of anything useful, everything else is destroyed, and the claim abandoned. The attackers have been pretty thorough up to now; there usually aren't any witnesses. But about three months ago—you hear about No Return?"

For a moment I couldn't place the name. "No."

"Hatsuko Matsumoro, 7871No Return."

Again, memory returned in a rush. The third stop on the rock hop Caleb, Leif, the twins, and myself had taken so long ago. The short, merry woman with the rollicking crew, sitting on a rock paying out high-grade silver, so glad to see new faces that they gave us their own beds, so pleased with our company that they had extended us an open invitation to visit again any time. It was an invitation I had not taken them up on, and now never would. "Oh, no."

"I'm afraid so. One of Matsumoro's crew survived long enough to give us a partial description. Archy did the rest." She looked at me soberly. "This is one of the bad guys, Star. The bodies he's left behind are—" She shook her head. "Never mind, it's almost supper time. Suffice it to say he doesn't always kill first. He's smart, too; every attack has been planned for when the Guard on the beat has been at the farthest point in his swing-through."

"What does he look like?" All I remembered were pupils expanded to cover the entire iris, black and impenetrable.

She dropped her feet and swung her viewer around. "Archy?"

A face topped with the Patrolman's dress beret stared out at me. Nothing went together with anything else: His brows were thick, his eyes were thin; he had a short nose and a long upper lip; his mouth was a slash of red flesh. Even in the standard, posed class photograph, the gaze was fierce and direct. Oddly, the more I looked at Kwan's face, the more his expressionless mouth seemed to widen in a smile, as if he knew something I didn't and would, one day, take great pleasure in explaining it to me, in detail.

My eyes met Perry's. She said sternly, "You see him again, you shoot first and ask questions afterward, you hear?"

"I hear."

—2—

Pyramid Building

Ancient astronauts didn't build the pyramids. Human beings built the pyramids, because they're clever, and they work hard.

—**Gene Roddenberry**

A week later we commissioned the first habitat to come off the assembly line of A World of Your Own, Inc.

I went over early to inspect the premises. From the outside, it looked like any other asteroid I'd ever seen, only this one was more regularly spheric in shape and was generating one gee on the interior equator with a 1.97-per minute rotation. Its original catalogue number was 12146, its original name Lucky Strike, a rock already hollowed out by a group of miners moiling for nickel. The vein played out and their fortunes made, the miners downed picks, sold us their claim for a pittance, and boarded the Cunard liner *Charles III* for home, riding in the Presidential Suite and ordering champagne with every meal. They were probably broke before the ship docked at HEO Base.

The rock's dull gray exterior was pockmarked with impact craters. Most of the craters had been filled in and smoothed over with silicon cement, maintaining the roughly even thickness of the inert shielding left in place by Whitney Burkette and his Meekmaker crew when they melted out the interior. At the sphere's Tropic of Cancer a long slender mirror was sliding slowly into its mounting. It was one unit of a ring of panels soon to be angled to reflect Sol's rays through the bank of windows circling the sphere, 23.5 degrees above where on the interior I hoped I'd find an equatorial river with no falls in it. I'd known Roberta McInerny a long time. I wasn't confident.

"Let's hit air!" Simon said impatiently, and I broke orbit and brought us down. The lock was easy to spot; it was one of the very few smooth, finished pieces of real estate on the exterior. I set the scooter down and hooked on to a cleat. We clambered out and pulled handholds across to the personnel hatch. One at a time, we rotated inside. Humberto Bengoachea waited for us to peel out of our pressure suits.

"Ben. How's it going?"

He shrugged. "Same ole, same ole. Except those engineers are saying they wanted a light rail system."

"So?"

Ben was a small brown man with a small brown face and small brown eyes. He matched his brown jumpsuit, which showed signs of having been slept in. He ran stubby fingers through already disheveled hair. "So we didn't plumb for one. The original design called for no vehicle more heavy duty than a bicycle."

I closed my eyes and tried to conjure up a vision of the contract between A World of Your Own, Inc., and the Off-Planet Engineering Company. It was only about 650,000 words long. I opened my eyes again and said, "Look, Ben, I'm sure bike paths and only bike paths were specified in the contract; get Archy to call it up and review the specific clauses. And let me know what the two of you find out."

"Can do."

I started to turn, and stopped. "Ben?"

"Yeah?"

"You're an agronomist; what're you doing dealing with this? Where's that traffic engineer, what's his name—"

"Dave Hauer," Simon said.

Ben gave us a hollow grin. "Him? Oh, he's down with Ceresian flu."

"Wonderful," I said morosely. "Half of Outpost is, too."

Ari Greenbaum and Maggie Lu were standing next to the model home in Village One, watching the carpenters beat on it with hammers. The place was a shambles, odd pieces of silicon prefab stacked haphazardly against bare studs, gaping holes in the kitchen and bathroom through which we could see as yet unconnected ceramic pipes, cable, and conduit underfoot everywhere. Simon accidentally stepped on the thin sheeting covering the airlock frame and sank in up to his knees. It took three of us to pull him out. The air was thick with sawdust; we both sneezed continually until Maggie gave us masks.

The front door did close. As if to compensate, the back door wouldn't open. "Why am I here?" Maggie asked the ceiling.

A panel of Leewall, tacked into place by one corner, slipped, and carpenter John Begaye jumped to catch it before the whole panel came crashing down. He readjusted the panel and drove in half a dozen staples. The panel protested but held, who knew for how long. "Pretty good all right," he decided, but then John was Navajo by birth and stoic by inclination, and if the entire sphere had been two minutes away from total collapse he would have said exactly the same thing.

"The kobolds it is," Dieter Joop said portentously.

"What's a kobolds?" someone, unfortunately, wanted to know, and before Dieter could get started yet again on the story of the malicious imps that haunt mines and miners in German folk tales, I looked a plea at Simon. He nodded. "Let's get out of here while we still can."

It took us twenty minutes to climb up to the axis, and when we got there we weren't even breathing hard.

It wasn't that much of a view, yet. We were standing inside a gray-brown ball with a monotonous interior relieved so far only by three flattish areas spaced more or less equally between the Tropics, the sites for the three villages. One of them would be located directly across from where we were standing, 450 meters away. Elsewhere, there were half a dozen groupings of smaller foundations spaced farther apart for the engineers and future colonists of the sphere to take advantage of the differing gravities on the interior shell. A shallow ditch marched its way around the sphere's circumference. I hated to admit it but Roberta was right; that damn river did look boring. Still, it wasn't my river, and it wouldn't be my World any longer than it took the check to clear on the last payment due.

There was no green to speak of, and the atmosphere was still so dry that there wasn't even the barest hint of cloud. The banks of lamps that lit the work areas inside the sphere lightened the interior to no better than dim; that would change when the last mirror slid into place outside and the completed array began to fill the interior with Sol's reflected glory. Solar power, solar heating, solar lighting—the solar virtue of this World was going to be one hundred and one percent. Always assuming the array worked once it was assembled.

I felt a sudden pang of nostalgia. The sphere bore little resemblance to Terranova, but as stripped down as it was, I could imagine the view in five years. The lush green vegetation, sucking up carbon dioxide and churning out oh-two; the blue of the distant river aerating the habitat's water supply; the polar skies filled with brightly colored wings as the colonists took their leisure in the air. I could almost smell the aroma of clover blooming, feel the moistness of the air after a rainfall, hear the rustle of rabbits in the undergrowth. "How far along are they in the machine shops?"

"Plumbing's in."

"Speaking of plumbing, where did the sewage treatment plant wind up? You never told me."

Simon had very white teeth that gleamed against his unshaven chin when he grinned. "They kept shifting it around from village to village, each village kept saying Not In My Backyard. They haven't even moved in yet and already they're fighting."

"So?"

"So we plumbed it into the biggest industrial complex." He pointed. "They don't want to live with it? Fine. They can work with it."

"They'll be furious when they find out."

Simon shrugged. "Not our problem. It's a turnkey operation. They move in, it's theirs, and that means all of it, including the problems that came with their infighting."

"You're such a hardass, Simon."

"True."

"I like it."

"I know." He grinned again. Simon had been my second-in-command for so long, our understanding was pretty near perfect. Maybe even pretty good all right. "I'm heading down to Ops. You coming?"

"No, I've got to find Roger. The genetechs were having trouble cloning the maples out of the geodomes on Outpost; I want to see how he's doing."

"Okay, see you later." With a lift of his hand he strode off. He tripped once and hopped three times in the low gravity before regaining his balance.

I found Roger mulching roots in a grove of saplings, each barely a self-respecting twig, although they looked healthy enough, and from little saplings did mighty maple trees grow. I hoped. "How's it going, Roger? The maples coming along okay?"

"Of course," he said, affronted that I would dare think otherwise.

"I'd heard there was some trouble with—" He looked at me, and I changed that to, "So, I take it there are no problems raising their nasty little heads in the biospherics department."

His lip curled, and he bent back over his twig. "Piece of cake. Those engineers are meat-eaters to a man. They want green, all right, but just enough to fill a salad bowl and soften the edges of the architecture."

"Glad to hear it," I said, a little wary. It was not like Roger Lindbergh to be uncomplaining. "Did they decide they wanted cows?"

He snorted. "Not hardly. They're not moving off-Terra to learn how to use a manure rake. Fixed-bed-enzyme milk'll do fine for them." He pointed with his dirty trowel. "We put in three of the FBE synthesizers, one per village, alongside the three meat vats. If all three are working, they run at half capacity. If one breaks down or needs maintenance, the other two take up the slack. Same with the mycoprotein vats."

"I've always liked redundancy in a habitat."

"Me, too." He worked compost into the roots of the tree. "Star?"

"What?"

He sat back on his heels. "Zoya lost the baby."

"Oh. Oh God." I sat down next to him. "Roger, I'm so sorry."

"Charlie doesn't seem to be able to fix whatever's wrong." He ran his finger down the trowel's edge, collecting a loose ball of the grayish dirt that had once been asteroidal pebble. He rubbed the grains between thumb and forefinger. "She says it could be the half gee on Outpost." He raised his head, his expression bleak. "We're going back to Terranova."

"What!"

"On the next TL-M ferry. Kevin Takemotu's reserved us berths."

First Perry, then Roger. It was beginning to look like a general exodus. My response was instinctive, if less than compassionate. "Roger, you can't leave. I don't know what I'd do without you, I—"

His voice was thin but firm. "We want kids, Star. We're willing to try anything until we get it right. You've got three of your own, you can't possibly know how we feel."

His shoulders were hunched, as if anticipating a blow. Roger was expecting me to argue with him, and it shamed me to realize he was right. I took a deep breath and said in a level voice, "You're right, I can't. You got a place to stay on Terranova?" He shook his head. "I've still got my house there. You need a place to bunk until you decide what you're going to do—" I remembered. "Right. Dammit. I forgot. It's halfway up the Rock Candy Mountains, in half-gee territory its own self. Sorry."

"It's okay. Thanks for the offer."

He set aside the trowel, and I watched him level the earth around the sapling with possessive pats. He worked as he always did, as he had for the twenty years I'd known him, with complete absorption, devoted to the propagation of the color green in any shade, in any climate, on any world. Roger Lindbergh never looked more at home than when he was up to his elbows in dirt. "You don't want to go, do you?" I said in sudden realization, and immediately cursed myself for my lack of tact.

He wouldn't look at me. "Ben's a good man. He's up to speed on the AggroAccel program, and he's been here on World One since we melted out an interior. He'll do a good job with it."

"Ben it is, then." I leaned forward to rest one hand over his clenched, grubby ones. "I'll miss you, Roger."

"I'll miss you, too, Star."

We sat like that for a long time.

The Ops center was a small, single-story building located at the World's equator, where the gravity was a full gee. I found Simon sitting at a U-shaped console surrounded by a forest of card frames and many swearing technicians. Computer techs swear a lot, but always in whispers, as if they're afraid the computer might hear them and in retaliation throw out another malf or glitch. "Sumbitch is a kludge," Sally Humboldt hissed at Simon.

"Couldn't find its way out of a silicon chip with ten megs and a flashlight," Will Noble muttered behind her, and a chorus of angry whispers agreed.

"Now, now," Simon said jovially, "another terabyte or two's worth of storage in the self-correcting program, and this problem will"—he grinned—"self-correct." There was a battery of raspberries and boos, and Simon's grin widened. Simon Turgenev up to his ears in megachips and data cards and actively hostile computer techs was a happy man.

Hung from the frame next to Sally was a length of wiring looped into a hangman's noose. "What's this?" I asked her, pointing at it.

She exchanged glances with Will, and following her gaze, I noticed a small plastic skull hanging from his keyboard. I looked around the room, and next to each programmer found other nooses and skulls, several miniature skeletons, some dressed in colorful costumes, and one tiny coffin.

In spite of myself, my imagination conjured up a picture of that little coffin tucked into the ground, consigning into the hereafter one or another of the various body parts we had found scattered across Ceres' landing field the week before. It would have been just the right size for some of them.

I shook myself. Those pitiful remnants, the shredded spoor of a pack of bloodthirsty killers, had gone the way of all flesh in the Belt, into the waste recycler on Ceres long since, days since, ages since. I was proud my voice was steady. "What the hell is this, guys?" A thought occurred. "It's not October already, is it?"

Will looked at Sally, who had her eyes fixed on the light-pen in her hands. "They remind us," he said softly.

"Remind you of what? Trick or Treat?"

He looked at me, his face solemn. "It reminds us of what happens if we leave a gate closed that should have been open."

"Or install a defective card," Sally said.

"Or give the software the right command at the wrong time," Bill York said, looking up from a keyboard.

I looked at the little skull with its little leer, and could find nothing to say.

"How'd the monitor program on the life support systems prove out?" Simon said.

"Five by," Sally said, albeit grudgingly, her voice rising up all the way to a mumble. "We threw a simulated atmospheric leak at it up near the North Pole. The diagnostic program located the leak and had a repair team on the scene in fifteen minutes."

"Good, good; that's what I like to hear, my brilliantly conceived, superbly written habitat programs functioning at optimum capacity." Simon flicked a few switches, pressed a button or two, and rose to his feet. "Keep up the good fight until 1400, children, when shall we gather at the river, the beautiful, the beautiful river. I love you, too," he said blandly, in the teeth of another barrage of curses.

Outside, I said, "I'm glad you're springing them for the ceremony. Maybe it'll cheer them up a little."

"Cheer them up?" Simon looked at me askance. "That's the best mood I've seen those byteheads in since Outpost put on spin."

Computer technicians, like architects, are another race altogether.

Halfway down to the dedication site we spotted Mother. She was with Roberta. They were arguing. Roberta looked stubborn. Mother looked patient. "I don't suppose there's any way of avoiding them," I said.

Simon gazed around the mostly bare circumference of World One. "Nope."

"I didn't think so." I braced myself and marched forward.

"Roberta, dear, I've identified and catalogued the recreational habits of each future colonist, and none of them has demonstrated any interest in running the rapids."

"Natasha, it's a matter of what the world should have."

"As opposed to what its inhabitants want? Really, dear, what's the point in constructing—Oh hello, Simon. Esther, dear, Roberta seems to think—"

Why was it, that by simply calling me by my birth name, my mother was the only person in the Solar System who could make me feel like I was back in braces? "That's Roberta's problem, Mother—thinking." I grinned at Roberta. She didn't grin back.

We came to a stop at the river's edge. The water in it was as yet only a few centimeters deep, mud-colored and sluggish. It was four meters from bank to bank; the channel was as much as two meters deep where the banks had been built up. I turned my head, following its course as the sphere curved up around us on either side, to meet eventually far above our heads. "It looks great, Roberta. Just like a river, and in fact, just like the picture of the river the engineers sent us. You done good."

Roberta stared off into the distance, her expression sour. I was tired of coddling her. I moved to where she couldn't avoid looking at me full on. "Roberta, it's a done deal. We're not putting the distillers on hold so you can reroute the channel or throw in some boulders to change its course. The engineers are happy with it, which means I'm happy with it, which means your job here is done. I want to see the preliminary blueprints of your designs for single-family housing in Village Two by next week. Okay?"

It wasn't. Three hours later Roberta still wasn't speaking to me as we stood in a crowd numbering all of the original shipmates of the *Hokuwa'a* and *Voortrekker* who could be spared from either their duties or the Ceresian flu. A small procession approached us, headed proudly by John Begaye and Maggie Lu. Roger was standing directly behind me and I caught the full force of his squawk on the back of my neck. "Where'd they get that tree? Star! Do you see that? Where'd they get that goddam tree?"

Zoya murmured something soothing. Next to me I could feel Simon begin to shake. "Star?" Maggie called, and I went gladly.

The tree was an eight-year-old hemlock, sturdy and thick, with healthy blue-green needles and purple cones. I kept one wary eye on a red-faced, furious Roger as it was brought forward to the river's edge. I steadied the tree as the members of the procession joined the crowd facing me.

I waited for the last whisper to die away. An expectant silence echoed off the inside of the sphere. Into it, I said, "Walt Whitman says that a leaf of grass is no less than the journeywork of the stars."

I smiled at the crowd, meeting Charlie's eyes for an instant. "I guess that makes us the stars' journeymen."

"But World One is much more than a leaf of grass."

"It is an entire new world."

"It is the first space habitat conceived, financed, and constructed out of Terran orbit."

"It's a world where a group of people of shared beliefs, professions, and lifestyles will come together to live, and grow, and prosper together in harmony."

"This World is the culmination of a dream that began long ago and worlds away, in the minds of a few, visionary dreamers, back in the days when Terrans didn't even have a reliable space transportation system, or the funds, or a bureaucratic structure to support the research and development for space travel, much less the construction of habitats and their colonization. The journey has been long, and difficult, and, for some of us"—my voice did not falter— "our last."

"Today, at journey's end, we pay tribute. To the dream, and to the dreamers."

I gestured towards the tree. "It has been the tradition of Terran builders for centuries that when the frame of a house is complete, they nail a tree to the ridgepole. World One has no ridgepole, and I'm not about to start driving nails through living trees when I know for a fact Roger Lindbergh would eviscerate me if I did." There was a ripple of smothered laughter in which Roger did not join. Zoya patted his arm.

"So today, here, now, begins our own adaptation of that continuing tradition. This tree comes from Central Park on Outpost." I heard a sound that I was pretty sure was Roger's teeth grinding together. "Archy and I have been looking into its genealogy, and from what we can discover, it is the offshoot of a hemlock planted in the Big Rock Candy Mountains on Terranova. That tree was seeded from a grove of mountain hemlocks in the Chugach National Forest in Alaska."

Settling the tree into the hole already dug for it, I filled in the hole, tamping the earth down around the little tree's roots. When I was finished, I stuck the shovel into the ground and stood back. "From Terra to Terranova to Outpost to World One," I intoned. "From the tree comes the wood."

"And the wood returns to the tree," they responded.

"Okay, Archy," I murmured into my commset.

Somewhere outside, a set of computer-driven waldoes made a final, minuscule adjustment. The last reflecting mirror was brought into line, and through the ring of tropical graphplex windows the World's first ray of sunlight slipped shyly inside, to glint off the motes of construction dust that danced through the air of the sphere, to cause the muddy ripples of the shallow (and still straight) river to gleam with a life of their own, to warmly caress our upturned faces. I looked down at the little tree, which, even as I watched, seemed to dig in its roots and shake out its limbs, the better to bask proudly in our approval and that first virgin ray of light.

There was a brief, sunstruck silence, followed by a thunderous, rolling wave of applause. The cheers from the crowd echoed across the equator, cheers for the little tree, cheers for the New World's christening by sunlight, but cheers most of all for themselves, and for the culmination of a dream.

Back on Outpost that evening, there was a smaller, more intimate, and infinitely more personal ceremony. Jammed into Charlie and Simon's living room were Charlie and Simon, Alexei, Axenia, Mother, Crip, and Paddy and Sean, looking so innocent I was immediately suspicious. With an agility that alarmed me as much as it awed me, they had managed to avoid, avert, deter, deflect, and duck any and all explanation of last week's presence in the train of Brother Moses' demonstration. I considered warning him, but I didn't know of what, and so left it for another day. A mistake, as it later turned out, but contrary to public opinion, I was only human.

Maggie Lu was there, as were Roger, Zoya, John Begaye, Helen, and Ari, Perry Austin attended by the Smith triplets (who filled up half the room all by themselves), and a slender young brunette with tilted hazel eyes and a shy smile, whom I did not know. Leif stood next to her, clasping her hand in his. I opened my mouth to say something, for example, Who are you? and, Why are you and my son holding hands? when there was a stir at the other end of the room. Mother produced a large box. I knew instantly what was inside.

So did Charlie. "Mother! You brought the candle with you?"

"Certainly I did, Carlotta," Mother said, austere and reproving. "If you will persist in dragging your family millions of kilometers from your native home, someone has to see to it that certain essential traditions accompany the family."

Charlie rolled her eyes at me as Simon fetched a small round-topped table on a slender base of leaf-shaped legs. He placed it in the center of the room and spread it with a white cloth. Mother opened the box and took out a piece of translucent green soapstone, short and squat and carved in the stylized likeness of a sea otter, after the fashion of Native Alaskan artists. It floated flat on its back with its paws in the air.

She centered the carving on the table, and between its paws placed Esther's candle, an equally squat, barrel-shaped taper some twenty centimeters high and twice that in diameter. The otter alone must have weighed five kays. Like Charlie, I had trouble believing Mother had lugged it and the candle all the way from Terra.

Between them, Crip and Simon brought forward a large, square, shallow tray and set it on the floor before the candle, filled with what appeared to be wet sand.

Mother smiled at us. "It is the custom for the youngest member of the family to light Esther's candle. Axenia?"

Charlie and Simon's third child came forward, chubby ten-year-old face puckered in concentration. A long, thin match—especially constructed by Outpost's openly incredulous prefab shop; there is no such thing as an open flame on a space station—was struck, and flared into life. The wick caught at once. The translucent wax began to glow, and the soapstone base with it, so that together they gleamed like a bowlful of pale Arctic sunlight.

"Please be seated." Mother curled up on the floor, Esther's candle behind her and the tray of damp sand before her. The rest of us settled into a circle at the edge of the candlelight. Leif smiled at the young brunette and released her hand to sit at our center, across the tray from Mother.

Slowly, ceremoniously, Mother drew the storyknife from a leather sheath stained and fragile with age, and held it high for us to see.

The ivory of the storyknife was yellowed with the patina of three hundred years' use. It was the size and shape of a small scimitar, thirty centimeters in length. The underside of the handle bore a row of tiny carved figures—a sun, a whale, an eagle, a salmon, a drum and, of course, the sea otter. Mother's totem, Charlie's, mine. Leif's totem, too, after tonight.

In the wet sand, with the point of the storyknife, Mother drew a house. "My family," Mother began, and the mere sound of that familiar invocation in the dim, flickering light was enough to transport me back in time to my own naming, so far away, so long ago. It was the last naming the family had held. Elizabeth, Charlie and Simon's first child, was only ten when she left, and had never had one.

"My family," Mother repeated, and drew a path from the front door of the house. "Good friends. Leif." She gave him a look both solemn and kind. "For three hundred years it has been the custom of this family that, in the year of their choosing, each child decide on the surname by which ever after they will be known."

"This custom was begun by Ekaterina Shugak, my great-great-great-grandmother." Mother drew the rounded symbol for woman next to the path. "She was born a Medvedev, which was her Russian father's name and her name at birth, as was the custom of the time. When Soloviev killed her brother and her uncle in the massacre of Umnak Island in 1766"—Mother drew two triangular male symbols and the X next to each that signified sleep or death—"Ekaterina repudiated her Russian husband, and with her three children"—the tip of the storyknife moved deftly, and three child symbols appeared, two male and one female—"boarded a kayak"—a single stroke, and the curved hull of a kayak appeared—"and paddled across twelve hundred miles of the most treacherous seas on Terra"—three wavy lines, one on top of the other, materialized beneath the kayak—"to Old Harbor, a village on Kodiak Island."

Mother paused. "Only she and one of the children survived the voyage."

She waited, long enough for us to picture Emaa Katya and her babies in an open boat on the Gulf of Alaska. "On Kodiak Island, Ekaterina took the name of Tlingit, in homage to the tribe of Alaskan Indians who kept massacring any Russian unfortunate enough to attempt to settle southeast Alaska." There was a ripple of laughter.

Mother raised the storyknife over her head again, displaying it between the tips of her fingers. "This was Ekaterina's storyknife. Her uncle carved it for her out of a walrus tusk when she was a child, so that she could tell stories in mud and snow to amuse her younger brothers and sisters and cousins. There is evidence that the storyknife was at one time a tool, a snow knife, used to cut blocks of ice to build temporary shelters called igloos, but by the time the custom passed to Ekaterina's generation, the snow knife had become a toy for children, more specifically a girl's toy, a storyknife."

With a single stroke of the flat edge of the storyknife, Mother swept the sand smooth. She drew the path again, from the top of the tray curving down to the bottom, and next to it, in the center of the frame, another woman symbol.

"This custom of taking a name continued with Ekaterina's surviving daughter, Elizabeth, my great-great-grandmother. At the age of sixteen she married Demetri Moonin and moved to Ninilchik on the Kenai Peninsula." The triangular symbol for man appeared on the wet sand, and next to it the symbol for kayak. "Demetri was lost at sea during a sea otter hunt not two years later, and at her naming the following year Elizabeth chose to take the name of Susitna, she who sleeps and dreams of her lover's return. Elizabeth Susitna inherited the storyknife upon her mother's death and was the first to use it during her naming."

Next to the woman symbol, Mother illustrated two child symbols. "Elizabeth Susitna had two children, Axenia and Demetri. Demetri was my great-grandfather."

"Like his father, Demetri hunted the sea otter"—the symbols for kayak, spear, and *ikamaq* were etched in—"and paid homage to its importance in his life by taking its name, Ikamaq." She held up the storyknife's sheath. "He made this sheath for the storyknife from moosehide. He wove the designs on its sides with rye grass picked in the Barren Islands."

Mother drew the child symbol next to Demetri Ikamaq. "Demetri Ikamaq had one child, a daughter, called Esther. Esther was my grandmother." The storyknife smoothed the sand; the path was redrawn, another woman figure inscribed. "Esther and her father were very close, and at nineteen Esther took his name to be her own, Ikamaq. She married Derenty Anahonak and moved with him to Seldovia. She brought the storyknife with her, made the candle from seal fat, and began the custom of lighting it during each naming ceremony."

"Esther had nine children." We waited as the tip of the storyknife inscribed five male and four female symbols. "One of them was a daughter, Elizabeth." The sand was swept smooth, and another female figure appeared, this time to one side of the tray. "Elizabeth was an artist and an activist determined to translate the traditions of both her cultures, Russian and Aleut, into her work. At nineteen she took the name Alutiiq, or Aleut, to be her own, as well as a middle name, Ekaterina, to commemorate both lines of her heritage."

"Elizabeth helped found the Alaska Federation of Natives, to write the Alaska Native Claims Settlement Act, and to establish the Ikamaq Fjords National Park and Wildlife Refuge. It was Elizabeth who made the base for Esther's candle from soapstone, carving it in the likeness of the family totem." In swift succession appeared the figure of *alutiiq*, or people, the roofed symbol for community, the branched symbol for forest, the three wavy lines for water, a hammer and chisel, and the ikamaq.

Mother swept the sand smooth again, and again inscribed the symbol for woman. "I am Natasha, daughter of Elizabeth Ekaterina Alutiiq and Enakenty Quijance. After the war, when the borders were reopened, I took my daughters to the Philippine Islands to meet my father's family. His father, my grandfather, was Alfredo Quijance."

She smiled, a gentle, reminiscent smile. "I spent all my time in Baguio sitting at his bedside, listening as he spoke to me of the Quijance family, of the leaders it has given to the cause of a free and independent Philippine nation, of its martyrs as well. He told me of leading the Battle of Pyongyang"—Mother drew the shape of a billowing mushroom cloud—"which action ended the United Eurasian Republic's eastward expansion and prompted the affiliation of the Philippines, Japan, and United Korea with the American Alliance."

Mother drew the Alliance flag, and paused. "Even as he spoke to me, he was dying of wounds suffered in that great and terrible battle, the last battle of World War Three, perhaps the last great Terran battle ever. We can only hope so. Decorated many times and by many nations, Alfredo Quijance was a general who grieved over the loss of each and every soldier under his command in that war. I think sometimes he was dying of the grief their deaths caused him, as much as he was of his actual wounds." Her eyes rested on me for a moment, before lowering again to the tray. The tip of the storyknife drew a field of crosses, row on row. "That the Philippines is a free state of the American Alliance today is due much to him. That the Alliance exists at all is, again, due much to him."

Mother's voice was very soft. "I remember his great pride in his family most of all, his pride in me. I chose my name late in life, but eventually I, too, followed the custom of my family, and chose to be known as Natasha Quijance, for my grandfather, so that I would always remember what I owed him, as his granddaughter, and as the citizen of a free and independent nation, on a planet made safer from war."

Mother sat with her eyes downcast. There was a brief silence.

Charlie stepped forward to squat beside Mother, taking the storyknife from her hand. Sitting next to each other, they looked more like sisters than mother and daughter, both tiny, with smooth brown skin, almond-shaped brown eyes, and thick, shining, absolutely straight and absolutely black hair. The only difference was that Mother's hair was cut above her earlobes, and Charlie's reached down past her waist.

My sister raised the storyknife and scrabbled in the sand as if she were writing out a prescription; her symbols were almost illiterate. "I am Carlotta Quijance, daughter of Natasha Quijance. On my nineteenth birthday I chose the name Quijance so that I would always remember my uncle Benigno."

"Uncle Benigno cooked." Something marginally resembling a stove appeared in the sand. "That's sort of like saying the Pope practices Catholicism or Shanghai Wang plays jazz. Uncle Benigno had a two-story house on the Seldovia Slough; for anybody else in town the bottom floor would have been a warehouse for fishing gear. Not for Uncle. He turned the whole thing into a kitchen, with industrial-size freezers and refrigerators, three separate ovens, and an eight-burner stove. He taught me to cook bagoong and adobo and lumpia for Aquino Day, and to make kulich and pashka for Russian Orthodox Easter, and turkey and dressing for Thanksgiving, and corned beef and cabbage and soda bread for Saint Patrick's Day." Crabbed symbols for food, a candle, a Russian Orthodox cross, a turkey, and a harp appeared in quick succession, only to be wiped clean with a single stroke of the storyknife. "Uncle Benigno could do more with a clove of garlic than any ten Cordon Bleu chefs could do with the spice cupboard of the entire Waldorf Hotel chain at their disposal. And his rice. Steamed, fried, in sushi." Charlie closed her eyes in momentary ecstasy. "He catered parties as far away as San Francisco, but what he liked best was cooking at home, for the family, for weddings and graduations and christenings, or for no reason at all—just to assemble a group of his nearest and dearest around a table and stuff them full."

Charlie shook her head, a slight smile on her face. On the sand, a small woman symbol was drawn next to a larger, man symbol. "I grew up in his kitchen, at his elbow. He had no children of his own, and once he decided I could be trusted with a rice paddle, he taught me everything he knew." She laughed a little. "He never wrote down a recipe in his life, and he was furious with me when I taught someone outside the family how to make sweet-and-sour spareribs. He was even angrier when I chose to become a physician rather than a chef. But he forgave me in time, and cooked banquets for all my graduations." Her smile faded, her face half tender, half sad. "Uncle Benigno always smelled of fresh ginger. I loved him very much."

There was a brief pause. Mother looked at me, and I rose and moved to kneel next to her. Charlie passed over the storyknife. It was warm from Charlie's hand, from Mother's hand. The carved figures on the haft pressed into my palm as I smoothed over Charlie's hen scratches.

"I am Esther, daughter of Natasha Quijance, sister of Carlotta Quijance. My father's name was Sven Ericson." I drew the man symbol and looked up at Leif. "Sven Ericson was tall and broad-shouldered, blond and blue-eyed, fair of skin. He looked like a Viking. He looked like you."

"And like you," Leif said gravely.

I inclined my head. "Yes. And like me. And like so many Alaskans, like so many of our ancestors, Sven was an emigrant, this time from Norway. He came to Alaska and signed on a fishing boat in Seward and went around the Kenai Peninsula, picking salmon and pulling crab pots. Eventually the boat came to Seldovia. Your grandmother was on the dock. He married her the next day." I looked at Mother, and she grinned a very un-Motherlike grin. It never pained Mother to talk of Dad. Not for the first time I wished I was more like her.

"My first memory is of sitting on his lap at the wheel of his crabber, the *Kaia*. It was late at night and late in the year, with a clear sky and a calm sea, and we were right out in the middle of the Gulf of Alaska, right in the lap of the Mother of Storms herself." I drew the kayak symbol and the sea symbol beneath it, and closed my eyes, the better to remember.

"You couldn't see anything but stars everywhere you turned. It was during the Geminid meteor shower, a meteor a minute. I didn't know what it was at first—I thought the sky was falling. Dad told me that our Earth was only one shore of a universal sea, and not to be afraid to catch the spray on my face."

I opened my eyes and looked at my daughter. "You come by your interest in astronomy honestly, Paddy. Your grandfather knew each and every star by name, their constellations, the Greek legends behind most of them. He taught them to me." I drew the Big Dipper and Polaris. "He taught me how to fish for salmon and for king crab in the Gulf. He taught me seamanship, from bowknots to red right returning. I know it was in his mind that I would step into his shoes when he was ready to retire, but he wasn't angry when I went into construction instead. He just kept on fishing. It was what he did. He was high boat in the Gulf for the last five years of his life.

"Then, in 1996, the *Kaia* went down off Dutch Harbor in an October storm. He went down with her." I reversed the kayak and water symbols so that the kayak symbol was beneath the three wavy lines.

I paused again. "I remember his laughter best of all, a deep, roaring belly laugh that seemed to shake the *Kaia* right down to her trim line. I still miss hearing it. I still miss him. At my naming I chose the name Svensdotter, so that I would be known as Sven's daughter, in his honor, and to keep the memory of him alive for as long as I live."

I swept the sand smooth and lay the storyknife on the tray, the hilt facing Leif. Mother said, "You have chosen today as your naming day, Leif. Have you chosen your name as well?"

"I have, Emaa," he said, very young, very dignified. He extended his hands, palms up, and into them Mother placed the storyknife. I saw his surprise at its smooth texture, his appreciation of its rich weight. He grasped the handle and began to draw, awkwardly at first. I was watching the tip of the knife score the sand when his first words registered. My head shot up and I stared at him with my mouth open.

"My mother's name is Esther Svensdotter, but she hates the name Esther the same way Auntie Charlie hates Carlotta, so everybody calls her Star. 'Star' is what Esther means, and it's sort of where she lives"—he stole a glance at my face—"and she's sort of the color of a red dwarf right now"—there was a burst of laughter, quickly smothered—"so I guess it fits."

My eyes dropped to the tray and the knife and my son's hands, and fixed there. The shaky but recognizable symbol for star filled the top of the tray of sand. Around it Leif drew the house symbol.

"I'm a Petri kid. You all know the song, 'born in a Petri dish, behind a Bunsen burner, in the lab on a Sunday afternoon.' Emaa fixed things so that Star would leave an egg on Terra when she took over at Terranova, and then Emaa finagled a donor for the sperm"—Leif skated smoothly over his father's identity—"and then she mixed them both together in a Petri dish, and here I am."

The smile in his voice encouraged us to join in his amusement. "Emaa raised me on Terra, and Star didn't know anything about me until we came out to the Belt. So I didn't meet my mother until I was ten." I could feel him looking at me. "I'd heard about her, though. Everybody had.

"Star Svensdotter built the track for the SuperShot from Anchorage to Nome, to connect up with what would have been the Siberian Express across the Bering Strait. She brought on line the first offshore oil field in the Navarin Basin. She oversaw the construction of Copernicus Base on Luna, and the Helios Early Warning System of solar satellites. She built Terranova, the space habitat in Terran orbit at Lagrange Point Five, practically with her bare hands. She led the One-Day Revolution to victory, and she held our first E.T. dialogue with the Librarians. In her spare time she skated in the Anchorage Olympics"—something resembling a duck on an ironing board appeared—"married Caleb Mbele O'Hara, and mothered three children, two of which she actually knew about." There was more laughter as Leif drew three child symbols, two male and one female. "Star Svensdotter has packed more living into fifty-nine years than most of us could into five hundred. It probably makes me more tired to talk about it than it did her to live it."

Leif drew the flat edge of the storyknife across the sand and paused. "Shall I tell you her secret?" He looked around the room. "She never gives up."

That was a lie, but only he and I knew it.

"Weather almost took out Navarin One a dozen times. During construction of Terranova she was the number one target for assassination on every Luddite terrorist's list. The American Alliance bureaucracy tried to subvert the construction of Copernicus Base and Terranova, and when they failed, the Space Patrol invaded and took over Terranova. Star took it right back. She never quit. I don't think she ever even slowed down. She had a dream, and she followed it to its end, and she didn't let anything stand in her way. It's because of Star Svensdotter that we're sitting here tonight, one point eight astronomical units out from Terra, celebrating a custom inaugurated three planets and three hundred years away."

I could feel him looking at me. I still couldn't meet his eyes. "I want to be like that. I want to live my life that way. I don't want to ever give up, I don't want to ever stop trying."

His voice firmed and rose. "I am Leif, grandson of Natasha Quijance, nephew of Carlotta Quijance, son of Star Svensdotter. I choose to be called Starsson, so that I will be known as Star's son all of my life, to remind all who know me that I wear my name in her honor, and to remind myself that my reach should always exceed my grasp."

I looked up just in time to see him return the storyknife to Mother, who sheathed it, and whose cheeks were wet when she rose to recognize and embrace him. "Leif Starsson."

Charlie, too, was weeping. "Leif Starsson."

Paddy and Sean and Alexei pushed up and were embraced in their turn. He kissed Axenia's cheek; Crip and Simon wrung his hand; Roger Lindbergh and Perry Austin and John, Joseph, and James Smith, Maggie Lu and John Begaye, all pressed forward to congratulate Leif in their turn. They were all shaken by the ceremony, but then guests always were, and in this place, millions of kilometers from home and family, it was especially moving.

No less so for me. I waited for the crowd to thin before stepping forward, face to face with my son. He was so tall, so straight. Steel-true and blade-straight. "Leif Starsson," I said. "You do me too much honor."

"Your name lends honor to me, Star Svensdotter," he replied, equally formal.

I embraced him. "You didn't tell me."

He hugged me so hard my ribs creaked. When had he gotten so tall and so strong? "I wanted to surprise you. Emaa knew, and her feelings aren't hurt, if you're worried about that. She understands."

I wished I did. I turned to the face the crowd. "Ladies and gentlemen, at this point the ceremony ends and the celebration begins. Charlie's laid on a spread that has to be seen to be believed. Eat, drink, and be merry."

I felt a nudge in the small of my back and turned to see Helen with a drink in each hand. "Way ahead of you, Star."

"Thanks, Helen."

She nodded at Leif, back to holding hands with the still unknown brunette. "That was quite a testimonial."

"He would have done better to take Mother's name."

"He didn't think so."

Her unshakable certainty annoyed me, and I said, "Let's hit the food before it's all gone, shall we?"

Charlie's table was laid with what passed on Outpost for linen and crystal, every plate, bowl, and pot filled to overflowing. As I heaped my plate Charlie came bustling up, beaming all across her duplicitous face, and said, or rather gushed, "Star, you know John Begaye, don't you? Would you steer him through the entrees? He doesn't know his way around Filipino cuisine yet." She bestowed a dazzling smile upon the two of us, somehow managed to insert my hand through the crook of John's arm, and bustled off.

Two things occurred to me simultaneously.

One, that John Begaye was male and unattached.

Two, that this time I really was going to kill my sister.

Simon, who is not a genius for nothing, headed straight for the bar. "Would anyone like a drink?"

"I think I would," John Begaye said.

"Attaboy. Scotch okay? Steve just brewed up a new batch."

"Scotch sounds fine."

"Water?"

John looked at me. "Neat."

"Me, too."

I bestowed a dazzling smile of my own in their general direction, discreetly reclaimed my hand, and doubled the amount of food on my plate. If I kept my mouth full, I might be able to keep myself from biting a chunk out of Charlie's ass.

The evening progressed, the conversation the usual mixture of business and pleasure, SOP when you live where you work and your work is your life. "We've received an inquiry from a group of bioengineers on Terra, Star," Ari reported. "They want to commission a World, and Archy says their credit rating—"

"A-one, boss!" chirped my communit. You couldn't beat Archy away from a party with a stick. It was, he had informed me once, an ideal opportunity to brush up on his social skills. It certainly increased his vocabulary.

"—is A-one," Ari repeated patiently.

"Do I hear a 'but' in there somewhere?"

He nodded. "They want their world to be absolutely antiseptic when they move in. No possibility of bacteriological contamination from anyone or anything but what they bring on board themselves."

"Are we having fun yet?" I said. "Neatniks of Terra, unite and move off-planet. Can we do it?"

We argued about it for a while, and decided we could do it but we wouldn't. "Sterile suiting for everybody who works inside? Decontam for every tool? Forget it," Maggie said.

Charlie snuck up behind me and cooed in my ear. "And how are we all? Everybody have enough food? John, you need a refill. Star, get him a refill."

A blunt instrument. A big, heavy, blunt instrument. No Outpost jury would ever convict. I got up and refilled John's drink. He thanked me profusely, until Simon's elbow in his ribs shut him up.

"Dear," Mother said, "we're having some difficulty with the miners on 6666Lucifer. They say they've found evidence of some kind of pre-disintegration religious icons, and if they let us come down for surveying and core sampling we'll be desecrating a shrine. They're saying they'll shoot on sight."

"Infidels beware," Simon said cheerfully.

Crip said, "We're getting the same kind of noise from the Save the Rocks League."

I caught sight of the expressions on the twins' faces, a kind of dreamy expectation, and wondered apprehensively what it meant.

Ari groaned. "Oh Christ, what're they up to now?"

"Not Christ, but the local equivalent. Brother Moses." Crip scratched his shaved head. "As near as I can figure, he's kind of absorbed the Promethean sect into his movement."

"What the hell is a Promethean sect when it's at home?"

"What is this crap?" I demanded. "Prometheus doesn't exist any longer, if it ever did. All we've got to show for it or them, or whatever the hell used to be in this orbit, are the remnants of a fuel storage facility, a couple of debatable artifacts that might once have been used to hold somebody's soup, maybe, and seventeen different theories about how the Asteroid Belt might once have been a planet." I avoided looking at Helen, who was being remarkably reticent and self-effacing. "We haven't uncovered any graven images so far as I know, let alone any evidence of organized religion."

Crip shrugged. "Tell that to the guys on Lucifer. All I know is Brother Moses is starting to figure Promethean deities prominently in his revival meetings."

"What Promethean deities!" From the corner of my eye I saw the twins become even more Sphinxlike.

Charlie joined us, pushing in between Simon and me, and in the process shoving me up against John and very nearly into his chicken adobo.

Speech trembled on the tip of my tongue but Crip beat me to it. "This isn't World business," he said, one wary eye on Charlie and the other on me, "but while we're all here—"

"Yes?" I said, my spine straight, my words clipped. "What is it?"

"We're getting crowded, Star. Outpost needs more room."

"Like how much more room?"

He looked at Simon, and Simon nodded. "I'd say go for broke and build on a second wheel, connected by axle to the first."

"The original wheel's getting a little shabby, too," Simon added. "If we're going to expand, we might as well do some R&M to the original station as well, get it all done with at once."

"Is Terranova going to sit still for a slowdown in World production?" Maggie asked. "Or, God forbid, an interruption in ore delivery, while Outpost adds on?"

I looked at Helen, who everyone seemed to have forgotten was there. "We'll start it up and tell them about it after, the way we usually do," I said. "We're on the spot, we know what's needed. If the work on Outpost begins to interfere with World production or ore shipment, hire on temps."

"With what?"

"With what we always hire them on with." Simon made a gesture that vaguely indicated a geodome down the rim from us. "A walk in Central Park." He hooked a thumb in the opposite direction. "A kilo of Outpost Kona Coffee." He waved his hands in the air in an all-inclusive gesture. "Free membership in the Outpost library."

"Free?" I said with revulsion.

"Get John some of that long rice, Star," Charlie purred. "I don't think he's tried it yet." She leaned around me. "Doesn't Star look nice in blue, John? That shade matches her eyes perfectly, don't you think?"

"Pretty good all right," John, who was no dummy, said through stiff lips.

"The League of Saint Joseph's talking strike," Ari said desperately.

Simon swore. "We just gave those damn riggers their third raise in eighteen months. What do they want, blood?"

"I think they want to stay home and have us mail them their checks."

The evening was almost saved when Charlie brought out coffee and the chocolate cheese mousse. She must have spent the last week down in the galley. The mousse was topped with whipped cream and a piece of bittersweet chocolate. When the first spoonful slid over my tongue, my irritation began to fade, and with the last bite I relaxed. Charlie might live to see morning after all.

Whereupon Charlie batted her eyelashes at John, whose expression indicated he was hoping for a massive explosive decompression event anywhere on Outpost, preferably within the next thirty seconds. "I don't know if I happened to mention it, John, but the twins are staying here tonight."

Charlie was saved only from certain death by the door sliding back and a breathless Renee Rothschild erupting into the room. "Star!"

Her alarm pulled me to my feet. "What?" Visions of the carnage at Dock 4 ran through my head. "What's wrong?"

She paused, panting. "Brother Moses is down at Piazzi City, calling for your head."

I looked at her, around the room. "So what else is new?"

There were a few chuckles, but Renee wasn't smiling. "It's not funny, Star; they've got weapons on their sleds and they're rounding up as many crazies as they can get to come up here and kill you!"

Blankly, I said, "Why?"

She looked me straight in the eye and said earnestly, "He's green, and he says you did it."

Surely I hadn't heard right. "He's what?"

She lost patience with me. "He's green! Brother Moses is green!"

I stared at her. She was dead serious. I couldn't help it, I started to laugh.

"No, Star, I mean he's really *green*—skin, teeth, beard, and everything in between—and Nora at Maggie's says *everything* in between, if you know what she means." She added, "It might just be reflection, but I think the whites of his eyes are going next. Everyone who's eaten or drunk anything on 55Pandora during the past week, all of them are turning green. Brother Moses says it has to be you trying to discredit his congregation. He says this has to be how you're getting back at him for the Save the Rocks League's interference with the latest ore shipments."

I gaped at her stupidly and she grabbed me and shook me. "Star, I'm telling you Brother Moses is down there arming for Armageddon! You've got to do something!"

Somewhere deep inside, a penny rolled down a chute and dropped with a firm, solid click into the right slot. Hydroponics. Mom and Pop. "Clap if you believe in kobolds."

My head, manipulated by an invisible wire, swiveled until I was staring directly at Paddy and Sean, sitting side by side against the wall. A Paddy and Sean who had abandoned the now passé look in Sphinx for the latest in seraphim, cherubim, and thrones. "Gosh, that was great adobo, Auntie Charlie," Sean said brightly. "May I have some more, please?"

Mute, Paddy held out her plate, too.

I took a deep breath. "Okay," I said. John Begaye backed up a step.

I blew the breath out. "That's it," I said. Even Charlie looked apprehensive.

"I quit."

I looked at Helen. "I'll go to Mars for you." I looked back at the twins. "So long as it's a package deal. The twins come, too."

The angels were abandoned to their own devices to be immediately replaced by astonishment and gathering dismay.

"I wouldn't dream of separating the three of you," Helen said, and her fleeting, ephemeral smile slid out of the room as quickly and unobtrusively as it had slid in.

—3—

Soft-Shoe Shuttle

Once more, once more, to go to sea once more
A man must be blind to make up his mind
To go to sea once more.

—old sea chanty

I felt more like Spam in a can than the god in the machine.

"How we doing, Crip?" He didn't reply at once. "Crip?"

"In a minute, dammit."

"What's the matter with you?" I demanded. "In thirty years and a kazillion launches, I've never heard you this edgy." He mumbled something, probably uncomplimentary. "What was that?"

"Hold on," he said testily. "I gotta make a course correction."

"What? Why? I thought we were plugged into insertion."

He didn't answer, and I waited, strapped into my deceleration couch, which on Mars would be my bed, and stared at the opposite bulkhead, which on Mars would be the ceiling of my stateroom. In a few moments Crip came back

59

on. "Friggin' IMU, nothing's worked right this trip. It's the goddam Great Galactic Ghoul, is what it is!"

Great Galactic Ghoul? "I beg your pardon?"

There was a pause. When Crip spoke again he sounded sheepish. "Sort of a legend around these parts. There's a history of spaceships going out of control on approach to Mars."

"So?"

"So it's sort of a Bermuda Triangle in vacuum. Spacers made up the Great Galactic Ghoul to account for the disappearing ships."

And disappearing ships' crews? I wondered, but didn't say. "You're the last person I figured to be superstitious, Crip."

"Superstitious my ass, Svensdotter," he snapped, "Mariner 4 had control problems, so did Mariner 7; Mariner 9's navigational system went haywire, fourteen Russian probes failed both orbit and/or touchdown; no one has ever found so much as a single nut off Fobos 1 or 2, and you want to tell me what happened to the Observer, the *Newton*, and the *Sagdeyev*?"

"I don't know," I said meekly.

"Nobody does," he said, triumphant.

I'd heard worse. I'd even heard dumber. I kept my mouth shut and let Crip stave off the efforts of the Great Galactic Ghoul to put a spin on our tail.

It had been a short, uneventful trip, thirty days door to doorstep, and now Crip and the twins and I had withdrawn to our respective ships; the twins and I to wait out the interval, Crip to perform all the minute, finicking, down-to-the-wire corrections in our vernier-assisted trajectory that would, hopefully, insert us into the Martian atmosphere at the proper angle.

I wasn't worried. Crip always got me from point to point in one piece. As sure as I was lying there, staring at the soon-to-be ceiling, he was sweating and swearing over the console in the *Pushmepullyou*, coaxing that little bit of extra thrust out of Starboard Vernier Number 23 that would make the difference between popping our drogue over Chryse

Planitia or, the way the planets were lined up that afternoon, the Huyghens Rift on Titan. Well, eventually Titan, long after any of us would be in any shape to appreciate it.

Not that I was worried about it.

"Sixty seconds to beacon detach," Crip said.

That meant we were right on top of Phobos. I counted the seconds down with him.

"—three, two, one, beacon away."

There was the distant thud of explosive bolts. The craft shuddered once. I waited, tense. Landing the beacon in exactly the right place on Phobos was critical. It would be the *Kayak*'s only means of communication, however delayed, as well as the primary means of data relay. If it missed its mark, at our present velocity Crip had about ten minutes to change the *Pushmepullyou-Kayak*'s mind about landing us on Mars, and maybe half an hour after that to get us re-oriented for a return to Outpost. There would be no second chance at the Red Planet. This, I told Helen mentally, is what comes of planning a Mars mission in such an all-fired, jet-propelled hurry.

I knew why she'd done it, of course: I was on board. If the mission had been delayed one day more, I wouldn't have been, and she knew it.

The minutes inched by like snails. "Bulls-eye!" Crip shouted. "Beacon on target!"

"Is it transmitting?"

"Stand by one."

I glanced at the digital readout on my communit. I wasn't sure we had a minute, but they continued to crawl by, with or without my permission.

And then Crip's voice came back over the headset. "Phobos Lander 1, transmitting, loud and clear, five by five."

I felt as relieved as he sounded. "Hooray."

"First thing that's gone right since we dropkicked out of the Belt."

I said nothing. Pilots swear, avow, and attest that they want each and every flight to go by the book and by the numbers, but around the bar all they talk about is how they brought that baby home to Mama with the IMU out, half a stabilizer missing, the rest of the crew incapacitated, and the ship running on empty. Pilots are weaned on the difficult and raised on the impossible, and they sulk when everything goes right, because afterwards there is no reason to brag about how smart and capable and talented and superhuman they are. Crip would drink for free on the past thirty days for the next three hundred and sixty-five.

The ship shuddered again. "Okay," Crip said. "We just dipped into the top layer of Martian atmosphere. All secure?"

"Okay here," I said.

"Five by five," Paddy said glumly over my headset, and Sean echoed her, equally glum. "Five by."

All the graphplex ports were shielded with an ablative bumper, but I knew from countless briefings what was going on outside. The *Kayak* was bottom down, its circular hull broadside to the Martian atmosphere. The *Pushmepullyou* crouched like a hairless, metal tarantula over the toroid's doughnut hole, connected to the *Kayak* by eight spidery legs that would detach by explosive bolts when the insertion maneuver was complete. Our large flat surface optimized atmospheric drag, which would enable air friction (such as it was on Mars) to slow us down. Crip, controlling the process with small, repeated firings of the *Pushmepullyou*'s verniers, would dip us repeatedly into the atmosphere, skipping across its upper fringes like a flat rock skipping across water, our velocity decreasing with every skip. Finally, and may I add, theoretically, our speed would slow from an arrival velocity of over 33,000 kph to a little less than 20,000 kph, in preparation for orbit, insertion, and descent.

Landing on Terra took a spaceplane. Landing on Luna, all you needed were retro rockets. To land on Mars, we were using the Martian atmosphere to ease on down the road with parachutes, three of them. If they popped too soon, they would burn up in the atmosphere. In that case controlling the speed of our entry would become academic, as would our rate of ablation, as would the length of our survival. The timing was precise, as the *Pushmepullyou* had to separate soon enough to escape Martian gravity itself, and at the same time remain connected to us long enough to ensure that that same gravity had firmly captured the *Kayak*.

The designers had saved on Delta-vee by making the command module a one-holer; I would have felt better if Crip had had at bare minimum a co-pilot. My subconscious reached out for a yoke, a throttle, a brake lever, rudder pedals—anything to make believe I was in even partial control of our descent.

I wasn't worried at all.

There was no sound from the other side of the craft, so I didn't know if the twins were worried or not. At this point, they would have cheerfully ripped their tongues out at the roots before they would have told me one way or another. I thought back to the scene around the galley table four weeks before.

"How am I supposed to study astronomy from inside a balloon that is itself inside the distorting influence of a planetary atmosphere?" Paddy demanded. "I won't have access to a telescope or star charts or Sam or anything else I really need!"

"You know perfectly well that Mars' atmosphere is barely worthy of the name," I told her, "and we won't be inside the balloon, we'll be inside the gondola. As for the telescope and the charts, we each get a personal freight allowance. I'm sure you can find a telescope to fit within that allowance, and if you go over I'm willing to give you some of mine. As for Sam's classes, if you ask I'm sure he'll be glad to set up a course schedule for you. We can load it into the computer and your education will suffer no significant interruption. Pass the rice, please."

"And what about me?" Sean demanded. "I suppose Mars is just lousy with arable acreage and irrigation ditches? I suppose I write my botany thesis on the seven different species of Martian winter wheat?"

"You'll be too busy tending to our grocery list to do much writing. Your thesis will have to wait, and," I added evenly, "considering where the study of botany and hydroponics has

led you lately, a brief hiatus at this time seems appropriate."
If not imperative.

They didn't even have the grace to look ashamed. "You
want to go to Mars, go!" Paddy cried.

"Yeah, unlike you, Mom, we have lives *here*, not on
Mars."

"You will shortly," I said.

"It's not fair! I'm not going!"

"I'm not either!"

"Yes, you are."

"Mom!"

"Why?" Sean said angrily. "Why do we have to go, too?"

I chewed and swallowed, deliberately taking my time.
"Because I say you're going, and because I'm bigger, older,
and tougher than you are, which means I can make it stick.
We're going to Mars. We're leaving at the end of the month.
Start packing."

For a moment I thought Paddy was going to throw her
glass at me. For a moment I thought Sean was going to
upend the entire table in my lap. If I'd known my announce-
ment was going to start World War IV, I might have recon-
sidered.

Mother cut across the ominous silence. "My very dears,
why all this fuss? You are going to enjoy yourselves thor-
oughly, I assure you. Imagine, a whole new world to discover and explore. You'll get to see the tallest volcano and
the longest planetary rift valley in the System, you'll have
the ruins of the ancients to wander through." She examined
a lumpia closely for flaws. "Although, lacking the education
and expertise of, say, someone of my background, you will
naturally enough be unable to understand and appreciate
them as they should be understood and appreciated."

"Why don't you go with her, then," Paddy muttered.

"Perhaps because I was not invited, dear," Mother replied
in her most excruciatingly affable tone.

"Natasha," Crip said.

She raised an eyebrow. "Is it possible, Crippen dear, that
you are about to instruct me as to my behavior?" She smiled
at him.

Crip shot me a look that said clearly, *You're on your own, Star*, and buried his face in his plate.

"Star, just tell me one thing," Charlie pleaded. "Just tell me you're not going to Mars because I tried to get you laid. You aren't, are you? I mean, what kind of reason is that?"

"It's no kind of reason at all," I said. "It's probably why I'm not."

The twins brightened. "Not going to Mars?"

"Not going to Mars for that reason," I explained, and their faces fell again.

It was like that for days, degenerating into sullen silence on the part of the twins and resigned acceptance in everyone else. What little time I could spare from handing Outpost over to Simon I spent familiarizing myself with our ship and packing it when it arrived the only way it could arrive, two days late. Packing a Martian year's worth of food and supplies for three people into the gondola of a balloon discourages materialism. So does having to label every single item in the gondola with its own weight, so us aeronauts would know its value as ballast. Not that that was anything I ever wanted to need to know, as it would indicate an immediate need to lift high and fast and a deficiency of either helium and/or hot air to do the lifting with. I must have tested the floor hatch on the gondola fifty times. If I had to pitch anything over the side, that hatch was, by God, going to work.

In an average man day, the average man consumes seven kays of food, eleven kays of water, and five kays of oh-two. Some of that we'd bring with us; much of it we were going to have to grow or make. Water, I devoutly hoped, we were going to find on Mars, in the permafrost layer frozen beneath the Martian surface. To these ends we packed seeds as well as vacuum-packed entrees, stasis-H as well as decaliter jugs, atpaks as well as molecular sieves and window boxes. The gondola had graphplex windows every second bulkhead panel all the way around. As soon as I found that out I showed them to Paddy, not without a trace of smugness. Making the best of a bad situation, she immediately appropriated the science station, with its pop-out bubble, for her astronomical observatory. Sean was slower at making himself to home; I found him muttering something—I hoped not incantations—over a box of seed packets one morning. Later that day I caught him helping Roger Lindbergh doing a practice install of a window box, although he naturally quit as soon as he became aware of my presence.

Charlie kept reminding us that we would be going from Outpost's half gee to Mars' one-third, and that we'd have to boost our exercise accordingly. Simon was reprogramming the gondola's computer for the seventh or eighth time and wondering out loud why so much space had been wasted on unnecessary things like exercycles when anyone with half a brain could see that with just one more storage rack, just ten more cards, he could make the environmental program foolproof. Mother was still sulking because she hadn't been invited along, and on every inhale reminded us that she was the one who'd been on her way to Mars when we insisted she stay on at Outpost to monitor the ongoing investigation into planet Prometheus. Archy had stopped speaking to me at all except when absolutely necessary, which was better than the twins hammering at me, but not much. Between Brother Moses breathing fire and smoke up one arm of the Belt and down the other, and the nearly mutinous conditions that prevailed across the station, I was actually glad when departure day arrived.

It was awfully quiet and awfully dark, strapped to my couch, hurtling toward the Red Planet at umpteen kph. I wasn't worried, though. With Crip on the stick, what could go wrong? And if worse came to worst, I could set us down. If I could get to the *Pushmepullyou*'s cockpit in time. I'd never landed on a planet with atmosphere and thermals and winds and things, though. But I knew my way around the ship's navigation console; Helen had made sure of that long before we broke orbit for launch.

"So what do you think?" Helen's voice over the p-suit headset was proud and invited me to be, too.

The silver, gray, and black tricolor doughnut that was the Mars lander was stuck on one end of the squat, spidery launcher. The dish-shaped pressure plate brought up the rear like an apologetic afterthought. What I thought was that the Mars Viking 3 looked like a solar-celled bagel in a stelatite skirt, as well as a menace to space traffic and every space traveler within a hundred light-years. I said so.

"I knew you'd love her," Helen said. "Let's grab a scooter and get up close and personal."

Up close and personal some of the rivets connecting the two vehicles of this Rube Goldberg nightmare were already beginning to back off. I pointed this out. "Just the wrapping on the package," Helen said soothingly. "Lock us on to the access hatch on the launcher and I'll show you around the inside."

Inside, Helen shucked out of her suit and went down the corridor that circumnavigated the hole of the doughnut, me on her tail. She pulled herself inside a room. "Communications and navigation. CommNav."

"Oh. So this is the control panel."

"Yup."

The high-back chair in front of the panel was still swathed in a packing sheet that crackled when I strapped myself in.

I scanned the gauges. "What the hell is a variometer?"

"Tells you your velocity up and down."

"Rate of climb."

"Yes."

"Then why doesn't it say so?" I searched further. "There's no compass."

"There's no magnetic field on Mars, or none to speak of."

"Right," I said, chagrined. "I remember now. All the better to kill us with ultraviolet radiation. So we're only going to know where we are at night?"

"Always supposing you have a clear sky," Helen agreed, "and are close to a geographical landmark you have plotted on the PlanetView."

I sat back and rubbed my eyes. "Does Mars have a pole star?"

"Deneb, but I think it's a couple degrees off true."

"Wonderful." Math was never my strong point; looking through a scope made me squint and see double, and back at astrogation class in Maria Mitchell I got lost between Hercules and the Pleiades more times than I would ever admit. A navigator, I wasn't.

"Paddy will be with you," Helen reminded me. "She's been better on a scope since she was five than you ever were in your life."

Helen was always such a comfort to me. "What's this?"

"Helium pressure inside the charliere. There's a He-maker mounted inside the charliere's throat; it should kick on automatically when the sensors show a depletion."

"And if they don't?"

"They will; they're backed up five times, and if it comes to it you can climb up inside the envelope with a sniffer"— Helen jerked her thumb towards a locker mounted next to the door—"and check it out in person. Same system for the montgolfier."

"And this red toggle?"

"That's your transponder, your emergency locater beacon. That's how you yell for help."

I looked at her. "We better not need help very bad, since it'd take an average minimum of two weeks for you just to get the word."

Unabashed, she said, "There's one on the hull, too. And here's fire extinguisher remotes, and these are the controls for the deflation port and the jibs."

I surveyed the array of knobs and gauges before me. "You know, Helen," I said slowly, "this is the first time I've realized that I'm going to be setting down on Mars in a vehicle of whose operation I have only the most rudimentary understanding. I'm not much more than an adequate pilot at the best of times, and that's on solar sleds and jitneys. What do I know about balloons?"

Helen waved an airy hand. "What's to know? The launcher injects the craft into the atmosphere, the drogue chutes pop the envelopes, and the Martian winds do the rest. All you have to do is sit back and enjoy the ride. And take pictures and keep a log," she added as an afterthought.

Somehow I just knew it wasn't going to be that easy.

Into the darkness, into the silence, I said, "Crip?" He didn't reply at once. "Crip?"

His voice snarled over my headset like a bad-tempered cat. "Whaddya want? I'm a little busy at the moment."

"You'll tell me, won't you? When we hit air? You won't just let us go without saying anything?"

"Svensdotter, sit back, shut up, and stop worrying. We're in the pipe. You'll be a flatlander again before you know it."

Nope. I wasn't worried. I was the head of an expedition with the full influence and considerable resources of the independent nation of Terranova at my disposal. Helen Ricadonna was behind me one hundred percent; I could almost feel her hand pushing at the small of my back. I had a crackerjack pilot and a taut ship with a proud name. What was there to worry about?

The night before launch Charlie threw a party. Everything had happened so fast and we were all so tired that it felt more like a wake.

"She still needs a name," Crip said, looking at me.

"Call her the *Kayak*," Leif suggested. "After Emaa Katya's boat."

"That sounds nice, dear," Mother said, nodding. "Sean? Paddy? What do you think?"

"I don't care," Paddy said.

"Call it whatever you want," Sean said.

"Esther, dear? What do you think?"

Emaa Katya made it to shore with one kid out of three. At this point the prospect of losing one or both of the twins was very appealing. "Sold."

And the *Kayak* she was.

She shuddered a third time, and I wished again for an unshielded window to see out of. Re-entry is always spectacular; it's the only time the moth gets to fly inside the candle flame and survive. The controlled erosion of our shield made a comet's tail of ionized particles and ablative material that, if you were its cause for being, put Comet Halley to shame.

Another bump, harder than the previous ones. "What the hell?" Crip said suddenly over my headset.

Now I was nervous. "Crip?"

A string of curses that sounded as if they were delivered from between clenched teeth was my reply.

There was a ripping, tearing, terrifying *cree-aaack*! from above, and a corresponding *thud* that sounded dull and deep from below—and the bumps starting coming, irregularly and all at once. I jiggled up and down in my restraints. From the other side of the craft one of the twins cried out. "Mom?"

"Mom, this isn't supposed to be happening!"

"Crip! What the hell's going on?"

Our only answer was a steadily building roar outside the bulkhead. There was a series of sharp *pops*! and then the separate bumps came harder and faster and closer together until they merged into one long vibration that rattled my teeth and forced tears from my eyes. Something broke free from its fastening on a wall across the cabin; I heard it clanking against something else, but my vision was so blurred I couldn't see what it was.

"Mom! What's happening!"

"I don't know! Stay strapped in!" *Oh shit oh dear oh shit*, but those last words were under my breath and strictly for my own edification.

The vibration increased, so that it seemed the *Kayak* was shaking apart around our ears, reducing us all to a state of speechless endurance. I was too scared to wonder if we were going to die. I lay where I was because there was nothing else to do, my hands knotted into the restraints, trying by sheer willpower to bring us safely down.

I don't know how long it lasted. It felt like days and was probably only seconds. When we finally broke through, there was one long, blessed moment of absolute silence, followed by a sinking feeling that increased to a fall and then to a plunge the likes of which I hadn't felt since taking wing from Orville Point back on Terranova.

"Mom!"

"Stay strapped in!" I yelled.

There were one, two, three more cracks, then another and, thank God, final jerk that jarred my teeth together.

"It's okay," I called. "Hear that?" The shrill waHOO of the drogue release siren echoed across the craft. "The drogues are out. We're inside, we've hit atmosphere."

I've never felt anything as good as the moment my deceleration couch hit me in the fanny and the *Kayak*'s plummeting descent first stalled and then, after a nearly motionless, midair pause, resumed in a much slower, steadier fashion. I've always liked slow in spaceflight; it makes for a longer trip but a softer landing.

We were well and truly captured by Mars' gravity; enough so that I could sit up, unstrap, and drop both feet to the floor and expect them to stay down. I stood up. My legs were shaky but they held.

The *Kayak*'s motion was odd, and it took me a moment to remember that we were swinging in simple harmonic motion at the bottom of our pendulum at the end of the drogues' vertical load lines. I wondered what our altitude was, and when the pressure-triggered explosive bolts would deploy the montgolfier. As if my thought triggered it, the bolts went off, it felt like right over my head, in a series of controlled explosions, one right after another, sounding like a 21-gun salute. There was a queer hissing sound and the floor hit the bottom of my feet and almost knocked me over. The *Kayak* swung hard and the floor tilted up behind me. I took a running step forward and in the dark tripped over a bulkhead panel that had shaken loose during our descent. The *Kayak* swung hard again and I danced around, grabbing futilely for something to hold on to. The only thing my clutching hands grabbed was air. I fell, heavily. The gondola swung hard in the opposite direction, and I slid rapidly across the floor and slammed into a bulkhead. "Ouch! Dammit!"

"Mom! Are you okay?"

The first thing my hand touched turned out to be the door into CommNav. I grasped the frame in both hands and pulled myself through with an assist from the pendulum. The pendulum swung like a pendulum do, and I slid rapidly and ignominiously across the floor of CommNav to collide with the bolted-in base of the console seat. "Shit!"

"Mom? What's the matter?"

I had to wait until the little blue cartoon birds stopped flying formation around my head before I could heave myself up into the console.

As soon as the seat cushion felt my weight, the instrument panel lit up, bathing me and the room in a red and green but mostly yellow glow. The green came from the montgolfier deploy, the red from the locater beacon, and the mostly yellow from all the *Kayak* systems on standby.

"Mom?"

"It's okay, Sean!" I yelled. "I'm in CommNav! Stay where you are until this thing settles down!"

"I don't think it's ever going to settle down," Paddy said sourly from the opposite doorway, "and it's me, anyway."

"Dammit, Paddy, I told you to stay put! Strap in!"

"There's only one seat in here," she pointed out.

I swore. "Then stay where you are and hang on!"

The *Kayak* swung back in the opposite direction, but I noticed the arc was not as wide. The return swing was shorter, too. Paddy, mindful as always of my age and authority, waited for the middle of the next arc and took three quick, short steps to clutch at the back of the chair. At the same time, somewhere behind us, something started with a whir. Another waHOO sounded, which I quickly silenced with a hard smack of one hand, and another light flashed green in front of me.

"The He-maker's on," Paddy pointed out unnecessarily.

"Uh-huh. Means the charliere's deployed and inflating." Another light blinked green. "And the legs are extending. Looks like everything's working. Everything important, anyway."

"So far," Paddy said skeptically. "I thought Crip said our entry was going to be smoother than decel in the scout. It felt more like we were riding inside a jackhammer in a silver mine on 2Vesta."

"Let's see if we can find out why." I punched up the standby net and raised my voice. "*Kayak* calling *Pushmepullyou*, *Kayak* calling the *Pushmepullyou*. Crip, you out there somewhere?"

The only reply was a burst of static. I repeated. More static. I called again. Again, static—in bursts, interspersed with dead air.

"Mom?"

"What?"

"Listen." Paddy was frowning, her dark blue eyes fixed on the squawk box.

"To what?"

"That static. It's—I don't know, it sounds almost metered, like . . ."

"It's CW," Sean said from the door. At our blank looks he elaborated. "You know. Morse code. Dit dah."

"You read Morse?"

"Dit-dit-dit, dah-dah-dah, dit-dit-dit," said my son.

"What's that?"

"SOS. That's about all I know in Morse. Seems appropriate right now."

"Great," I said again. Well, I used to know Morse in another life. I swiveled back to the console and concentrated. Sean was right. Now that I knew what I was listening for, I could hear the rhythm in the bursts of static. Dit-dah-dah-dit, dit-dah-dah-dit, dah, dah-dah-dah, dah-dit-dah, dah-dit-dah. "P, P again, T, O—that's easy—K this time, K again. Okay, PP is probably *Pushmepullyou*, KK is *Kayak*. What the hell is TO?"

"To?" Paddy suggested. "As in *Pushmepullyou* to *Kayak*?"

The same code sequence repeated itself, once, twice. "If he's sending CW, that must mean his transmitter is knocked out. Or our receiver." I didn't care for that idea. "Maybe his receiver's still up." I punched in the standby net. "Crip, this is Star. Can you hear us? Is that you sending CW?"

The code sequence continued for a moment. Then it was abruptly interrupted by a series of dah-dit-dah-dit dah-dah-dit-dahs. I blew out a relieved breath. "CQ back at you, buddy. Is your voice transmitter out?" Dit-dah, dit-dit-dah-dit. "A, F? Affirmative? Okay, stand by one, I'm going to switch in the translator." I reached across the control panel and accessed the computer. "*Kayak* computer, boot up."

There was a long silence. The hair on my neck stood straight up. I re-entered the code and said sharply, "*Kayak* computer, boot up."

There was another silence, broken by a tinny voice from the ceiling pickup. "*Kayak* computer, on line. Voice ID, Star Svensdotter, access all programs. Proceed."

My sigh of relief nearly took out a bulkhead. "Computer, run communications program."

"Running."

"Analyze incoming transmission and translate into System English."

There was a brief, almost ruminative silence. "Transmission is broadcasting in Morse code."

"We know that, what's it say?"

"Unable to comply with that command."

"You can't read it?"

"This unit equipped to communicate in System English and Russian only."

I said blankly, "You can recognize Morse but you can't translate it?"

"Affirmative."

"I have said it thrice; what I tell you three times is true," Sean remarked.

"Just not in Morse," Paddy agreed.

"Thank you, Helen Ricadonna, you cheap bitch," I said furiously, forgetting for the moment the reasons behind our hurried departure, and my audience.

"That command is not recognized. Please rephrase."

"I miss Archy already," Paddy said.

"Computer off," I said. I pulled my chair down the panel to the keyboard and switched on the screen. "Crip, you still there? Okay. Our computer isn't equipped with a translator. My code's rusty, so send slow. What the hell happened?"

He transmitted, I tapped out the message on the keyboard,

and it appeared on the screen. His fist wasn't the cleanest I'd ever heard and it took a while to get the rhythm, but the message was short, succinct, and chilling. We'd suffered a sudden, unexplained course change—he might have said two, but I wasn't sure. The timer on the explosive bolts had triggered prematurely. The *Pushmepullyou* had let the *Kayak* go too soon, and the command module had only just managed to insert us into the Martian atmosphere.

I exchanged glances with the twins. Neither of them looked as scared as I thought they should. "So where are we?"

On Mars, was the increasingly faint reply.

"Thank you, Crip. And not quite. Where on Mars?"

Don't know. Gotta go. Time for course correction. Love. Bye.

"Wait! Crip! Where are we coming down? Crip? Crip, are you there?"

There was a final burst of static. Dah-dit-dah, the letter K, the standard EOT for ham operators. And then, nothing.

"Crip?"

Dead air was my reply.

Nothing echoes like an empty radio net, except maybe a train whistle or a cathedral with no choir. From now, for the next year Martian and two years Terran, our only communication with Outpost would be on two-week delay, bounced off the beacon on Phobos. Which meant that until we reached the surface of Mars and made contact with the archaeologists at Cydonia, we were essentially mute.

This time when the *Kayak* thumped, she thumped down hard enough to make my stomach lift up into my throat and knock both twins off their feet. She rose up on one side, and for one terrible moment I was afraid she was going over. We hung there for too long, as if she were making up her mind, until with a queer sighing sound she began to fall back. It was the twins' turn to slide across the floor, as I rode my chair with the grim determination of a bronc rider at the Calgary Stampede.

Whumpf! Down she came. She rocked once, up off the opposite side, and settled back, into a position that had her listing heavily, maybe 15 degrees off horizontal.

There was some creaking as the structure settled around us, then silence.

Releasing my death grip on the console, I took a deep breath.

The ablation panel covering the CommNav port fell off.

Just fell off, as if the air pressure caused by the rate of our descent had been the only thing holding it on in the first place.

Just fell off, as if the thump down had been the last straw.

Just fell off.

And wasn't it lucky that the graphplex panel in the port beneath it held. The compartment was flooded with bright pink light and my eyes instinctively narrowed against it. Someone's breath sucked in but I was already in motion, up and out of the chair and through the door into the companionway that circled the inside of the doughnut and housed the equipment lockers. The floor tilted in that direction and I tripped and started to slide, picking up speed as I went. There was nothing to grab hold of, nothing between me and the lockers except a slick floor, and I smashed into them with a crash that resounded around the ship.

"Mom? What are you doing?"

Locker doors crashed open one after another until I found the right one. "Sean! Paddy! Out here on the double and into your suits!"

The twins slid into view, their palms smacking into the lockers, eyes wide with alarm. "Mom, what—"

"Move it! Into those suits! Hustle! NOW!"

The barked command galvanized them and they leaned up against the bulkhead and climbed into the white suits, stamping their feet into the attached boots, shoving their hands into the gauntlets, pulling the clear bubbles of the helmets forward over their heads. With rough hands I locked their helmets down, ran the zips on the front of the suits up until the twins choked on them, and sealed the zipper flaps. I spun them around one at a time, so fast they staggered and almost fell on the tilted floor, and checked the life support packs built across the shoulders of the suits. One was running a tad rich in nitrogen; I adjusted a valve on one of the tanks mounted horizontally below the pack. When the last checklight on the second pack flashed a steady green, I took my first real breath in five minutes.

I climbed into my own suit and turned so one of the twins could check my pack to see how long I was going to keep breathing. A fist knocked less than politely on my helmet and a gloved finger pointed at my ear. I chinned on the helmet's headset, and the blast of indignant sound had me reaching hastily for the volume knob on the back of my left gauntlet.

"What's going on, Mom? Why did we suit up? Are we going outside?"

"Pipe down, I'm not deaf. What's going on is the ablation shield fell off the CommNav port. The *Kayak* appears to be disintegrating around our ears. We suited up in case she does. And, yes, we're going outside, to see if there's any other damage."

A ruminative silence. One of the twins said slowly, "I thought the shields were supposed to come off."

"Come off, yes. Fall off, no."

The suit locker faced the hatch. In spite of all the time I'd spent practicing on it back at Outpost, the tilting floor made leverage difficult, to say the least. I was wishing for a crowbar when it finally popped.

I wedged myself inside, retaining just enough ease of motion to hit the switch that rotated me to the exterior of the hull. I broke seal and grabbed a handhold to haul myself out again, dangling feet downward in the center of the craft. That there was a hole told me that the telltales on the CommNav panel weren't lying and that the envelopes had deployed, but hanging from the hatch I couldn't get my head back far enough in my helmet to see. Enough light came through the material of the envelopes to observe that the inside of the hole looked solid enough. The hull's ablative shield was still in place, stretched across the bottom so that the ground wasn't visible.

"Mom! Can we come out?"

I activated the lock, and while it was rotating back, felt around for the locker that held the rope ladder. By the time the lock had rotated a second time, I had the locker open. One swift tug and the ladder was unrolling swiftly, to fall with a sullen thud against the shield. Two white-suited figures emerged from the lock to cling to handholds.

They looked at me, waiting. "The hell with it," I muttered, and jumped.

I'm 193 centimeters tall and built sturdy. Back on Terra, back about a hundred years, I would have weighed 170 pounds. On Terranova, I would have weighed the same, but in kays. On Luna, I weighed a sixth that. On Outpost, half. On Mars, a third.

On Mars, a third was enough. The shield gave with a smart snap; I had a split second to feel it fall out from under me and a nanosecond to enjoy weightlessness before my heels hit and the rest of me followed, hard, smack down on my butt.

"*Oooff.*" My breath expelled on a startled whoof.

Something hit my helmet with a slithery thunk and I yelped and dove out of the way. It was only the rope ladder, which rolled out a good twenty-five centimeters short of the surface of the shield, now lying flat on the ground in several crisped pieces.

Someone giggled.

I got to my feet and felt gingerly for broken bones. The only apparent injury was to my matronly dignity, which couldn't afford it.

"Can we come down now?" someone demanded.

"Stand by one."

"Mom!"

"Stand by one," I repeated, and walked over to the *Kayak*'s nearest leg. The pink glow of the Martian horizon was enticing. Something about its shape bothered me, but it would have to wait while I focused on the essentials. The *Kayak* hunched over one leg like a dog lifting hers, but all three legs were fully extended into landing position and firmly imbedded in the surface, the crossbars down and locked. For all her rakish tilt, she wasn't going anywhere.

When I was sure the ship wasn't going to fall on the twins the instant they stepped foot on the ground, I went back to the rope ladder and laid hold of it with both hands. "Okay, one at a time." I bent backward and watched one white-suit launch itself from the side of the doughnut hole to the ladder. "Careful, dammit!"

Paddy jumped down next to me, bouncing once before catching her balance. Sean positively scampered down the ladder, landing between us. I turned them around to check their readouts one more time before they wriggled free to dash out onto the surface of a new world.

They were brought up short just beyond the edge of the *Kayak*'s hull, no less short than myself, a step behind them.

The sky was a hazy salmon pink. The ground was rust-red, but there all expectation ended.

"Holy cow, Mom," one of the twins whispered.

"We're in a lot of trouble," the other agreed.

Our scheduled landing site had been Callirrhoes Sinus, a nice boring piece of flat real estate to the north and west of Cydonia, and from concentrated perusal of all the pictures transmitted over the years by various Terran, Lunar, and Terranovan probes, I was pretty sure this wasn't it.

The surrounding landscape wasn't boring and it sure as hell wasn't flat. We had come down in what appeared to be the exact center of a narrow canyon. Its head was lost behind the *Kayak* in a supple twist of ridge. We were facing its mouth, a gaping grin of canyon walls a hundred kilometers in front of us. Beyond that grin, an edge dropped off into another, larger canyon, a canyon running perpendicular to ours whose distant opposite wall shelved abruptly into a mesa just touching a pink horizon.

Everywhere I looked were surfaces even less flat and boring than that. On our right, less than a meter away, a series of slender spires stood grouped together and yet separately, carved into a set of colossal chessmen from a sheer, vertical face of layered stone that thrust straight up out of the ground; three hundred meters of slip fault in reverse. A crimson butte stood square and stolid, casting a square, stolid shadow over a merry tumble of stout little stone sausages. Vermilion sandstone mushrooms grew in profusion from a heap of boulders sliding down the left side of the canyon's mouth. Four bulging, maroon balloons surrounded a rectangular platform with a weird superstructure in a tumble of various geometric solids that stood six meters high. A single scarlet tower, almost perfectly cylindrical in shape, rose up regal and alone, the grounds around it scoured clean of the merest pebble, waiting for the imam to mount upon high and call the faithful to prayer.

Landscape by Venturi, commissioned by Disney, with advice from Salvador Dali. Who says Mother Nature doesn't have a sense of humor?

With the part of my mind that was still working I wondered what direction I was facing. I realized I had no idea. It scared me. I hate being lost.

What scared me more was how close our botched descent had brought us to disaster. I'd spent all my time worrying about bouncing off Mars' atmosphere and into orbit around Capella. The spires nuzzling our starboard bow were jagged and menacing, with sharp promontories and purposeful-looking outcroppings. That the *Kayak* had not shish-kebabed itself on one of them, had not tangled in the chessmen or smashed itself upon the butte or been skewered by the mosque or disappeared into the abyss lurking at the canyon's mouth, had in fact come to rest so sweetly, so neatly in the only acreage unencumbered by rocks with points on them within a half dozen hectares, was almost enough to make me believe in God.

Belatedly, I turned to look at the twins. They had been born on Outpost, actually on the *Hokuwa'a* before it became one half of Outpost. They'd been on and off and in and out of a hundred asteroids before they could walk. They'd grown up with the infinite, glittering backdrop of space. It was anyone's guess how they were going to react to a finite horizon. They were both still upright, which I took to be a good sign.

"Wow," Sean said.

"Wow," Paddy said.

"Wow," I agreed. No visible signs of agoraphobia, at

least not yet. I was relieved until I turned back to the view and saw that the maroon balloons had begun to move.

The balloons were down at the mouth of the canyon, where rays spilled inside from the setting sun, touching everything within reach with ruby gilt. It was a dazzling sight to behold, especially since it had been a decade and more since I'd seen anything like it. I watched the balloons glimmer in the distance, thinking the atmosphere was distorting my line of sight since they looked larger than they had seemed at first. Then I realized they weren't larger, they were closer. Closer and getting more so with each passing second.

"Mom?" said one of the twins.

"Mom?" said the other. "Do you see that?"

I blinked. The balloons were rolling over each other. Was the wind blowing into the mouth of our canyon? I looked up and saw that our envelopes weren't rising exactly straight off the top of the *Kayak*, but that was because the *Kayak* had landed crooked. I didn't see any dust. So no wind.

I looked back at the balloons. They were closer, maybe a kilometer away.

"Mom?" Both twins moved nearer to me.

I am ashamed to admit that I didn't even think of the arms locker. I stood there with my mouth open and watched it come.

It was either a bug-eyed monster or some kind of vehicle. It didn't look like something the Librarians would use to get around, so I decided it was a vehicle. "It's a vehicle," I said, as if by saying so out loud would make it so.

Neither of the twins moved an inch from my side.

The four balloons rolled over themselves, hauling their bizarre platform of cubes and tubes and cones on a directional bearing that had us as their objective, and the closer they got, the more bizarre they looked. I relaxed a little. One of the cubes was an Eddie Bauer Atpak; I recognized the goose emblem on the side. The Librarians weren't, I was pretty sure, patrons of Eddie Bauer. "It is a vehicle," I said. When it turned to avoid a boulder and light glanced off the ladder bolted to one side, I was relieved to see that it was a vehicle for humans. One Librarian encounter per lifetime is all I recommend.

The balloons resolved themselves into wheels made of sections of overstuffed bags, the superstructure into a cabin of interconnecting, segmented shafts and elbows made of some transparent material, maybe graphplex. The whole thing looked like a perambulating gerbil cage, and it might have been the absurdity of the entire structure that kept me mute and immobile when a four-alarm fire should have been nothing to it.

The twins were no better off, and the three of us stood there, speechless, as the vehicle pulled up before us with a distinct flourish. A moment later the top half of the cone sitting in the forward section of the chassis popped its top, and a gray pressure suit clambered out and down the ladder, landing solidly on both feet in a puff of pale pink Martian dust. He might as well have appeared in a bolt of lightning and a billow of smoke for all the gawking awe we accorded him.

Our expressions must have been clearly visible through our helmets. Undaunted, the gray suit marched up, and a thin, lined, leathery face with a grin that split it in two looked out at us. He said something. I was still too bemused to produce even a shrug. He waved a reassuring hand, twisted a knob on the side of his helmet, and spoke again. Still nothing. Another twist, another, and suddenly a voice crackled in our ears.

We all jumped, and a chuckle emanated over our headsets. "Scared you, did I? Bet you weren't expecting to see anyone round these parts. Saw you come down, thought I'd come over and say Hi. Nice tub, even if she does look like a drunk on her way home at closing time. I reckon I'd shine up some on my landings, though, were I you." He gave out with a hoot of laughter that rang off the insides of our helmets and had us all reaching for our volume knobs. "Balloons, is it?" He leaned back and gave the exterior envelope a long, assessing look from bright, sharp eyes. "The Chamont design, be my guess. Practical yet elegant." He gave an approving nod and started around the toroid.

Like automatons, we followed him.

"Toroid for the gondola, is it? Well, an efficient form, I suppose, although it is kinda hard to build on to, and then there is all that wasted space in the center. I purely hate wasted space. Still, I suppose now I think on it you'd need it to pack the balloons into, wouldn't you? Not a get-around I'd pick myself, though; too little say in where you go. Wait a minute, where the hell are my manners?" He smacked me on the back hard enough to dislocate a vertebra. "I'm Johnny; who're you folks?" He gave another of his laughing hoots and me a second smack on the back, which this time nearly knocked me over. I hoped my rebreather was still connected.

I felt like I needed to sit down, but there wasn't anything to sit down on. "Ah," I said, my voice sounding weak in my own ears, "I'm Star Svensdotter. This is my son and daughter, Sean and Paddy. Our ship's the *Kayak*."

"The *Kayak*, is it?" He thought it over, frowning, and I felt myself holding my breath. At last he nodded. "Good name. Short, easy to remember, easy to hear. Important for Maydays. I approve."

"Thank you," I said meekly.

He gave the *Kayak*'s hull a farewell, approving smack. "Well, it's been nice visiting with you folks, but you'll have to excuse me; I've got work to do."

"Work?" Sean said.

"What kind of work?" Paddy said.

Johnny bent a stern eye on both speakers. "Come along, and I'll be pleased to show you."

Like sheep, we followed him out of the shadow of our hull and over to his vehicle. From a locker bolted to the rectangular chassis he produced a small metal object made of, it looked to me, every size nut and bolt and washer ever produced from a tool-and-die machine in the history of man, shaped into two skinny pyramids, one larger than the other, attached at their bases.

"What's that?" one of the twins asked.

"An ozone-maker," Johnny replied, in a matter-of-fact tone of voice that squelched any response, disbelieving or otherwise. He squinted around at the landscape. His eye lit on a nearby hollow at the base of a cliff and he gave a sharp, satisfied nod, produced a small shovel presumably out of a hat, and marched off. We trailed along behind.

We reached the hollow in a body and the three of us stood around, watching, as our new friend carefully rearranged the loose soil at the base of the cliff into a small hole, into which he planted the thick end of the gadget he had brought with him.

"This here's an ozone-maker," he repeated. "My own design." He paused to beam up at us expectantly.

"An ozone-maker," I said. "How, ah, interesting."

" 'Tain't just interesting," he said reprovingly, "it's necessary. I been moseying across Mars for, oh, getting on ten year, must be, planting these out. Plan to keep on doing it till I keel over. Probably won't be any time soon—you've probably already noticed how easy it is to get around on Mars; not much strain on the old ticker." He held his gadget erect with one hand and patted dirt around it until it was buried up to its base line.

Sean broke out of his stupefaction long enough to say, "That thing makes ozone?"

"Yup."

"How does it work?" Sean asked, a mistake, as this launched a lecture. Ozone—he called it oh-three—was made up of three oxygen atoms per molecule. There was ozone in Mars' stratosphere in minute quantities, necessary to absorb short-wave UV radiation, "or," Johnny grunted, "it did before those blankety-blank, deleted, unprintable idjits downstairs started mucking up the air." He did not tone down his invective out of courtesy for his audience, and I could see the twins' ears growing points inside their helmets. Eventually he ran out of breath and waved a sarcastic hand, taking in the general area of the entire, not as lifeless as we'd thought, planet upon which we stood. "You see what can happen from that kind of foolishness."

Ozone, Johnny said, was produced above twenty klicks when short-wave solar radiation was absorbed by molecular oxygen. He had just begun a pungent description of oh-three's irritating odor and strong oxidizing properties when one of the twins interrupted him. "How does your ozone-maker work?"

He shrugged. "Simple. Surprised you can't figure that out for yourselves." Sean looked annoyed, Paddy affronted, and Johnny gave a malicious grin that warmed my heart. "You need oh-two to make oh-three, right? My oh-three-maker plugs into the permafrost and boils it out of the ground. The oh-two molecules bleed up through the structure and into the atmosphere. As it climbs, the solar radiation agitates the oh-two into oh-three." He stooped and twisted a bolt on the side of his gadget. A small, faceted sheet unfolded from one side. It looked like a solar collector, which it proved to be. "Power," he explained in an aside, and twisted another knob. "Eureka, like that Greek fella said. Instant oh-three!"

He sat back on his heels, clearly expecting applause.

"Remarkable," I said with perfect truth.

Sean looked at Paddy, and Paddy said, "Why? I mean, why are you doing this?"

Johnny stared up at her. "Well, now, missy, that's about as dumb a question as I've ever heard."

She blushed and he relented. "I have a fondness for Mars, missy. To paraphrase the late, great Daniel Webster, it's a small planet but I love it. All it's lacking is a little matter of atmosphere, and I don't plan on going to my just reward until I've got these little devils churning out that sweetheart of a UV-eating gas all over. Once we get us some protection from the UV, why, I figger it'll be just a matter of sticking a seed in the ground and stepping back quick before it jumps up and pokes me in the eye."

He chuckled at his joke. The twins exchanged a long, silent glance, and I nudged them both, once each, sharply, in their backs.

Johnny groaned a little as he got to his feet, and stamped the dirt in firmly around the gadget's sides. He brushed the dust from his gauntlets and said, "Well, I'd stay and visit a spell, but you know how it is, a fella gets used to his own company. Be seeing you!"

He turned to go and I found my voice. "Wait! Mister—Johnny, wait up a minute!"

He paused, looking over his shoulder, his expression impatient.

I came up next to him and stopped, somewhat at a loss. "Can we offer you something? Are you low on any of your supplies?"

"Naw, I grow what I need and trade with Vernadsky for the rest."

Vernadsky? "Well, books then? Or I know—maybe we can run you a copy of the latest news from downstairs."

He snorted, the expression denoting a wealth of disdain. "Don't need no book but the Good Book, and there ain't been any news fit to listen to since the UER overran the EC." He cackled. "How long'd that last?"

"They are still the United Eurasian Republic."

He gave me a sardonic look. "But?"

"Well—" I hesitated. "You know the French."

He cackled again. "Figgered. Them Russkies might's well've taken on Satan himself; they'd'a had a better chance. Well, I'm off. Been nice meeting you folks." He gave a jaunty wave and climbed back into his vehicle. The cone snapped back down, the wheels began to roll, and we scattered to get out of the way. For the first time I noticed the name, lettered clumsily on the side of the chassis, *Runamuck*. Beneath the name its home port was listed as New Peoria, Mars. Not a location I'd found on any map generated from Maria Mitchell Observatory, but I'd guess real enough in Johnny's mind.

The *Runamuck* turned up a previously unnoticed ramp-like fall of rock and disappeared over the rim of the canyon. We watched him until he was out of sight.

The twins broke the spell to crouch before the metal contraption jabbed into Martian soil. "Look." A finger pointed at the tip of the pyramid. I bent over. It might have been my imagination but I thought I saw the barest wisp of steam before it boiled out into the atmosphere. My son the skeptic fetched a sniffer from the *Kayak* and confirmed a minuscule quantity of oh-two present in the emission.

We never saw Johnny again. Occasionally we ran across one of his ozone-makers, dotting the landscape like the spoor of some exotic Martian beast, and I may say right here that every one of those little devils we came across was still working, still churning out that sweetheart of a stinky gas so essential to life as we know it, one molecule at a time.

If we left it up to Johnny, Mars should have an atmosphere in time to welcome settlers around, oh, 2342658 A.D.

Or so.

— 4 —

Lost in the Horse Latitudes

It is a mistake to allow any mechanical object to realize you are in a hurry.

— **Ralph's Observation**

The sun went down and darkness fell with the shock of a blow. Suddenly and completely exhausted, we stumbled back to our cockeyed craft, nuked something to eat, and spent a restless night in suits, strapped into our uncomfortably tilted bunks.

The next day was spent assessing damage to the *Kayak*, which was extensive. After our rough descent, about the only thing working were the legs. The more we looked, the more amazed and grateful I was that the hull was capable of holding a seal. I could see a minimum of a month's worth of repairs and maintenance before we could lift out of our canyon and make air for Cydonia, wherever our canyon was, and wherever Cydonia sat in relation to it. "Let's get to work," I said without enthusiasm, and without enthusiasm we got to work.

We broke the stepladder out of its locker and assembled it, and I climbed up and fumbled the railing out of its recess. When I descended, the top of the ladder ran smoothly back and forth along the railing. "Pretty good all right," I said. I climbed back up and began the process of removing the ablation shields. Some of them, like the one on CommNav, were already so loose they nearly fell off in my hands, and all were so badly burned that there was no hope of salvaging the material against any future need. I didn't say anything as we worked our way around the *Kayak*'s keel, but I saw the twins exchange one very eloquent glance when I let the first buffer fall and in Mars' one-third gee it shattered into a thousand crisp, charred pieces.

The task, new to us, took a while to get down right, and we didn't finish it until the following day. For lunch we popped some Enertabs—I could hear Charlie fuming about proper nutrition and adequate rest periods—and finished the job, in time to nuke another pre-packaged meal from our store of Space Services Rations and fall exhausted into bed, this time sans suits. I forgot to strap myself in and fell right out again.

I spent the next three blasphemous days balanced on the top rung of the ladder exposing the solar cells layered over the top third of the gondola. Not before time; the batteries were as close to being dead as made no never mind. It took two days for them to recharge, and we ate our meals in the dark until they did.

We were still careening into morning from our off-kilter beds, but leveling them and the *Kayak* required lift. The exterior balloon, the montgolfier, was limp from rips and leaks; small rips and slow leaks to be sure, but the fact remained that it had ruptured during the descent. I wondered how it was going to stand up to the yearly Martian dust storms.

The balloon was actually two balloons, a charliere inside a montgolfier, a gas envelope inside a hot-air envelope. The envelopes were designed to remain inflated all the time, but as the sun set, the atmosphere cooled and the montgolfier's hot air contracted; lift decreased and the craft settled to the surface. The helium in the charliere contracted as well during the evening, but enough of a lift-to-weight ratio was maintained to keep the envelope's soft structure upright. The exterior of the montgolfier was coated with a graphite composite to attract and absorb Sol's rays; it was slick, too, so that any ice that formed during the subzero Martian night would slide off. It worked fine for ice, as I would soon discover; it also worked fine to keep us from grabbing hold in mid-patch, further lengthening the process and shortening my temper in about the same ratio.

We had to repair the exterior envelope before we got to the interior one, and you haven't lived until you've tried to patch one balloon from inside another, perched on a merrily swinging, jury-rigged jumpseat controlled by a running line usually in the hands of an idiot on the ground (it didn't matter who was in the seat; whoever held the running line was an idiot), in subzero temperatures, wearing a goonsuit, which due to Mars' gravity and joke of an atmosphere was lighter in weight and more maneuverable than a pressure suit but didn't seem like it after an hour's worth of patching.

Still, I didn't let up until we'd examined every square centimeter of every single slick, black, 30-centimeter-square panel of graphabric that made up the montgolfier and charliere, as well as each and every horizontal load tape and vertical load line, from crown to throat and back again, and then one more time just to make sure. We deployed both jibs, inspected them for damage from entry—wonder of wonders, found none—and repacked them. We checked the jib sheets to see that they were intact and ran free. I hauled myself up hand over hand to personally examine the running blocks and the rest of the tackle. "Check the rip cord," I called down, "and I mean yank on it. I've got it on belay up here."

Someone took hold and gave the line a sharp tug, and I bumped into the exterior balloon. My weight depressed the surface and the helium inside it. It was helium instead of hydrogen because helium was cheap and easy to make in the Belt. Hydrogen lifted less than one percent better, and if we ran out of nitrogen we could mix helium with oh-two and breathe it. Plus, hydrogen burns. Helium doesn't. As Helen had pointed out to me with exaggerated patience, there wasn't much chance of fire in Mars' oxygen-starved air. I didn't care. Hydrogen fires had been the norm rather than the exception in the Belt, due to careless handling of explosives and the do-it-yourself gas refineries found on every other rock. If I never saw another hydrogen fire again in my life, I'd die a happy woman.

It took two weeks to locate and patch all the tears, and another two days for the He-maker, red-lined, to make enough helium to inflate the charliere to its performance pressure. Judgment Day came almost a month after touch-down. I picked us out a new campsite, a level plot of red gravel half a klick up the canyon. We weren't going any farther until I was certain the *Kayak* was in full fighting trim.

We waited until noon to move so that we could take advantage of the midday breeze. After the solar cells powered up the instrumentation, I'd begun logging the local weather conditions. In spite of our protected position and the small size of the canyon, a breeze came up almost every day at about eleven, usually between two to four kph, usually steady, usually lasting until about three in the afternoon. If it held true to form, it would be enough to move us to a less lopsided location.

I squinted, watching the telltale tied off to the pole stuck in the ground at the mouth of the canyon. The thin strip of yellow paper hung limp. Between the *Kayak* and the pole stood Sean, safety line wrapped once around a stanchion fixed to the ground, the end clutched in both hands, feet braced.

"I don't know why you had to use my washi paper," Paddy grumbled. "I've only got a ream of it with me, and it's not like I can get more when I run out."

Then again, if the breeze failed me, I was just tired enough of sleeping strapped into my slanting bunk to pick the goddam doughnut up and pack it across the canyon on my back, balloons and all.

"There," Paddy said. The paper stirred.

"Okay," I said. "Is the jib deployed?"

"For the third time, yes."

"Is the anchor up?"

"For the third time, yes."

"Okay."

And it was as easy as that. The gentle little zephyr drifted into our canyon and curled inside our triangular jib. Two of the *Kayak*'s legs were already free of the gentle slope we had landed on; the third had jammed itself so securely into the ground on impact that it had resisted every attempt with shovels to loosen it, and I was too afraid of damaging the water-recovery gear inside to insist. The only way out for that leg was back up the same way it had come down. I held my breath as I felt the gondola sway, tugging at the buried leg. I strained with the motion of the balloon, pushing my feet against the floor, pulling at the edge of the control console.

It must have worked. The leg relaxed its grip and slid free with an almost audible click. We began to move.

"Sean?"

The goonsuited-figure outside waved, and with the end of the safety line he held took an extra loop around the stanchion. That line was the only thing holding us down. From the port in CommNav I could see the foot of the jib bellied out.

"We're moving too fast," Paddy said.

The ground slid beneath us.

"We're moving too fast! That stanchion's not gonna hold, Mom!"

"Okay, drop the jib."

Before the words were all the way out of my mouth, I heard the sound of a fist slapped down, the click of a switch. The jib snapped tight, spilled air, went limp, and slid down the throat of the montgolfier to drape itself in untidy folds on the gondola, thankfully not over the CommNav port.

At the same time, the line from the gondola to the stanchion went taut. Sean dug in his heels and leaned back against the pull of the line, but it wasn't necessary. We floated, stationary, less than a meter from our new campsite.

"Talk about dumb luck," Paddy said. "We couldn't do it that right again if we tried for the next year."

I had purposefully inflated the envelopes to less than half their maximum load, hoping that it would be unnecessary to deflate them once we got where we were going, but the montgolfier was still too full to let us sit all the way down. I activated the deflation port and bled some air out, just a little, and we made the gentlest three-point landing in the history of aeronautics.

That night I rolled into bed and stayed there.

Up till then we'd been using water from the storage and recycling tanks, but the *Kayak*'s life support systems had been designed around the assumption that we were going to be able to recover water from Martian permafrost through the extractors in the ship's tricycle gear. Of course, that assumption was based on the Viking probes in the late twentieth century, the Ares roving probes in the early twenty-first, and some iffy data from unverifiable reports published by the New Martians at Gagarin City. From the available data, our worst-case scenario required drills three meters in length, and ours extended to four. We took a core sample with an opticannon and found permafrost a little over one meter below the surface.

In the galley Sean and Paddy beat the core sample into pieces and dumped them into a pot and nuked them. When six centimeters or so of liquid lay on the bottom of the pan, I scooped out a mugful and ran it through the manual filter. It tested safe for human consumption. "Big surprise," Sean said. "The only thing more antiseptic than Mars is Auntie Charlie's clinic." It was flat and tasted kind of minerally, but it was indubitably water, cool water, clear water; we weren't going to have to face the barren waste without a taste of water. "Okay," I said. "Let's start the leg drills."

There was a life support instrument panel on one bulkhead in the galley. I pushed a button and shifted a lever and prayed that the gauges were reading right and that the *Kayak*'s drills really were grinding into permafrost, passing electrical current generated by the solar cells to melt said permafrost and thereby provide us with water. The next morning we retracted the drills, pumped the evening's melt-off into the scrubber for desalinization and de-bugging. The aerator kicked in and ten minutes later we had running water in the kitchen and both heads.

"How about that?" I asked no one in particular. "Something actually worked, first time." I switched on the solar water heater, and half an hour later took my first hot shower in 500,000 kilometers.

I had to give Helen credit; once the *Kayak* achieved her proper orientation, she was one sweetly designed craft.

The gondola hung beneath the two balloons, a doughnut-shaped cabin forty meters across. The top third of the exterior was sheathed in solar cells; the middle third alternated rectangular graphplex ports with water storage compartments built into the bulkhead, both following the curving side of the toroid; the bottom was solid lockers all the way around the ring, storage for equipment we needed easy access to for work outside.

Inside, the gondola was divided into wedge-shaped compartments; the galley/recreation area, the sciences station, which came equipped with a pop-out bubble for its viewport, the twins' suite, including two bedrooms and a tiny sitting room between, the storeroom, the CommNav center, and my bed-sitter, with the galley/rec area on the other side. If I raised my hand, the tips of my fingers just brushed the ceiling.

The first thing we did after setting up shop at our new campsite was find Deneb, Mars' pole star, even if it was a couple of degrees off, and even if we did have to wait all night before it came into view between the steep walls of the canyon. Paddy ran a sun sight the next day.

"So where are we?"

"Valles Marineris, where else?" she replied.

I ignored the barely concealed scorn in her voice. "Do we know where in Valles Marineris, exactly?" She shrugged, and I resisted the temptation to take her by the shoulders and shake her until her head fell off. "Well, wherever we are, we're half a planet away from where we're supposed to be. I can hear Crip now."

"He didn't even get the right hemisphere," Paddy said.

Sean, looking over Paddy's shoulder, snickered. "The Great Galactic Ghoul strikes again."

"Okay, let's bounce a message off Phobos and tell Outpost what happened and that we're okay." I paused. "Let's set up a loop on the transmitter, too, to bounce a message off Phobos back to Mars, say every hour. Maybe the guys at Cydonia look up once in a while. At least they'll know we're okay."

"And if they don't?"

No answer for that one.

We each had our own life support chores, assigned on a rotational basis, although each crew member had his or her own favorites. Paddy unpacked her telescope, growling ungracious refusal when offered help. The three of us broke out the window boxes from their hull locker and stuck their brackets into the slots mounted next to every window on the gondola. We brought in pail after pail of Martian dirt, sterilized it, watered it, fertilized it, and even ground some of it finer.

Sean, every bit as protective of his precious plants as Paddy was of her telescope, started seeds for lettuce, carrots, radishes, and sugar snap peas. In square, shallow flats he germinated strawberries, tomatoes, broccoli, cauliflower, zucchini, and green peppers; eventually these would be transplanted to the larger planters fixed in odd corners in every room on our craft. We were going to be a floating hothouse. It reminded me of those days when Caleb used to infest our quarters with every living species of orchid known to man. I stuffed that thought back into its sack as soon as it popped out.

Four of the larger planters already contained a couple of self-pollenizing dwarf fruit trees (one mandarin orange, one midget Granny Smith apple) as well as, hurrah, *Coffea arabica* and *Solanum tuberosum*; thanks to Roger Lindbergh's AggroAccel program all four were close to bearing. I liked hash browns in the morning, home fries for lunch, and mashed potatoes for dinner, and I wasn't conscious in the morning until my third cup of coffee. I hovered behind Sean as he carefully unwrapped each planter; I winced as he cut into a branch to see if the sap was still running on the coffee tree; I groaned audibly when he pinched off a leaf of the potato bush, rubbed it between his fingers, and sniffed at it. He turned and gave me a look. I retreated, reluctantly, to the kitchen, where Paddy was setting up the meat and milk vats. "Any problems?" I liked cream in my coffee, too.

She gave me a look the twin of Sean's. "What kind? You think I can't get the lid off the MCP vat, or that the enzyme switch on the FBE synthesizer is too tough for me to throw?"

We went back outside and started banging on the hull, locating and opening every hatch and inventorying its contents. "Three Eddie Bauer One-Man Survival Kits, 14D-FWS, expiration date January 1, 2051," Paddy read from the label of a bundle in one locker. She shoved it back inside and started to close the hatch on the locker.

"Open 'em up," I said.

She looked martyred. "Mom."

"How do we know one of those kits isn't filled with seeds for pansies, giant, variegated?"

"They weren't on Outpost," she muttered.

"Do you know that, your own self? Did you stock this locker personally?" She didn't answer. "Open them up, Paddy, one at a time, and enter the contents on the computer. When we're done, we'll check Outpost's inventory of what they packed against ours of what we find."

Her lips moved but I heard nothing over the headset. She began emptying the locker onto the ground and opening the bundles up, one at a time.

"What're these?" Sean said, staring into another locker a little farther around the hull.

"What?" I peered up, following his pointing finger, and grinned to myself. "Them're wings, flyboy."

He was quick, was my son. "You mean like on Terranova, and in the Bat's Cave on Luna?"

"Exactly like that. I had Crip build us each a set when I knew for sure we were coming to Mars. I figure in one-third gee we ought to be able to log a few hours in the air."

Paddy's hands had stilled in their task. "Flying, Mom? Really?"

"Really."

I saw excitement spark in both faces, but then their eyes met and they remembered how determined they were to dislike Mars and everything to do with it, and the spark died.

It hurt. I was surprised how much, and determined not to let it show. They wouldn't let me be Mom again yet, fine. I stayed captain.

I would have yanked out all ten fingernails without benefit of anesthetic before I'd admit I was taking the easy way out. Discipline is always easier than love and of the two far less dangerous. By the time I realized how much this enforced mental and emotional separation hurt me and my children, it was almost too late.

There was still a lot of work to be done before the *Kayak* would be shipshape enough to lift off, although after I assured and reassured myself we weren't going to spring a leak and that we were going to have enough water to drink, I cut back our work hours to eight. That may have been a mistake.

For me, the free evenings were long and quiet. Far too quiet. A creak from either envelope, a rasp of a line against the side of the gondola, a murmur from either twin, and I was instantly on my feet, alert, ready to respond. One morning I woke to a horrendous cracking, tearing sound far above my head. I was heading for the hull breach alarm in my birthday suit when I realized the sound was merely a night's worth of ice cascading down from the crown of the montgolfier as the coated surface of the envelope heated beneath the rays of the rising sun.

I was an efficient and dedicated sleeper. On Outpost this had been no problem, as Archy had screened all my calls and knew not to wake me for anything less than an armed revolt. Now I had enough peace and quiet to keep a dead man happy and I couldn't sleep through a little ice falling off the roof.

After three decades of so many people, so many department heads and employees and employers having first dibs on my attention, my time was my own.

I didn't have the faintest idea what to do with it.

I spent one evening hanging over Sean's shoulder in the darkroom, until I switched on the right light at the wrong time and inadvertently overexposed a whole series of shots of some strata in the canyon wall Paddy was interested in. I've never been shown the door with more icy politeness.

I went around to the science station and offered to help Paddy reconstruct the series on the spectrometer. I didn't know Martian strata from spumoni, but I was willing to try. Finally Paddy said, "Mom, give it a rest, will you? If you'll get out of my way I'll have the series back on disk in an hour."

I couldn't pace; there wasn't room. One morning at breakfast I noticed that the cuticles on one hand had begun to bleed freely into the reconstituted scrambled eggs. Shocked, I examined the tips of my fingers. I'd been biting my fingernails without knowing it. In my life I'd never bitten my nails. I raised my head and found both twins regarding me with identical expressions of apprehension.

"Maybe you should read a book or something, Mom," Paddy suggested.

"Yeah," Sean said. "You brought enough of them with you."

"I did?" I tried to remember.

That evening I broke out my own personal luggage allowance. I hadn't given a lot of thought to spare time, since it'd been so long since I'd had any. I hadn't read much since Terranova, and after I married Caleb . . . well, if I were truthful, I told myself briskly, I hadn't read much since those days on Norton Sound, trying to poke holes into a hydrocarbon reservoir that, for a change, turned out to be there. I wasn't all that sure I remembered how.

In the rush to pack the *Kayak*, filling my personal baggage allowance was just another task in a long line of Things That Must Be Done Before Dropkick. Personal baggage allowance? I'd said to myself. What'd I tell the twins? Right, a hobby or something. Well, I used to read. I rooted out my supply of cartridges and tipped them into a bag sitting on a scale. The red numbers on the digital readout ran up. My eyes wandered while the readout made up its mind and encountered the guitar hanging on the wall of my cabin. I walked over and struck a chord. The resultant jangle made me wince. I hadn't played it in twelve years. But it was just about the right weight. I set it on the scale along with the bag of cartridges. I looked at the readout. I added another handful of cartridges, took out one, and sealed the bag. There. All done.

I might as well have packed with a shovel.

On the *Kayak*, I picked up the cartridge on the top of the pile without reading the title, and curled up in a comfortable chair in the galley. I slipped the cartridge into the headset, settled the headset around my ears, and flipped it on. I hung my legs over the opposite arm of the chair and doggedly began not to bite my nails.

The cartridge hadn't been rewound and the projection on my corneas began in mid-scene, the words sliding rapidly up the page. I adjusted the scroll speed and the letters came into focus. "Go bind thou up young dangling apricocks, which like unruly children cause their sire to stoop with oppression of their prodigal weight."

Old Bill not only knew about unfit kings; he knew all about surly kids, too. I changed cartridges to something a little less close to home and restarted the headset.

Pawing through that knapsack of tapes was like rediscovering the Seldovia Public Library when I was five. For history I had Branch's witty two-volume biography of Martin Luther King, Nordhoff's irreverent look at the causes of the Third World War, Mattingly's you-are-there account of the Spanish Armada, the log of Christopher Columbus (he'd had his problems with ship's crews, too), Rhodes's fascinating histories of the atomic and hydrogen bombs,

Foote's eerily empathic trilogy of the American Civil War, and every acerbic, exasperated word Barbara Tuchman had ever written about imbeciles in power anywhere. Johnny Ozone would have liked Barbara Tuchman.

For poetry I had several anthologies as well as the collected works of Frost and Don Marquis—I'd almost forgotten who Archy had been named for. For literature I had Thoreau, and for fun I had a variety of popular authors, Georgette Heyer and Nevil Shute and John D. MacDonald and Ross Thomas and Margaret Atwood, as well as some more recent works by Braz Albana and Julitta Mistral, writers Helen had recommended, whom I had never gotten around to reading.

Not bad, I decided, for packing with a shovel.

My cuticles healed and my fingernails grew back, but I was still restless. The atmosphere inside the gondola persisted in being colder than the atmosphere outside. We were plugging into enough permafrost to mine an adequate supply of oxygen to resupply the tanks on our goonsuits; I started taking long walks between dinner and dusk. I followed the tracks of Johnny Ozone's *Runamuck* up over the rim and followed my nose from there.

The terrain was always magnificent, if not always easy going. I saw massive mesas of smooth, vertical slabs of stone, striated in layers of ages above, tumbled mounds of epochal debris below. Chasms opened up suddenly beneath my feet to slam together again a meter away, next to rusty red landslides the size of Rhode Island, next to smooth slip-faults of stone flat enough to hit a racquet ball off of. So much evidence of ancient activity somehow soothed the jagged edges of my nerves, and the walks tired me enough to sleep through a glacier rolling off the roof.

All in all, I think it would be fair to say that our first six weeks on Mars did not go well. Sean sulked (there is no other word), until he reminded me of the Andy Capp cartoon character who all the time ran around beneath his own personal rain cloud. Paddy was so efficiently noncommittal as to be almost invisible, her main purpose being to draw no attention whatever to herself, no matter how trivial or transient. I was unrelentingly perky, a self-proclaimed cheerleader without a pep squad. The Good Ship Lollipop we weren't.

It was partly our situation: The three of us hadn't spent this much time alone together since their father was alive and, simply put, we got on each other's nerves. I'd told Helen I'd wanted people to stop looking to me for all the answers; I didn't have them, I never had. What I didn't know then was how much I'd miss the questions.

I was aware (had been made most painfully aware) that I had uprooted the twins from everything and everyone that was familiar to them, and I retained just enough common sense to realize that they had every right to be angry and resentful. Nothing would be accomplished by trying to force them not to be. I waited, patiently, for overtures that never came.

It wasn't fair. The twins had each other. I had no one.

I was lonely.

The Sunday afternoon this realization struck me I was pretending to read Shelby Foote, but was really listening to the low hum of muted voices coming from the stateroom opposite mine, wishing I was part of the conversation, knowing I would not be welcome. And there, slipping in between the second battle of Bull Run and Chancellorsville, Caleb's dark face looked up at me, grin wide and white, green eyes amused, black hair a riot of tight curls, one eyebrow twisted up by an old scar. I leapt to my feet as if stung by a bee, made a beeline for the goonsuit locker and the hatch in that order, and was beating feet for the nearest horizon shortly thereafter, striking out recklessly, choosing a previously unexplored path at random. My stride ate up the ground, and unfamiliar landmarks slid rapidly past. "Lonely," I scoffed, panting up a slope of loose talus. "Poor baby, can't handle a little solitude. Hah! Probably just can't stand your own company! Of all the pathetic, adolescent—"

I reached the top of the slope and halted, breathing hard. It was because Caleb had been a soldier, and I'd been reading about soldiers. It was because Caleb had been black, and I'd been reading about the Civil War. It was because Caleb's death had been absurd and useless, and I'd been reading of absurd, useless battles that ended in 25,000 casualties a day. It was *not* because I was lonely, it was *not* because I was grieving; I was all over Caleb's death, I *was*. "Goddammit, men have died and worms have eaten them, but not for love!"

It does not do to yell inside the helmet of a pressure suit. My voice echoed off the inside of the smooth, hard surface, beating against my eardrums in ringing waves, and it drove me to my knees. I shut my eyes and clenched my teeth and waited out the echo.

When I opened my eyes again, for the first time I focused on what was at the top of the slope.

My first thought was that, against all expectations and assurances to the contrary, Mars was proving to be awfully crowded.

It looked like a toppled column of thin, rounded silica, but the colors were all wrong, dull brass and steel-gray and leaden silver. So were the surfaces, polished to a metallic gleam only partially masked by a thin accumulation of red, powdery dust.

It was a habitat, an artificial, man-made dwelling. Or it had been. I took an involuntary step forward for a closer look and tripped over something.

It was a body.

Numbly, I knelt down, careless of the loose rock beneath the knees of my goonsuit. The body's torso was almost severed at its waist. It was no longer a man or a woman, just a mummified husk, with all the life-giving moisture boiled out of it, the cardboard skin sunk into the bones, the head a grinning skull with an incongruously tousled mop of reddish hair, the hands curled into claws, the synthetic material of its clothes its only pitiful protection from the pitiless Martian atmosphere. Against my will, I was transported back in time and space to that horrible scene on Ceres and the memory of the dead weight of a dismembered hand. My breath came in shallow pants; a bead of sweat rolled down my nose. I felt a wave of nausea and checked it by sheer force of will.

"Chalk another one up to the Great Galactic Ghoul, Crip," I said, determined on composure, if not nonchalance.

I looked further and had my worst fears confirmed. There were other bodies. Too many bodies, too many limbs from too many bodies, scattered haphazardly across the level ground in front of the burst structure like so much flotsam cast up by a plus tide.

It took me a minute to realize that none of them were suited up for outside work. It took another moment to realize that that couldn't be right. What were these people doing outside in inside clothes?

I tried to think. A once-in-a-lifetime direct hit from a meteor, maybe? But that wouldn't account for the way the hull of their habitat had been opened up.

A chill chased up my spine. Great Galactic Ghoul, my ass. I'd seen dead bodies in my time. I'd caused more than a few, if it came to that. There had been explosive decompression here, but all of the bodies had also taken current or post-ED hits from what must have been laser weapons at full charge, at close range. The edges of every wound I looked at were as neat as the open wound on the habitat itself, which had been sliced down its horizontal axis with almost surgical precision. That alone would have been sufficient to destroy all life inside, but that hadn't been enough. These people had been sliced up like so much meat.

Like the freighter's crew on Ceres.

The echo of Kwan's amused, maniacal laughter was faint but clear.

I lumbered around the torn length of the bulkhead and was brought up short by letters, standing out stark and bold against a whole section of fuselage shaped down to a blunt point. Like the bow of the ship.

Of course. The cylindrical shape, the thinness of the metal bulkhead, the rectangular plastigraph tanks between the plasteel sandwich that must surely have held water and doubled as UV shielding. My head cleared a little. Of course. Not a habitat, a ship.

Then the letters registered. Without volition one hand came up and touched the neat block figures, and I forgot to breathe.

The bow of the *Tallship*.

—5—

Certainties

For certain is death for the born
And certain is birth for the dead ...
　　　　　　　—Bhagavad Gita

I broke the Martian land speed record getting back to the
Kayak, and made enough noise coming up the hatch that
both twins were standing next to it with inquiring expressions when I slammed in. I popped my helmet and shoul-
dered between them, making straight for the arms locker,
and their eyes widened.

The sonic rifles I left racked, reaching instead for the
laser pistols, cursing when I had to pause to loosen my
gauntlets to pick them up. The chargepaks read full and
gave a satisfying smack as I loaded them into the butts
of the pistols. Just in case, I checked the paks on the sonic
rifles, too. Over my shoulder I said, "Suit up. Sean, are the
shovels still in the Number Two exterior hatch?"

"Yes, why?"

Paddy's hands came up to catch the holster before it hit her in the chest. "What's wrong, Mom?"

I told her the truth. I think I wanted to frighten her, to frighten both of them. "I found a wrecked camp a couple of klicks north of the ramp. It used to be a spaceship called the *Tallship*." I paused and fixed them both with a look they flinched from. "Suits. Now."

They began pulling them on. "Is the crew—"

"The crew is dead." I corrected myself. "The crew has been murdered. Whoever did it opened up the ship like a tin can and then took potshots during the explosive decompression." Paddy was fumbling with the catch on her holster, and with impatient hands I brushed her fingers aside. The tongue ran easily through the buckle and clicked down solidly. I tugged on it to make sure it was seated securely around her waist. "Remember the drill?"

Paddy nodded, reaching to pull her helmet forward, her voice muffled. "No pulling a weapon unless I mean to use it, no aiming unless I mean to fire, no firing unless I'm aiming to kill."

"Good girl." They both seemed to have grown a foot since touchdown on Mars, not enough, not ever enough to grow into the slender, wicked-looking weapons now strapped to their sides. But there was simply nothing else to be done. I'd trained them myself, and they were their father's children. I jammed that thought ruthlessly to the back of my mind. There was no time to think of Caleb now.

"Wait a minute," Sean said slowly, one hand pausing at the fastening at his throat. "Wasn't the *Tallship* the sister ship of the *Conestoga*?"

Paddy's head snapped around inside her helmet, and she said sharply over her headset, "You mean Lavoliere's second ship? The guy who killed Dad?"

"Get your helmet on, Sean!" I barked. "Now!"

I led the way up the slope and back to the wreckage at a trot. More secure with a weapon strapped to my side and my children within arm's reach, I inspected the scene with an eye less clouded by panic.

The Tallshippers had picked a good place for their settlement, a long, level shelf on a south-facing slope. There was a circular blast mark a few meters off the stern; they'd set the ship down on her tail like the textbook said and then let her down easy on her side, probably with lines and pulleys. I looked and found holes drilled where they'd fixed eyebolts for the guys. There was dirt piled high, wide and handsome over the bulkhead facing north. Not that they'd had much work to do there, as they'd set her down to within ten centimeters of the slope. Reluctantly I admitted that their engineers had done more than play with chromosomes. That much luck doesn't just happen, it's planned.

Burying the north side let them open up the south side to the sun, as witness the series of square holes cut into the fuselage. All that was left of the windows were shards of a grainy kind of glass, in which, when I held it to the light, I could see bubbles. It had a pinkish tint, but that might have been the ambient light. I investigated further and found wreckage that might have been a smelter and a kiln. A hole in the ground was all that remained of what I presumed had once been a permafrost well. If there had been a thermal unit plugged in at the wellhead, it was gone now.

The inside of the ship had been stripped of anything useful. What had been too big or too awkward had been destroyed where it sat. I found no trace of weapons, no ammunition, not so much as a rifle bracket. I remembered that day on the *Conestoga*, and the antique with which Lavoliere had killed Caleb. No, the geneticists on Lavoliere's ships were not what one could call well-armed.

If any of them had known how to use a weapon, Caleb might still be alive.

In a voice louder and harsher than I'd meant it to be I said, "Paddy, Sean, neither of you go out alone or unarmed again, you got that? You're either together or with me, and you are always, I say again, *always* armed." I added, "We're starting target practice again, too, first thing tomorrow."

"Is it true, Mom?" Paddy said, her voice uncertain. "Was the *Tallship* the sister-ship of the *Conestoga*? Are these the people that killed Dad?"

"Dig," I told her.

"But Mom—"

"Dig!"

We dug, a wide communal grave. I gave up trying to match the body parts after the first three; it took too long and I felt enough in the cross hairs as it was. It wasn't until we were filling in the mass grave that I caught a sound over my headset. Half-gasp, half-sob, and I looked up to see where it came from.

Sean was digging next to me. Our helmets were very close, and through his visor I saw a tear spill from one blue eye and leave a wet, shining track down one dark cheek.

I looked across the open grave at Paddy. She was crying, too.

They were sixteen years old, and during the last three hours I'd had them witnessing the results of a massacre, collecting and burying body parts, and arming for all-out war. They'd had the temerity to inquire about their father's death, and in reward had had their heads bitten off.

"Sean," I said.

Another tear slid down his cheek, and his glove smacked into his visor when he tried to wipe it away. He straightened up and squared his shoulders and looked as if he were trying to suck the tears back up beneath his lids, as if he didn't dare display such appalling weakness before his commanding officer. That hurt worse than all the rest.

I tried to speak gently. "Sean, Paddy, that's enough. Go stand watch on the edge of the shelf. Sing out if you see anything move. Shoo. Take your shovels with you."

"But—"

"I'll finish up here. Go on now."

But when the last shovelful of sand covered the last obscenity, Sean was once again at my elbow. "I want to say something. Give a blessing."

I stifled a sigh. "If you must." I leaned on my shovel and prepared to be patient.

The shovel was jerked out of my hands. "What the—" I lost my balance, staggered a step, and regained it in time to see the blade of the shovel coming up from the ground in a silent, deadly arc. "Sean!" I ducked out of the way just in time.

Sean had my shovel and he swung it with silent, single-minded ferocity. "Sean, what are you doing? Put that down! I said put that down, dammit!" The blade came up again. I danced out of the way, not fast enough, and the blunt side connected with my elbow. The resulting harmonic tremors shivered all the way up my humerus and down my spine. "Shit! Ouch! Sean, cut it out! Paddy! Help!"

Paddy waded in from Sean's blind side and made a grab for the shovel handle. Sean jerked it free; the handle thumped into Paddy's diaphragm and she slipped and fell and used her fanny to bounce off the Martian surface and back to her feet.

"We can bury the bodies, is that it?" my son screamed at me. "But we don't have to do anything for their souls? Damn you, Mom! Damn you, I hate you, I hate you, I hate you!" The last words were sobbed out, accompanied by jabs with the business end of the shovel that decreased in force and mercifully failed to connect with anything else. When Paddy tried the second time to disarm him, Sean yielded the shovel without resistance. He bent over, uncaring now that tears were fogging up the inside of his visor.

I stood there, breathing heavily, feeling the sweat trickle down my spine, listening to my son sob over the headset on our goonsuit helmets. "I'm sorry," I said. "I'm sorry, Sean."

"You sure are," Paddy said, a tremor in her voice. She stood shoulder to shoulder with Sean, squared off against the world in general and me in particular.

"Shut up, Paddy," I snapped.

"Shut up yourself," she snapped back.

"Shut up, both of you!" Sean yelled.

He was sobbing again and I couldn't bear it. "Sean, please, baby, don't cry."

"I'm not a baby and I'll cry if I want to," he said, his voice breaking. He caught himself in mid-gulp, it sounded to me as if by main force of will stifling his tears and getting his breathing under control. He marched forward to plant himself smack in front of me. I looked down at the determined, tear-streaked face glaring up at me through a graphplex bubble that was altogether too clear. "You had us bury the bodies, Mom. Why do you have to make fun when I want to say something that maybe might make their souls rest a little easier?"

"I—I—" I flopped around like a landed halibut. "I don't know, Sean."

"You don't think we have souls, do you?" he accused.

A theological discussion in the middle of a newly dug and already entirely too well-populated graveyard was not my idea of fun, but my son's distress held me rooted to the ground. "Truth, Sean? I don't know. I haven't thought much about souls. I've always been more concerned with the life I was living, to waste—to spend a lot of time worrying over the one to come."

He pounced. "Then where's Dad?"

"What?"

The voice, thin, wavering, and oh so very young, demanded, "Where's Dad? If he's not with God, then where is he?"

"And why won't you ever talk about him?"

It wasn't a comment, it was an accusation. Even through her helmet I could see Paddy's chin stuck out. "What?" I said.

"You never talk about Dad, Mom."

I looked at her with real disbelief and perhaps even anger. "What do you mean? I talk about him, I talk about him all the time."

"No." Paddy was positive. "You don't."

Next to her Sean nodded confirmation. "You think about him all the time, maybe. But you never talk about him."

"He's not just dead, Mom," Paddy said, and the desolation in her voice chilled me to the bone. "It's like he never existed."

• • •

It was a long, quiet, thoughtful walk home. By the time
we reached the *Kayak*, I knew what I had to do.

The morning of our departure from Outpost Mother had
drawn me to one side and held out a small, slender package.
"Here, take this with you, dear."

The unmistakable weight of old ivory filled my palms.
"What? But, Mother—"

"You may find occasion to use it, dear." She had hugged
me and kissed me. "Safe journey, my very dear. Come home
to us soon."

There had been no time before transfer to the *Kayak* for
me to ask why she had given it to me.

How could she have known how much I would need it?

The rich weight of the storyknife rode now at the small
of my back; I put it on every morning beneath my jumpsuit.
Truth to tell, I was frightened of the responsibility of caring
for it. It was a 300-year-old family heirloom, and I needed
the security of knowing it was by me at all times.

How could Mother have known?

I boosted the twins up the hatch. "I'll be up in a minute."

I rummaged through the exterior lockers until I found a
small, collapsible bucket. There was a patch of blood-red
sand fifty meters south of the ship; I filled the bucket and
brought it on board.

After dinner I closed the door to my stateroom and busied
myself with some thin, flat sheets of graphplex, a ripsaw,
and a thermal soldering iron. In half an hour I had knocked
together a square, shallow pan. I shook sand out of the
bucket into the pan and smoothed it over. It had to be
ground down before it would soak up enough water to hold
a cut with the storyknife. Before I went to bed I set the meat
vat for turkey.

Sunday evening I cooked elaborately, or as elaborately
as I was able: bioturkey, dressing out of a prepak, potatoes
out of a window box, and rehydrated pumpkin pie. The
whipped cream out of the synthesizer was a pale imitation
of the real thing, and I could see both twins drawing mental

comparisons between my cooking and Auntie Charlie's. I forked the last of the pie into my mouth and said around it, "You two clean up in here. In fifteen minutes I want to see you both in my room."

Paddy opened her mouth. "But I was—"

"Fifteen minutes. My room."

Fifteen minutes to the second later there was a knock on the door so tentative I nearly missed it. "Come in."

The door slid back and the twins filed in, to come to an abrupt halt immediately inside the doorway.

I was seated on the floor of the room, my back against the edge of the bed, my legs crossed. The tray of Martian sand was directly before me. We didn't have a candle or anything remotely resembling the ingredients for one, but I'd turned all the lights down and rigged a makeshift wick to float in a tiny cup of Outpost olive oil, a small jug of which Charlie had insisted on including in the galley supplies. The tiny flame cast a flickering glow over their wide-eyed faces.

"Welcome," I said. "Please. Sit down."

They exchanged one of those impenetrable glances they specialized in—us in, everybody else out, and don't let the door hit you in the fanny on your way. "Please," I said again. "Sit down."

They hesitated a little longer and then complied, sitting across the tray of sand from me. My palms were open in my lap, and the storyknife lay across them, an ancient gem carved from a walrus tooth, gleaming from the grasp of six generations. They saw it, and their eyes widened.

I'd never begun a naming ceremony before, and I strove for the sense of calm purpose and absolute certainty that always radiated from Mother when she began one. For a while I was afraid it wouldn't come, that I wasn't worthy enough.

The wick of the little candle flickered. The twins didn't move. It did come at last, quietly, padding in like fog on little cat feet, to curl up in the corners and beneath the bed, a force that comforted and reassured and strengthened. It was almost like speaking to the Librarian, hearing a voice without words, seeing pictures without form, a presence that seeped into my skin, though I remained Star Svensdotter. I was not so much forced onto a path as I was shown the way and left to take the first step on my own. The decision was mine.

Once, at another naming long ago and a hundred million klicks behind, my grandmother had told me the storyknife had its own spirit, that the hand holding it was only a medium for the truths it had to impart. I believed her then. I believed her now. I believed her because I wanted to, because I needed to, because I had to, and I willed my children to believe, too. The haft of the storyknife slipped into my right palm and my fingers closed over it. The carved figures pressed into my skin—sun, whale, eagle, salmon, drum, otter—the ivory warm and tactile. Two houses appeared in the tray of red sand. "It was not the custom of your father's family to choose their own names. His parents gave his names to him. Therefore I will tell you of his mother, and of his father."

I drew the figure of a woman in one house. "His mother, your grandmother, is Uhura Mbele. Uhura means freedom, I think. She is a tall, slender woman, and beautiful. Her skin is black and polished. Her hair is thick and dark. Her eyes are large and brown and they look right through you to the truth behind. She's the daughter of one of the oldest Zulu families of New South Africa, and serves the government as minister without portfolio, specializing in foreign affairs. Occasionally, New South Africa loans her out to the United Nations as an arbitrator. She negotiated the settlement that put Cyrus the Second of Persia on his throne." I had to smile. "I only know her to talk to over the tri-vee, but even secondhand she seems a competent and formidable person. Very controlled, very dignified. The first time I talked to her from Ellfive, I was glad she was downstairs and I was up. Sometimes, Sean, when you're especially determined, you look a lot like her. Sort of paralyzingly dignified, and, I don't know, ungetatable, I guess."

That surprised a giggle, quickly stifled, out of Paddy. I drew the figure of a man in the other house. "Caleb's father, and your grandfather, was Sean O'Hara. Sean is John in Irish; it means 'God is gracious.' Sean was a mercenary in the New South African War of Independence, and in the Diamond War, in which he was killed leading the liberation of Mandelaville. He was a soldier, like your father. He died before I met Caleb, but I've seen some tapes. Big man with a bigger laugh that reminded me of my father when I heard it. He looked like someone who took only big bites, and made sure to sample everything that came his way. Sometimes, Paddy, when you laugh that belly-laugh of yours, you look and sound just like him."

I drew a path from the door of each house and brought them both together to form a single line. Beside it I drew another figure, a male. "Caleb Mbele O'Hara was their son."

Sean's breath expelled on a long, queer sigh. Paddy reached for his hand and gripped it tightly.

"Caleb is a biblical name. It means faithful." I drew the symbol for friend, as close as I could get to faithful in storyknife.

"Mbele is an African name. It was your grandmother's family name. It means forest spirit." I drew the symbol for anua.

"Like a kobold?"

I shook my head. "A German kobold is more like an Irish leprechaun, mischievous, malicious, often dangerous. An mbele is like an Aleut anua, a thing more of the heart, and of the soul, and of the essence of all living things."

"O'Hara is an Irish name. It was your grandfather's family name. It means Irish chieftain, or that the first O'Hara was one—I'm not sure which." I drew the symbol for chief.

"Caleb was a soldier, like his father, and then a minister, like his mother. He was a friend of your Uncle Simon's downstairs, before either of them came upstairs to work for me." My grip tightened on the storyknife.

"We met in January of 2006, on Ellfive, the habitat now known as Terranova. We were about to commission, a month away from the arrival of the first Terran colonists."

I told them of my first sight of their father, my new security supervisor, spiraling out of control in free fall across the warehouse lock. "It was not a sight to inspire confidence," I said, smiling a little. "As first impressions go, it wasn't very accurate, either. Your father was the best at whatever he did."

I told them how Caleb charmed their cousin Elizabeth with limericks.

"Limericks?" Paddy exclaimed.

I nodded. "When we first met, he used to make them up. Bad ones. His life was threatened from time to time over them."

"Tell us one," Sean demanded.

"One about you," Paddy agreed, nodding.

I couldn't remember any about me, but I could remember one about Elizabeth, and I recited it for them.

> At Ellfive the resident elf
> Put her gravity one day on the shelf
> In a single bound
> She reached the speed of sound
> And inertia ran away with herself.

"Whew," Paddy said, and Sean looked pained.

"I warned you." I told of the evening Caleb came calling and found me skating alone on the tiny lake above my house in the Big Rock Candy Mountains on the South Cap, of the orchids he seduced me with. As I drew their outlines, I could see their burnt-orange blush, could smell their bittersweet fragrance. *Cattelya labiata biensientes.* October orchids.

"Dad was a gardener?" Paddy blurted. A tiny smile curled the corners of Sean's mouth.

"An amateur one. He specialized in orchids. He used up most of his baggage allowance to bring them upstairs."

"Most of?" Sean said. "What did the rest go for?"

"A Remington scattergun. Your father was always practical." I laughed, surprising myself and, from their expression, the twins as well. "I was furious with him. At that time there were no weapons allowed on the habitat. My orders. But, unbeknownst to me, Helen and Frank had sent Caleb up as my bodyguard."

"Bodyguard?"

I shrugged. "There was some trouble with Luddites and other crazies. Helen and Frank were worried, so they sent Caleb up to keep an eye on me. I thought I was getting a new security supervisor, when in reality I was getting my very own personal Doberman pinscher."

"Mom?"

"What, Paddy?"

She hesitated only a moment. "What's skating?"

I must have gaped at her, because she flushed, but she continued to stare at me challengingly out of my eyes and her father's face. "You said Dad caught you skating. What's that?"

I floundered. "Skate on the ice, uh, on metal blades attached to boots. It's a sport, on Terra. There are different moves, jumps, spins . . . Paddy, I know I told you about my skating." She remained uncomprehending. I shifted uncomfortably. "I, uh, well, I even made it to the Anchorage Olympics."

Her eyes widened and she sat up straight. I held up a hand. "I didn't win; I barely placed." Ruefully, I added, "Even then, I didn't have a whole lot of finesse. I was too big and too slow and I had a fatal tendency to skate from jump to jump. I doubt that I would have made the Olympic team at all if Harriet Dabney hadn't fallen three times in the nationals."

"Yes, you would," Sean said. He shifted beneath our stare. "At Leif's naming, he said something about your being in the Olympics," he mumbled. "I was curious. I had Archy look it up." He raised his head and said earnestly, all embarrassment aside, "Archy has you on tape. You were *good.*"

Of all the compliments I had ever received in my life, that was unquestionably the sweetest. Paddy's expression was harder to define, and took me a moment to recognize. It was pride. And she was looking at me.

"So Dad caught you skating," Sean prompted, "and he brought you orchids. Then what?"

At first I wasn't going to tell them, and then I thought, Why not? It was the truth. "And then we practiced making you."

Sean blushed to the roots of his hair, but Paddy demanded, "And all he did was bring you flowers? Boy, Mom, you were easy."

But I heard her tone, and we exchanged our first woman-to-woman grin.

Thoreau said most men lead lives of quiet desperation. I'd always lived, or wanted to live, a life of noisy joy. The noise had always been there, but the joy had been made conspicuous by its absence for some time. This was what Helen had tried to tell me, back on Outpost. This was what Charlie had been trying to tell me for the last ten years. This was why Mother had given me the storyknife. She hadn't known I would need it, but she had hoped.

That night, for the first time in twelve years, I opened up the floodgates to memory, and Caleb's presence became a living, breathing force on board the *Kayak*, until I could almost see him, standing straight and stocky, the wide, teasing grin splitting his dark face in two, the scar drawing his right eyebrow up into a satanic twist, the green eyes serene. Caleb never got excited about anything.

Well, not often. I told the twins of the first visit to the *Conestoga*, which I was glad to learn they didn't remember, when Captain Lavoliere had removed patches of their skin to add to his colony's genetic pool. "It was the first and only time I saw your father lose his temper. I had to tackle him on his way back to the *Conestoga*, and believe me, your father didn't tackle easy. He didn't speak to me for weeks."

Until the night before he died. The memory hurt. I faced it, accepted it, and kept talking.

An hour passed, two. In all that time neither twin moved from their position or tried to stem the flow. Silent tears dripped into the tray of sand, wiping out lines even as I drew them, smoothing over figures until they softened and blurred. Neither twin moved to stop the tears, either. I talked until my voice was hoarse, until I ran out of words, until the makeshift wick burned up the last of the oil and the room was plunged into shadow.

"I'm glad you killed him, Mom," Paddy said suddenly, passionately. "I'm glad you killed Lavoliere."

Sean squeezed her hand. I took a deep, shaky breath. "It didn't bring your father back, Paddy."

Sean spoke. "Tonight did, though. Didn't it, Mom?" He gestured. "He was here. Dad was here. I could feel him. For the first time since he died, I could really feel him." His hand tightened on Paddy's. "He was here."

The storyknife was warm in my hand. "Maybe he was," I whispered. "Maybe he was."

We sat still for a moment, before Sean rose to his feet, moving stiffly after all that time sitting on the floor. He tugged Paddy around the tray of red sand to stand before me, and reached out one square hand, already calloused, already capable, to cup my cheek. He leaned down and kissed me, as much of a salute as a caress. "Thanks, Mom," he said simply. "I love you."

He looked at Paddy. Something slid down her cheek. She erased it with an annoyed swipe of her hand. "I guess you really did love him, Mom."

"I guess I really did," I replied.

We stared at each other. "Okay," she said at last. "Okay, Mom." She leaned over and kissed me, too, twice, once on each cheek, and again, like her brother, there was as much tribute as affection in the gesture. She leaned her forehead against mine, just for a moment, eyes closed, before allowing Sean to pull her towards the door.

"Guys," I said as they turned to their room. "What I said before still goes. We operate on the assumption that whoever killed the Tallshippers is still out there. Outside this craft we go armed. We start standing watches tomorrow, too, and from now on the infrared sensors are set every night at sunset. And target practice for all hands at 1700 hours every Monday."

All my little homily on crew safety and ship's security got me was two identically raised eyebrows. "Don't spoil it, Mom," Sean said, a little smile kicking up one corner of his mouth.

"You can't anyway," Paddy added.

"Good night, Mom," Sean said.

" 'Night, Mom," Paddy echoed. "Sleep tight, and don't let the bedbugs bite."

The door closed behind them. I went to my own bed and fell straight to sleep and didn't wake up until the alarm blared in my ear. If ice slid off the roof, I didn't hear it. If Kwan tried breaking into our airlock, he did so quietly. I had no dreams, either. Or none I remembered.

I guess I really did love him. I guess I didn't know how much, until then.

—6—

Playing Tourist

For my part, I travel not to go anywhere, but to go. I travel for travel's sake. The great affair is to move.

—**Robert Louis Stevenson**

I'd been keeping a log, partly because that's what ship's captains do during voyages, partly to fill in time between walks and books. And let's face it, if you work at it hard enough, just being in motion can disguise, for a while at least, the dismal fact that you aren't getting anywhere.

At any rate, the following morning, a Monday, I made an entry in my log: "Taking the day off. Maybe tomorrow, too. Maybe the whole week. Don't call us, we'll call you." I saved it and bounced it, and wasted at least a full minute savoring Helen's reaction when she read it two weeks from now. I sat at CommNav for a while longer, scanning the horizon for signs of life, and was relieved to find none. Kwan was on Mars, of that I was convinced, but from

121

the dust that layered the devastation of the Tallshippers' habitat, he was long gone from the area. The freighter he'd hijacked on Ceres wasn't capable of planetfall. I wondered how he'd achieved the surface, and in what, and who he'd stolen it from.

I tried not to imagine what would have happened if it had been Kwan who had seen us come down instead of Johnny Ozone, and succeeded most of the time.

We had our backs to a wall, albeit a fractured one, and a clear view of the only direction anyone could come at us from, except from above, and the canyon was deep enough that, properly anchored, we were invisible from the surrounding plateau. It was a quiet harbor, out of wind and sand, but saw double duty as a position defensible in case of attack. We needed some time off, and I was going to see that we took it, crazed killers loose on the planet or no.

The twins were cleaning up after breakfast when I poked my head in the galley. "You about done? Good. Suit up."

Paddy groaned, this time a sixteen-year-old groan I thrilled to hear. "Again?"

"But I wanted to prune the herbs today—" Sean began.

I interrupted him. "The herbs can wait until tomorrow. Come on, suit up. And don't forget your pistols."

Identical martyred sighs, but they suited up and followed me out of the lock. When I popped the exterior portside locker, they perked up. I grinned inside my helmet and parceled out wings for three all around. "Okay, kids. Let's go flying."

The airfoils and harnesses had survived the journey intact. We lubricated the moving parts with a moistureless graphite solution, and packed the pieces up the ramp and out of the canyon to a stubby cliff that rose out of the landscape like a squat, square bookshelf, a bookshelf fifty meters high. Three sides went straight up; the fourth sloped just enough to walk on and no more.

The airfoils were made of a plastic and graphite composite, the harness of graphabric, and the journey up might have been sweatier if Mars had not been so obliging in its low gravity. As it was we were all panting by the time we made the summit. The top of the Bookshelf was as level as I could have wished; I cleared an edge of loose gravel and a few larger rocks, stuck a telltale on a collapsible pole at one end, and we had a launch site and a landing strip.

I snapped my airfoils into the harness and donned both. Everything fit, no chafing of shoulder and body straps, the hand controls for the wing flaps fitting cleanly over goonsuit gloves, my helmet and shoulders locked securely into the extended wing. I tried the toe controls for the rudder one at a time; my boots snugged sweetly home, and the rudder shifted easily.

I shrugged free and assisted the twins. When I was sure the twins had Introduction to Martian Aviation 101 cold, I looked at the telltale. It stood straight out to one side, so I knew there was a steady breeze up on the plateau— I didn't really care from which direction—and the sun was rising higher in the sky every moment, warming the Martian surface and generating thermals even as I thought. I looked at Paddy and Sean with a wide grin that materialized of its own free will. "Okay, I'm going to take a short test flight, check out the equipment and the conditions. You stay put."

"No fair," somebody muttered.

"Stay put," I repeated, "and watch me." I circumvented further discussion by the simple expedient of stepping to the edge and falling off. I fell straight forward, arms/wings straight out, hooking my boots into the toe controls almost by habit, as if I were back on Orville on Terranova, as if I'd never left. It was like riding a bike; once you've mastered the technique, you never forget how.

At seven millibars pressure there wasn't much immediate lift, but at one-third my Terranovan weight there didn't need to be. I didn't fall for long, with pressure gathering beneath my wings even in that skinny Martian air. I grabbed for all I could get and banked right, swooping for a dark patch of ground I'd spotted earlier, and caught the first thermal of the day to spiral rapidly up and over the Bookshelf. The controls responded like they were my own nerve endings. I pulled rudder and came in low and clean, a meter over the top of the little butte, scattering twins before me.

"Whoopee!" somebody yelled over my headset. "Ride 'em cowgirl!"

These kids had never seen a bird in flight before and I got a little cocky, pulled up too sharply, and stalled. Nose down and around and around I went, leveling out well before impact but considerably chastened in spirit. Not chastened enough not to come in hot on final, though, and the expression on the twins' faces, even through their visors, was worth it.

"Wow, Mom, that was incredible!"

Sean didn't waste time with words, shrugging into his harness and stepping to the edge. I grinned over at him. "Ready? Okay, go!"

We spent the whole day falling off the Bookshelf. Atmosphere wasn't vacuum, and a rudder wasn't a vernier jet, but the twins had been on friendly terms with the basic principles of flight since first-grade science. They caught on fast, and before dark Paddy had taught herself to snap roll, reminding me so sharply of Elizabeth and all the hours spent in the air off the North Cap of Terranova that the memory was like an actual physical pain. This time I didn't run and hide. Where was Elizabeth now? What was she doing? Was she happy? Was she lonely? Did she miss us? I had in the space of ten minutes trusted the Librarians to provide for her every need, halfway across the galaxy from the globe that gave her birth, so far away from everyone and everything that was familiar to her. Had they?

"Hey, Mom, watch this!" Sean stalled and recovered, all in one smooth movement, homesteaded a thermal, and began a smooth, circular climb. In an instant Paddy was on his tail, and I on hers.

The sun was setting by the time I called a halt, barely making it back inside the *Kayak* before the last light failed. We were all sore through the shoulders and our calf muscles ached from the stretch it took to operate the rudder, but we assembled huge sandwiches and ate two apiece, slept ten hours straight through, and were back in harness an hour after daybreak the following morning. I declared a school holiday and cut back our daily chores to the absolute, basic, must-do life-support minimum. For the next week, we flew.

It was the best week of my life.

We'd figured out our approximate location, the great canyon just south of the equator. On Terra, Valles Marineris would stretch from one side of the North American continent to the other, long enough for it to be day on one end and night on the other. You could tuck Everest inside one of its deeper channels and never miss it, and in some places it would take Crip a hundred hours to trundle a 15-kph solar scooter from one side to the other. It was the gaudiest tourist attraction in the Solar System this side of Saturn's rings. We'd come down at or about midpoint, near Melas Chasma. It made for incredible air time.

There were canyon walls etched like crystal, entire mountains worn down by wind and sand to mere mesas, hundreds of pedestal rocks carved into weird and wonderful shapes. No two were the same; here an hourglass, there a judge's gavel, the hammer of Thor, a stately, ridged column that but for its pigment would have looked more at home holding up the frieze on the Parthenon. One morning, impatient, we took to the air immediately after sunrise and I saw a rough red shape like the spindle off a spinning wheel, its base surrounded by a puff of mist that looked like clean, white, freshly carded wool.

"Have you ever seen anything like it?" Paddy said, her voice hushed.

"It's like a temple," Sean murmured.

"Have you, Mom?"

In our three-man crew I was the admitted planetary expert, but this . . . "Once, in the American Southwest. A place called Monument Valley. The Grand Canyon, of course. And there's another canyon on Kauai . . ." I shook my head. "No, Paddy. I've never seen anything like this, anywhere, ever."

• • •

Sunday afternoon we packed the foils and harnesses away for the first time in a week. Dinner that evening was eaten to the accompaniment of much laughter and many swooping hand gestures describing impossible feats of derring-do aloft. Crip would have felt right at home. For the first time in a long while, so did I.

Over dessert (fresh strawberries from the barrel outside the sciences station) Sean said, "So we're leaving in the morning?"

"Yeah," I said. "It's time. It's been almost two months since we landed, and"—I gave the bulkhead an affectionate pat—"the *Kayak*'s shipshape."

"You figure on heading us northeast right off?"

I stretched and grinned at Paddy. Like Sean and myself, she was sunburned and more relaxed than any of us had been in years. "I don't know. There's an awful lot of Valles Marineris we haven't seen. Plus, I was wondering, how do you feel about mountain climbing?"

Sean sat up. "Olympus Mons?"

"Well, it's just down the, er, street. Biggest mountain in the Solar System. Be a shame to get this close and not take a look."

"A shame," Sean echoed. "What about Cydonia?"

"The ruins at Cydonia have been there for five thousand centuries. I imagine they'll still be there when we get around to them."

Paddy said with undisguised glee, "Helen is going to be *furious*."

"We'll tell her we took the scenic route," Sean suggested.

"It's her own fault, anyway," I said, as piously as Brother Moses on a Sunday morning. "She's the one who sent us here in a balloon. It's not our fault if we have to go where the wind blows."

When the laughter died down, I judged the time ripe to ask a question I'd been dying to know the answer to for three months and the last million kilometers. "Guys? How *did* you turn Brother Moses green?"

They sobered, and their eyes met. They had stoutly denied

all knowledge of the incident, but I wasn't a mother for nothing. "Why do you think it was us?"

"A lucky guess," I said dryly. "Might have something to do with the mystery datatech who reprogrammed the Outpost galley menus to require a daily half-kay of chocolate for all hands in November."

"I don't know what she's talking about," Paddy told Sean. "Do you know what she's talking about?"

Sean, the most notorious chocoholic on two planets, three moons and 100,000 asteroids, spread his hands wide, innocent bewilderment writ large upon his countenance. "I haven't a clue."

"Or it might have been that study on physical fitness in zero gravity commissioned by and forwarded to Outpost from the Terranovan Institute of Physical Health last September." When they said nothing, I added helpfully, "You remember. The one debunking the beneficial effects of prolonged exercise in a zero gravity environment. The one with the statistics that put your Auntie Charlie into orbit without benefit of spacecraft. Only it turned out there was no Terranovan Institute of Physical Health, so they couldn't have commissioned a study, or compiled statistics, or forwarded them to Outpost."

Paddy, whose favorite physical position was prone, clicked her tongue. "How dreadfully irresponsible of someone."

"Simply dreadful," Sean agreed sadly.

"So tell me about Brother Moses."

They looked at each other, turning on the twin high-beams. Sean raised an eyebrow. Paddy gave a faint shrug and decided to talk. "It wasn't our fault," she said, with a piety to match my own.

"It sure wasn't," Sean agreed. "We meant to turn him blue."

"Blue?"

"Well, we were running this experiment in the physics lab, and we rearranged a set of atoms into coal tar."

"Coal tar?"

Paddy nodded. "Uh-huh. After we figured out what it

was, we looked up what it does. And one of the things it does best is indigo dye."

"Oh."

"There were a lot of possibilities," Sean said.

I held up a hasty hand. "Don't tell me. It's better I should not know. You made indigo dye from the coal tar."

"Uh-huh."

"And you put it in 55Pandora's plant food supply," I said, and was gratified to see their jaws drop.

"How did you know?"

I faked an elaborate yawn. "You were studying hydroponics that month. I figure you made a chemical adjustment that made the plants think the fake indigo was chlorophyll. Second, the people on 55Pandora turned green from the inside out, so it had to be something they were ingesting. Third, you wanted to make a trip out to Mom and Pop's, also known as the Apothecaries to the Asteroids. If you needed something refined down to a substance palatable for organic consumption, without losing its original dyeing capabilities, they would be the ones to see."

Sean's face darkened. "Yeah, and if you'd let us, Brother Moses would have been blue."

"Instead of that tacky green," Paddy said, equally accusing.

"And fourth and last, I saw you marching in the procession behind Brother Moses the day of his demonstration." I looked at Paddy. " 'Honk if you love asteroids'?" I looked at Sean. " 'Clap if you believe in kobolds'?" I gave my head a slow, mournful shake. "And I thought Caleb's limericks were bad."

I stopped Paddy's furtive giggle with my best stern, maternal look. "I would like to make one thing perfectly clear. There will be no turning of mothers, grandmothers, aunts, uncles, or cousins green or any other color. Is that clear?" I paused. "Well, maybe we could make an exception for aunts. But definitely not mothers."

"Oh no, Mom," Paddy said virtuously. "We wouldn't think of such a thing."

"Certainly not," Sean agreed.

Yeah, right. "Good," I said. "Glad to hear it. Go to bed, you monsters."

The next morning I turned on the He-maker and by the time the breakfast dishes were done the pressure gauge on the inner envelope had climbed 10 degrees. The sun rose, the air in the outer envelope expanded, and it was time to retract the drillers in the gear before the *Kayak* took off without them. The gondola, tethered to a small, collapsible anchor, began an almost imperceptible sway beneath our feet.

"Paddy, stand by the anchor."

"Standing by the anchor, aye."

"Sean, you're on watch. Stand by the port in the sciences station."

"Standing by sciences, aye."

The *Kayak* strained at her slender leash as the nav board blinked green all the way across. "Okay, Paddy, release the anchor."

"Anchor released."

"Roger anchor released. Reel in the line."

"Reeling." I waited. "Line in, anchor up, flywheel locked."

"Roger anchor up and locked. Stand by."

"Standing by." Her response was prompt and very crisp, and I smiled to myself. Paddy was enjoying herself. For that matter, so was I.

Something moved outside the port. I looked up from the board, and through the curved graphplex panel saw the walls of the canyon descending. No, we were ascending, and gaining momentum with every meter we climbed. I put a hand on the deflation port lever, just in case, and my fingers tightened as we gathered speed.

We burst out of the top of the canyon like the cork out of a champagne bottle, only rather more controlled, and the cracked and chasmed expanse of the Martian landscape rolled back beneath us in every direction, as if someone had taken hold of the edge of the planet and shook it out flat for our inspection. I knew the horizon curved, but on first sight that first day up, the wrinkled landscape seemed to go on forever, folds of pachydermal Martian skin with blood and heartbeat frozen just beneath the surface. The sight so overwhelmed us that I don't think anyone said a word for the rest of the day. We just looked, and looked, and looked.

We kept on looking during the days and weeks that followed. We drifted all that third month, at the whim of the Martian winds, maintaining a discreet altitude so that there would be no emergency deploying of jibs or red-lining of He-maker to get us out of sudden ends to any box canyon we might have taken a fancy to wander up. "Wind-surfing," Sean called it, using the leading edge of the nearest available weather front to keep us afloat on an endless, rust-red sea. Somedays it was our friend the zephyr, others a laughing gust, but it was always there. We could feel it herd us on our way, we could measure it on our instruments should we disbelieve our senses; it was a palpable force with which we had to reckon each and every day. In the Belt, to get from rock to rock you moved yourself or you didn't move. On Mars, you moved whether you would or not. Or at least you did if you were hitching a ride on a balloon.

Landscape, and weather, and then there was all that sky. Tucked away in the bottom of our canyon, the sky had not seemed quite so omnipresent, but once we were up and out, our perspective changed. As thin and insubstantial as the Martian atmosphere was, it hung over us with a tangible presence that wrapped us about and made us feel somehow snug. The Martian moons, too, hovered over our journey, constant guardian angels. Phobos did not so much rise as it did spring into the western sky, a pale oval that looked like Luna's little sister, so curious as regards our presence on her planet that she checked in on us every eleven hours.

Phobos' orbit was decaying, Paddy informed us, as usual overcome with the romance of our situation. In a hundred million years or so, it would break up and crash to the Martian surface. For now, it traveled around Mars in 7.7 hours, 6,200 klicks above the planet's equator, in an almost perfectly circular orbit. If and when the Martian winds took

us above or below 70 degrees Martian latitude, we would
not be able to see Phobos at all.

Deimos, on the other hand, was barely ten kilometers in
diameter and over 21,000 kilometers from Mars in synchro-
nous orbit; it looked like a bright star and, in comparison
with Phobos, a very slow one. It was so far away, in fact,
Paddy informed us, still in that didactic tone, that it teetered
on the edge of escaping Martian gravity and leaving the Red
Planet's orbit altogether, which it would do eventually anyway. It orbited in the Martian equatorial plane, and remained
in our view for as long as sixty hours.

Phobos and Deimos both turned on their axis in the same
time it took for rotation, showing the same face always to
Mars, as Luna did to Terra. "This view could get old,"
Paddy had said disparagingly back on Outpost, but then
Paddy had never looked anywhere but up, and had no soul
besides. How could anyone not fall instantly and irrevocably
in love with the hurtling moons of Barsoom?

God, Mars was gorgeous!

Let's face it, when vacuum isn't scaring the hell out of
you, it's pretty dull to look at. I mean, how many different
ways can you look at black on black? Even the myriad
different stars superimposed on vacuum's black backdrop
begin to look alike after a while; they don't even twinkle
when you're not looking at them through an atmosphere.

I'd forgotten how beautiful a planet could be. The surprise
of colors in the strata of rock formations, the difference in
texture between the corded remnants of riverbeds old when
Terra was young, the sheer, solid surfaces of cliffs, the
exhilarating rise and fall of flatland to foothill to peak to
gorge. There were columned buttes, Doric and Corinthian,
the abandoned cities of some race of prehistoric giants.
The desiccated fingers of old riverbeds clawed into the
upthrusting bulks of stolid plateaus. The tortuous switch-
backs of Lowell's canals isolated massive, table-topped
mesas, huge and square and indestructible. Delicate pillars
reached for the stars between sheer-walled canyons cutting
deeply into the sides of the Valley. Above them all, there

was an endless horizon at the edge of a sky that began its day flushed with the pink of good health, faded to a clear, bright peach at zenith, only to meld into a subdued ocher landscape with the setting of the sun. The sun looked larger from Mars than I remembered from Terra, because of the amount of dust in the air and the diffusion of light. The subsequent moody effect Sol had on the Martian landscape was as unexpected as it was enchanting. Sunrises were intimate and secretive, zeniths brassy and boisterous, sunsets sleepy and a little sad.

Our first sunrise was a complete surprise. We'd forgotten curtains. There were shutters on the windows of private quarters on Outpost because of all the activity going on non-stop outside. On Mars, we assumed there would be only us and a few hundred Russians we hadn't run into yet, and we had taken our privacy for granted. After our strange encounter with Johnny Ozone, which felt as if it had occurred in a dimension beyond sight and sound anyway, and then the horrible wreckage of the *Tallship* colony, I realized Mars was determined not to be treated as if she were harmless. I still never thought of curtains.

That first morning my side of the *Kayak* faced east, and I got it first: a sharp spill of bright light right through graphplex, covers, eyelid, cornea, pupil, lens, vitreous humor, and up the optical nerve into the cerebral cortex. Without consciously moving, I found myself standing in the center of my stateroom, heart pounding, short of breath, blinking into the dawn's early light and wondering what the hell was *that* and who forgot to turn down the cabin lights the night before?

I'd been working off-Terra for almost thirty years; I hadn't set foot on Luna in sixteen; in their young lives Paddy and Sean had never been closer to Sol than Ceres. It was an adjustment for all of us.

Once we became accustomed to being up with the chickens, the days fell into a pattern. There was a real danger in being so far removed from any authority, in being accountable only to yourself for the work that must be done. It was a hard lesson learned in hiring personnel to babysit asteroid refineries for the long haul to Terran orbit. There was a potentially fatal and always economically disastrous tendency on the part of the crew to let things slide, to drift from day to day, week to week, month to month, to procrastinate until well inside the range of Terranova Traffic Control. In the interim, skills deteriorated and morale waned. The rock jockeys called it mental mañana.

The only effective preventative for mental mañana was a strict, rigorous, daily schedule. During the admittedly brief planning stages of this mission, Charlie had pointed out to me that even our method of transportation would meander; the challenge lay in not allowing the *Kayak*'s method of transportation to dictate our actions, or in this case, inaction.

Of course back then we had not been aware that we would be doing quite so much traveling; at any rate it was impractical to rely on the constant newness of our surroundings to keep us continually at a point of enthusiasm; the twins and I had already seen too much of the Solar System to be forever awed by new sights, although from the first day we never slept through a sunrise, nor were we ever very far from a port during a sunset. The solution lay more in the assigning of responsibilities to each crew member, and then holding each one accountable for his or her duties.

A kid on a space station grew up smart or didn't grow up. Sean and Paddy had been rabid overachievers from the age of two, and vacuum is a great disciplinarian. That sense of discipline paid off in spades on Mars.

We rose with the sun and ate breakfast as the air inside the montgolfier heated. By the end of the meal the helium inside the charliere had warmed and expanded. I retracted the rotary drills up into the legs, and by the time the galley was cleared and locked down, we were aloft. For the first still hour or two following the dawn we rose slowly, straight up, and remained more or less stationary above the campsite of the night before. Our lack of motion combined with the long shadows cast by the rising sun made this the best time for photography. Each of us had been trained in the operation of every machine the gondola carried; as time passed, Sean displayed an increasing facility with wide angle, high-definition photography. He got so he could assemble a collection of pixels and come up with a recognizable topographic feature with little or no help from the computer. He started testing himself against the imaging program and beat it often enough to give me a mild sense of alarm.

Paddy's affinity seemed to be for the spectroscope, which I should have been able to guess would happen, considering the waking hours she spent glued to the ocular of her telescope. The spectroscope examined the optical spectra of Mars, as emitted by the various topographical formations over which we were passing. Paddy identified and charted deposits of calcium carbonates, zinc, magnesium, phosphorous, and, of course, iron. "It's the Red Planet, all right," she remarked one day. "There's almost nothing but Fe on this rock." After six weeks she could identify the bluish-white crystalline of zinc at a single glance, and began using the scope more for confirmation than identification.

As the need to oversee photography and spectroscopy grew less, I began spending more time at the cartography station, plotting our course and speed, making sun sights and polar fixes, and plugging new topographical information into the PlanetView.

The value of a map is to put things in perspective. Where have you been? Where are you going? Where are you now? Good question, on any given day during those first months on Mars. The Martian prime meridian, comparing to zero degrees longitude through Greenwich on Terra, passed through Airy-o, a small, well-defined crater near the Martian equator. Once we signed on with Deneb and got our geographical bearings, I fed the data into our cartography program. It already contained major geographic features such as Olympus Mons and Valles Marineris; all I had to do was fill in the blanks.

But no flat map could show a globe without distortion. I could have encoded flat maps until the cows came home and transmitted the data to Maria Mitchell for compilation into a global representation, but this would take time and Helen didn't want to wait; she wanted an accurate scale diagram of Cydonia ASAP. She fussed over this problem until in self-defense Simon and Sam developed the HT PlanetView. The PlanetView was little more than a keyboard and a holographic tri-dee projector connected by a little black box, one of Simon's better efforts, that translated the keystrokes into contour lines. Its lens projected a scaled globe with the lines of latitude and longitude already drawn. Depending on which key you hit, the globe displayed Martian geography, geology, or meteorology. Other modes could be programmed in at need, including a to-scale close-up of what we knew thus far of Cydonia, at which I had yet to look.

Our tasks had the gratification of immediacy: We saw a butte that morning, Sean had registered its photographic representation by noon, Paddy had a spectral analysis of its composition in the computer before dinner, and I had the butte on the PlanetView before we went to bed that night. It was very satisfying work.

We broke for lunch at noon and afterward retired to our respective cabins for some alone time. At two we met in the galley for the twins' lessons. There were syllabi and course schedules already laid out on the computer; I tried to jazz things up by playing devil's advocate and giving the twins something with a pulse to ask questions of, a privilege they generally disdained. They were both very, very bright, a fact I occasionally deplored and frequently cursed.

School got out at five. We rotated the chores of cooking, housekeeping, and tending the crops. Dinner was at six. At my insistence we ate together; if Paddy'd had her druthers she would have crammed food in her mouth as she leaned into the bubble port, peering through the ocular at the approaching dusk. I made them sit up at the table like civilized human beings, use knives and forks and napkins, and maintain a conversation consisting of more than single-syllable grunts when their mouths weren't full. Mother would have approved, but I wasn't sure either one of the twins would ever forgive me.

By seven the galley was clear again and available for reading, playing board games, watching tapes, and general recreation and pursuit of hobbies. Roger Lindbergh had slipped a disk with a lot of medieval herbal texts stored on it into Sean's personal luggage. He spent a lot of computer time trying to decipher them, and wowed us at mealtimes with statements like "Ye bay leaf boiled with ye peel of orange maketh a water for the washing of hands at ye table" and "Take parsley and hyssop and sage and hack it small and boil it in wine and in water and a little powder of pepper and mess it forth; it will heal all manner of evils of the mouth," not to mention "Ye maidens make garlands of marigold when they go to feasts or bridals because it hath fair yellow flowers and ruddy."

Sean started another flat germinating with the seeds Roger had included with the disk, and even I had to admit the herbs smelled wonderful when you rubbed the leaves. I started to experiment with them in the cooking. Thyme improved the flavor of biopork tenfold, oregano covered a multitude of sins in spaghetti sauce, and spearmint grew like a weed and was wonderful dried and brewed for a sweet tea. I immediately sat down and bounced Charlie a message off Phobos to the effect that I now knew how to cook. Four weeks later came her reply: "Did you pack any baking soda?" I was pretty sure she didn't mean as an ingredient.

Paddy had been vitally interested in astronomy since before she could walk; she spent most of her free time in the bubble port peering up at what stars she could find with the 3-inch telescope and the astronomical calendar that had been the major portion of her personal luggage allowance. The same dust in the air that caused our spectacular sunrises and sunsets frequently obscured the telescopic view, and Paddy cursed Mars' bad seeing loudly and often. I wondered what she'd do when we had our first real dust storm.

Paddy wasn't one to sit around twiddling her thumbs, though, a character trait she shared with her sibling. Thank Christ none of my children were the kind who sat around moaning, "There's nothing to do!" When it became evident that the roiled-up Martian atmosphere would balk regular attempts at observing, Paddy simply lowered her sights.

She called up all the available information from our ship's computer on geology and soon her conversation was peppered with references to "the erosional work of the wind" which was "preeminent in arid to semiarid regions" such as Mars in shifting "dust, silt, fine and coarse sand" and creating features such as "sand dunes, deflation hollows, and pedestal rocks." She seemed especially fascinated with the sandblasting effect on the latter; during our long run down Valles Marineris she never let a spire or a monument get by her.

For fun she folded origami. Kevin Takemotu had taught her how on Ceres, someone else had invented reusable washi paper, and Paddy had included a multicolored ream in her personal freight allowance. One day Sean found a tiny golden crane sitting serenely among the cherry tomatoes, a brown hippopotamus grazing through the hyssop, a silver samurai helmet perched on top of a cucumber. Another morning we woke to a galley ceiling papered with a galaxy of stars—yellow giants, red supergiants, brown dwarfs, silver globular clusters. A rocket ship stood poised to enter this array over the door into the science station. Paddy must have used up all her paper, though, for the exhibit remained only a day before vanishing, to reappear on the galley wall ten days later as an intricate, many-towered castle with a blue moat and a dragon breathing fire and smoke over all.

Between Mars and the twins, waking up on the *Kayak* was always an adventure. I didn't mind, as long as I woke up the same color I went to sleep.

We reached the mouth of Valles Marineris two months out of Picnic Harbor, and came more or less by accident upon Gagarin City. Less because we had its coordinates locked into the computer and had been planning a visit since touchdown. More because we got caught in a dust storm, the first of the season, and could have been dumped anywhere from Chryse Planitia to the South Polar Cap.

Once every Martian year the planet approached perihelion, or a little over 200 million kilometers from Sol, the closest it got to the sun in 687 days. At least once during that time, the entire planet was blanketed by a dust storm of hurricane-force winds, theoretically created by the 150-degree difference in temperature between day and night, in turn created by the planet's proximity to Sol. Let me tell you right here and now that while Martian air at rest may be the 98-pound weakling of planetary atmospheres, when it wakes up it hits like a heavyweight. We'd been experiencing winds no stronger than 60 kilometers maximum; during the storm, our anemometer broke off at 114.2 kph. I would have, too.

And it caught us on the hop. We weren't at perihelion— we wouldn't be for another month—but in that perverse way any planet's weather has of confounding all expectation and prediction, it blind-sided us. One minute we were floating innocently at a thousand meters, sighting in on Deneb to check the IMU's calibration. The next we couldn't see a centimeter outside the CommNav port. The winds shrieked. Lightning flashed. The sun was a half-hearted, fading glow. We couldn't tell how fast we were going because our instruments couldn't see through the dust to measure our ground speed. We battened everything down including ourselves and rode it out because there wasn't anything else to do. It wasn't that rough a ride, surprisingly, but we were flying blind, coasting on the crest of a wannabe Force 10 gale.

And then as suddenly as it had started, six hours later it stopped. The skies cleared, and a breeze hardly worthy of the name wafted us gently north, and we forgot the storm when we saw what was outside the port.

Paddy, barely breathing the words, said, "Olympus?"

I shook my head. "I don't think so," I said softly. "We covered a lot of ground, but not that much."

It was immense, a mound of Martian earth that climbed up, up into the sky, slowly, gradually, so that its height was deceptive to the naked eye. It reminded me of the gradual slope of Mauna Loa on Hawaii, until you were at the peak and 4,169 meters, with the world at your feet and no recollection of how you got there.

"Arsia?" Sean suggested.

"I don't know. Let's take her up."

We made helium until we reached 12,000 meters and gave up. Before we blew air to descend, we saw Arsia rising in the southwest and Ascraeus almost directly north. "Pavonis, then," Paddy said, looking up at the great volcano with something approaching awe on her face, an expression usually reserved for natural wonders viewed through a telescope.

"The Middle Spot," Sean agreed. "Wow."

"We must be right on the equator," I said, and reached for the deflation port switch. "Let's see if we can find us a place to camp for the night. I'd purely love to watch the sun set behind Pavonis this evening."

We set the *Kayak* down on the first level patch of ground we came to and spent the next week watching sunsets and cleaning dust out of various exterior orifices on the gondola. The rock bug shared locker space with a kilo of the stuff. Each and every one of the ports had long, thin grooves scored into their graphplex surfaces by wind-driven sand, and we spent another day filling those in. Our outside instrumentation needed extensive repairs (including a new anemometer) before we would know precisely where we were, but I called a day off and we went flying instead.

We'd been lucky, and I knew it. The Martian dust storm seasons usually last for months and cover the entire planet, and I didn't think for a moment we'd seen the end of this one. It was time we went to ground.

On my first glide, I saw it. Another of the ubiquitous splosh craters, almost at the periphery of our range of vision, at the extreme edge of the eastern slope of Pavonis Mons, just far enough off to escape the mountain's five o'clock shadow. The sun glinted off something. I grabbed for altitude and there it was, an obviously man-made structure with square, flat surfaces in geometric solids.

The *Kayak* was a taut ship. When she broke down, she always picked a good place to do it.

—7—

The House by the Side
of the Road

To know the universe itself as a road, as many roads,
as roads for traveling souls.

—**Walt Whitman**

The first thing I saw on settling the *Kayak* inside the crater
were flashes of light resulting in little explosions from the
side of the habitat. "What the hell?"

"What is that, Mom?"

"I don't—is it—damn!"

"What?"

If I could believe my eyes, it looked like hits from small-
arms fire, the same kind of hits we'd seen on those pieces
of the *Tallship* left big enough to identify, the same kind
of hits on the freighter back on Ceres. They were getting
too damn familiar to me, and it was starting to piss me
off. I tried to raise Gagarin City on the net; no answer.
No surprise, they were busy. I made a tape identifying and
describing ourselves and our ship, said we were friendlies

141

and please not to shoot us, and had the computer translate it into Russian and set it to transmit in Russian and English every five minutes. I set the *Kayak* down safely out of range and began to suit up. "What are you doing?" Sean said.

"I'm suiting up. I'm sick of this shit. I'm going out there and help the Gagarins shoot back."

They stood watching in silence for maybe a millisecond, and reached for their own suits. I paused half-in and half-out of my goonsuit and demanded, "And just what the hell do you think you're doing?"

"We're sick of this shit, too, Mom," Paddy said. "We're going out there and help you help the Gagarins shoot back."

I stood up straight. "You're doing no such thing. Get those suits off and go stand by in CommNav." They didn't move. "Did you hear me? Go stand by in CommNav!"

"No," Paddy said.

"No," Sean echoed. "We'll give the Gagarins help, but we'll *all* give them help."

"All or none, Mom. Besides, why have you been making us practice with small arms and hand-to-hand for, if not for a situation like this?"

"We're fighting men, Mom," Sean said, "and you made us that way."

"You have no combat experience," I said.

"No," they agreed, and waited for me to work it out for myself.

And they never would have, if I had my way. But the world being what it was, they would get it whether I let them or not. In the meantime precious seconds were ticking past. The horrible ruin of the Tallshippers' habitat flashed before my eyes. "All right," I said, the most painful words ever to come out of my mouth. "But only one of you goes. Somebody has to stand watch here, keep the ship safe."

To my infinite relief, the common sense of that observation penetrated two stubborn heads. Sean looked at Paddy. "I'm older."

"By two minutes!"

"I'm better at hand-to-hand."

"I'm a better shot!"

"I can—"

"Hold it!" I said. "Scissors-paper-stone."

They played and Paddy "lost." "All right, Sean, suit up. Paddy, you're responsible for the safety of this ship. If the fighting comes this way, you lift fast and high."

"What about you and Sean?"

"You *lift*. Got it?"

She paled, but said steadily, "I got it, Mom."

"And you lift, regardless, the instant Sean and I hit dirt. Don't leave the crater, just get high enough to be out of range."

This time her response was immediate. "Aye, aye, Captain. I lift when you hit dirt."

Sean and I suited up. Paddy locked down our helmets and strapped on our holsters. Sean went through the lock first. Paddy, her young face set in stern lines, gave my shoulder one hard smack before closing the hatch. I slid down the ladder and hit the ground, running lightly, head and shoulders hunched against an expected blow.

There was none, for either of us. From some kind of ports high up in the structure, the habitat was returning fire, and as we poked our heads up for a first, close-up look at the situation, one figure took a direct hit. The front of his suit exploded, and I heard Sean gasp over the headset. I counted eight figures remaining, all attired in the awkward pressure suits worn in vacuum as opposed to our own lighter weight and infinitely more flexible goonsuits. An advantage. Good.

"Sean?"

"What?"

"See that pile of rocks? Get behind it. I'll go left. Don't fire until I tell you to. They still don't know we're here, so our first shots will be a gift. Make them count. After that, keep your head low and don't take any chances." I grasped his shoulder and gave it a shake. "You hear? No heroics! Gagarin is returning fire, and between the both of us we can run them off. Got it?"

"Got it," he said, and he sounded so young I nearly quailed and ordered him back to the ship.

"Okay," I said. "Go." Without looking back, I ran left. I'd already picked out a frost heave for myself, and landed behind it at the end of a long skid that would have made any third baseman proud. When I'd wriggled up the back side of the little rise enough to see over it, I strained to see the figure of my son. "Sean?"

"I made it, Mom? Now?"

"Not yet." A movement caught my eye farther up the crater floor. A rover crawled into view, a vehicle with a cab made of assorted geometrical solids mounted between four enormous wheels made of individual, inflated bags. "Sean! Do you see it?"

"Yes," he said, his voice excited. "Do want me to—"

"Maintain your position! It's not Johnny!"

"What? How—" His reply was interrupted by a figure, also clad in a p-suit, which clambered all the way out of the rover's top hatch, raised a weapon, and began firing at the city.

The besiegers weren't aiming, just firing off shots at random. They weren't even doing that much damage; the surface areas they connected with exploded in the yellow flash we'd seen from the gondola, leaving behind holes not neat but small. Behind them I saw the outlines of the inhabitants scurrying to patch those holes. There were a lot more people inside than out, and I wondered why they hadn't mounted a counterattack.

I drew my laser pistol and checked the load. The sonic rifle had a longer range but was ineffective against a pressure suit unless you had the muzzle pressed right up against it. I sighted in on the broad back of a pressure suit, finger on the trigger. "Sean? Now!"

I squeezed. A small round burned area appeared over the sixth vertebra. The arms of the p-suit flew up, the weapon dropped from one hand, and the figure fell face forward to lie unmoving. I sighted in on the next figure over and shot again, and missed. I could just hear Caleb chiding my poor marksmanship. "Squeeze, Svensdotter, don't jerk." And I could see his wide grin and his dropped voice as he murmured, "When we're in bed, you don't jerk, you squeeze, right? Just like that." I blew out a breath, held it, and sighted carefully. This time I connected with an elbow.

One figure on Sean's side of the shooting gallery was crawling toward the rover; three were already running in that direction, a fifth must still have been inside because it was moving toward them. The sixth turned, slowly, surveying the field behind him as if he had all the time in the world. He swung a little too far toward Sean to suit me, and I chinned on Channel 9, universal stand-by. If they had their ears on anywhere, it'd be there. "You sons-a-bitches attacking Gagarin City, you're surrounded. Lay down your arms, now!"

There was a brief silence, broken by an amused drawl. "Well, well, well. Did you miss me so much you had to chase me all the way to Mars, darling Star?"

The voice echoed inside my helmet. "Who is this?" I said weakly, but I knew.

A low chuckle was my only answer, and the standing figure broke and ran for his vehicle. "Kwan!" There was no response and the running figure didn't check. "Sean! Shoot for the rover! Aim for the solar panel!" I lit out, pounding down a futile pursuit that inevitably fetched up too short of its goal. The distant figure scrambled up the ladder of the wheeled vehicle and had barely disappeared inside before the segmented wheels began to roll. It climbed through a spot where the crater's rim was lowest and vanished from view.

I swore, loud and long, and turned just in time to to catch Sean, running full tilt, against my chest. The collision rocked me back on my heels; I caught him by the arms and held on. Through his visor his face was congested, his eyes blazed. His voice over my headset sounded urgent and intense. "Come on, Mom, let's get back to the *Kayak*! We can follow them and—"

"And what?" I said in my coldest voice.

In the middle of his first firefight, flushed with the bloodlust of his first victory, he didn't want to hear it. "And wipe them out! Mom! We have to! That was Johnny's rover! They probably killed him! We have to get them!"

"With what?" I said, at my most blighting. "The *Kayak* isn't armed. You want to shoot at those guys through the ports, which are not gun ports, while they're shooting back and taking out the envelopes?"

His flush began to subside. "But, Mom—"

"But nothing. It stops here, at least for now."

"But—"

"No buts." I held his gaze, my own stern. "Take a beat, a couple of big breaths. Do it," I said, when he would have argued.

When reaction set in and he began to shake, I caught his weapon before it fell and helped him to a boulder. My own heart rate was 100, according to the vital signs I chinned from the inside of my helmet. I waited until it had dropped to 90 before calling the *Kayak*. "Paddy? You there?"

"I'm here, Mom."

"Is the ship all right?"

"No problem, those guys didn't come anywhere near us. Mom?"

"What?"

"That was Johnny's rover, wasn't it?"

"It looked like it. Have the Gagarins responded to our message yet?"

"Negative."

I thought for a moment. "Okay. Paddy, we still got a breeze?"

"Yes, three knots southwest."

"Do you have our location?"

"I can see you out the CommNav port."

I waved. "Did you see that?"

"You just waved."

I measured our distance from the habitat. "Okay, pop a jib and bring her over nice and easy, and drop the ladder." Thirty minutes later Sean and I were inside and stripped down to our jumpsuits. "Still no response from Gagarin?"

Paddy shook her head.

"Okay, we drop the anchor and stay put in full view until we get one. After what they've been through today, they're liable to be a little trigger-happy with people marching up to the front door."

It took them until the following morning to respond to our taped message. "Vernadsky Habitat to *Kayak*, Vernadsky to *Kayak*, come in please."

The words were in System English, a relief. "This is *Kayak*, Star Svensdotter speaking. Is this not Gagarin City?"

There was a slight hesitation. "Yes and no. Will you come inside?"

"Be happy to, ah, er, whoever you are." I punched out of the net and looked around at the twins. "Come on. Let's go meet the neighbors."

The entrance to Gagarin City was a large lock reached by a broad, well-defined avenue packed solid from the passage of many feet and some kind of tracked vehicle. The whole habitat was backed up against the north side of the crater. It looked as if it had been built a dome at a time, each dome a different size and with a different level of roof, clustered together like kernels of corn and banked with red dirt. Many of the domes were misted over, behind which we could see bulky and interesting shapes. A tall, slender building, the only one I could see with four sides, rose up from the rear. I assumed it would house a sentry, but it wasn't until we got right up to the lock that we saw any signs of life.

There was a handle which wouldn't turn. There was a buzzer next to the lock and I held it down. At almost the same moment, the shield on the viewport next to the lock slid back. Sean said, "Mom. Over there."

There were three people staring out at us, two men, one enormous and one not so enormous, and a diminutive woman. "Hello." The big man pointed to my left, where next to the viewport there was a plaque with a radio frequency on it, which I chinned my transmitter to. "Hello again. I'm Star Svensdotter. These are my children, Sean and Patricia. We are on an exploring and mapping mission for the American Alliance." I felt Paddy look at me, and plowed on. "You can see the *Kayak*, just inside your crater."

The big man looked confused for a moment; then his face cleared and he nodded. "Your ship, yes?"

I had to smile. "Our ship, yes." I gestured at the charred pockmarks of battle dotting the habitat. "You saw us yesterday?" They all nodded. "There has been trouble elsewhere. Perhaps we could exchange news."

There was a vociferous argument which looked as if it almost came to blows. It ended with the smaller man stamping off in a rage and the big man and the woman looking relieved. "I, Nikolai Yevtushenko. This, Tatiana Tchiakovsky. You go to the airlock, Star Svensdotter, yes?"

"Yes," I said. I turned, and he said, "Wait." I looked back at him. He patted the holster strapped to his side. "Weapons you must leave outside."

My reaction was instinctive and immediate. "No. We keep our weapons with us."

"Then you don't come in."

I didn't like it, not one bit. Paddy broke the staring match, unstrapping her belt. "Mr. Yevtushenko? We'll take them off and you can store them inside for us. Would that be all right?"

Yevtushenko looked at her. He smiled suddenly, a wide smile full of perfect white teeth that split his flowing black beard and gave him the twinkly look of a youthful Father Christmas. "It is all right, Patricia Svensdotter. Your weapons we will hang by the lock."

Paddy looked at me. "All right," I said, still reluctant. "By the lock."

The lock popped and we stepped inside. It closed immediately behind us, and I got that panicky, claustrophobic feeling I always get in a lock when someone else's hand is on the cycler, but air hissed in, and after a few moments the red light on the ceiling blinked green and the interior door popped. As we stepped inside, the little man who had stamped off in a rage came stamping back, this time carrying a small tray. He thrust it at Yevtushenko and snapped off a terse sentence in Russian, if anything in Russian can ever be terse. Yevtushenko gave a small, grave bow. The woman hid a smile behind one upraised hand. The little man favored us all with an impartially hostile glare and stamped off again.

"Grigori reminds us to mind our manners," Yevtushenko said solemnly, and held out the tray, laden with the traditional Russian greeting of bread and salt. "Welcome to Vernadsky, Star Svensdotter."

It was real bread, round loaves of brown rye, and real rock salt, in lumps smaller than peas but not by much. "I thank you, Nikolai Yevtushenko," I replied. The bread had a slightly bitter aftertaste, and the salt was, well, salty. We nibbled politely, and the amenities observed, Yevtushenko relieved us of our side arms, hung them on pegs next to the lock, and led us at a brisk pace through a bewildering labyrinth of corridors constructed of panes of a thick, plasticky material that was by turns opaque, translucent, and transparent, held up by a triangle-based webbing of gray tubular frames. The design was muscular yet delicate, a bow to Shelob and at the same time a salutation to Charlotte. I winced away from a bright ray of sunlight that stretched in through one of the transparent panes. Yevtushenko noticed. "Not to be afraid. The panels are polarized."

He led the way into the mess hall, a serving line at one end and tables and chairs scattered across the floor, most of them occupied. Conversation halted as we entered, to resume again sotto voce. We followed Yevtushenko through the serving line, loading our trays with borscht and blini. Their coffee was terrible; their fresh fruit, including three kinds of grapes, was sweet and firm and juicy; the water tasted vaguely of chemicals but was drinkable.

We sat down and Yevtushenko salted and peppered everything with a lavish hand and dug in. We followed suit, ignoring the curious stares directed our way. No further word was spoken until Yevtushenko pushed his tray to one side and leaned back in his chair. "So, Star Svensdotter." He regarded the three of us. "You have information to share, yes?"

I pushed my tray to one side. "Yes. But first, do you know who was attacking your habitat yesterday?"

His face darkened. "No, we do not. Do you?"

"Yes," I said, "but tell me what happened first."

He frowned. "They came in the rover, a day before you. We thought they were a friend who visits here sometimes, so we are not suspicious." Except for a few mixed-up tenses, his English was very good. "When we saw there is more than one, we locked them out and demand they identify themselves. They try to force entry through the main lock, and when we drove them off, they try to come in through one of the emergency vents on the second lung."

"They didn't make it inside?" He shook his head. "How did you stop them?"

He threw back his head and laughed, a big, booming laugh that shook his several bellies, turned every head in the cafeteria, and probably ran the air pressure all across the habitat up at least one millibar. "We waited until they were inside the entrance to close off the other two lungs and direct all the air in the habitat to Number Two. By then the sun is up and the air expands inside the habitat. The exhale from Number Two Lung was, how do you say, healthy, yes, healthy. Viktor was watching from the tower, and he said that when those"—here he used a Russian word that probably meant just what it sounded like—"managed to pick themselves up, they were half a kilometer from the vent."

The more I thought about it, the more I liked it. I grinned, and he said, his eyes twinkling, "It is no more than you would have done, Star Svensdotter, yes?"

"It may even have been much less," I admitted, and he whooped and struck his hands together. "So that's when they started shooting?"

"That's when they start shooting," he confirmed, nodding. "We made them angry, I think. But their weapons were small, and did little damage."

I looked at the hundred or so people seated around the room. "Why didn't you counterattack? You definitely had them outnumbered."

"The patching crews were keeping up with the damage." He shrugged. "And then you came, and there was no need."

This was entirely too relaxed an attitude to take, in my opinion, but it wasn't my habitat. "So who are these people?" he said.

I told him everything I knew about Kwan, including the earliest meeting, which I had kept from Paddy and Sean. I ended my story with our landing and the meeting with Johnny Ozone. "That was his rover, wasn't it?"

Yevtushenko nodded, frowning. "He was a friend. Do you think—"

I shook my head. "No, he's dead. It's a habit, with Kwan. If there is anyone left alive after one of his attacks, it is strictly an accident." I told him of the *Tallship*.

"I see." Fingers stroked his beard. "And then?"

I recounted our subsequent wandering, the dust storm, our involuntary arrival off the southern slopes of Pavonis Mons.

The mess hall was backed up on what looked through the translucent partition like some kind of giant terrarium, and as I spoke, every now and then I heard noises I couldn't put a name to. As I finished, there came a flurrying sound, as if air were being beaten together in a bowl, and half a dozen loud, indignant, and definitely inhuman calls. Paddy cocked her head and asked, puzzled, "What is that, Nick?"

"What's what, my little Padrushka?" he replied before I could reprove her for her familiar address.

"That noise. Listen."

We did. There were three long, clear notes on a descending scale that I had heard before. I looked at Nikolai, incredulous. The notes were repeated, from farther off. "That," Paddy said. "What is that?"

Nikolai smiled at me. "That, Padrushka, as your mother well knows, is a golden-crowned sparrow."

Paddy looked blank, and I realized neither she nor Sean had heard a songbird before. The geodomes on Outpost had no animals other than the bees, halibut, and oysters we engineered into their ecosystems and harvested for food. The seafood in the New World showcase aquarium was just beginning to mature when we left. The only animal I remembered seeing around Outpost or down on Ceres, or for that matter anywhere in the Belt, was the ubiquitous *Felis catus*.

Nikolai rose to his feet and led us into the next room. It was immense, the ceiling twice as high as the room we had just left, and so crowded with vegetation that I felt instinctively for a machete. Nikolai marched over to a bin, thrust a hand inside, and came out with a fistful of grain. "Do as I do," he told the twins, "and be very still and quiet."

They followed him out into the middle of the forest, a collection of palms, bamboo trees, and what I thought I recognized as rubber plants, maybe. In a small clearing, Nikolai scattered some of the seed and sat down in the middle of it, motioning to the twins to follow suit.

We waited. A three-note trill broke off into an inquiring chirp. There was a rustle in the branches, a whir of wings, and suddenly we were surrounded by little brownish birds with yellow-gold streaks down their heads, pecking up the grains, moving ever closer to Yevtushenko, and to the twins.

Cautiously, so as not to frighten the aviary, I leaned forward to look at Sean's face. He was mesmerized, his eyes fixed on the tiny birds. Paddy was similarly entranced. It was the first time in what seemed like years that I had seen them looking exactly and precisely like what they were: children. In that moment I wanted Caleb back, to see what wonders we had wrought, to share my pride, and, I admit freely, to share my fear for their future. It would be a long time before I forgot how frightened I had been the previous afternoon, watching Sean light out for cover. Not for nothing do they call children hostages to fortune.

I blinked my eyes clear and looked back at Nikolai. One of the sparrows was eating out of his hand. In another moment a second had hopped up onto his wrist, a third to his shoulder. Beneath them, Nikolai and his many chins and bellies sat like a benign, very hairy Buddha. Moving very slowly, very carefully, Sean rose and returned with a double handful of grain that he split with Paddy. He sank down to the floor and divided the remaining grain between both hands and rested them palms up on his knees. A tiny bird with greenish-yellow feathers and black markings and a slightly curved beak watched him, head tilted first to one side and then the other. He hopped cockily forward to perch on Sean's wrist and peck up a seed. Sean turned to me, his smile blinding. A bluebird came tenderly up to alight on Paddy's knee, and she sighed, a long, drawn-out sound of pure enchantment.

When the food was gone, the birds chirped and marched around for a bit longer, looking expectant. When Nikolai didn't move, they gave what appeared to be a collective sigh for all good things past and flew back into the surrounding trees in a blizzard of wings. A moment later, a three-note scale rang out.

For the rest of the time we remained at Gagarin City the twins walked in Nick's shadow and quoted him verbatim, Paddy as if he were Maria Mitchell, Sean as if he were God.

Only it wasn't Gagarin City to its inhabitants, it was Vernadsky. Gagarin City, Nick explained, was a name wished on them by the UER's Department of Space. The twins looked at me and smiled, and I knew they were remembering the naming ceremony. "Why Vernadsky?" I asked him.

"Vladimir Vernadsky," Sean said, "born 1863, died 1945. He was the first Terran scientist to envision the planet as a whole and entire ecosystem, self-correcting and self-sustaining. He's called the father of biospherics."

Nikolai was delighted with Sean. Paddy pouted a little. Nikolai noticed, and promptly became equally delighted with her. A man not to be underestimated.

Whatever they called it, the New Martians' habitat was a model of successful communal effort, a mini-city with a fully functioning environment, all enclosed beneath a series of domes. New domes were added as adequate material was distilled, cultivated, hacked, mined, and refined out of the raw materials Mars provided. They'd made a good start by choosing the right location, the south-facing inner slope of a splosh crater, two kilometers above mean datum surface and half a minute off the equator. They had continued in the right direction by building out into the crater's center. They bored their wells horizontally, into the north cliff, to avoid endangering the habitat's foundation with possible subsurface subsidence. At least half of each dome was buried to protect it from ultraviolet radiation, the exposed half treated to deflect UV back into space.

Since planetfall twenty-five years before, the first three hundred colonists had tripled in population, and some of the first children were now hard at work on the 15-hectare farm that was projected to double in size within the next decade, enabling the habitat to support an increased population, currently projected for two thousand people. The ecosystem was modeled after experiments in the Arizona desert on Terra and the Luna habitats at Copernicus Base and Orientale. It included a miniature salt water ocean, in which Paddy and Sean had their first swim. There was always a waiting list for the beach, Nikolai said. It was understandably the habitat's most popular attraction, and the marine biotechnologist was very firm about the number of people he would allow in the water at a time. The health of the seafood stocks came first, which included oysters, clams, and mussels. There were angel fish, too, which I think got by mostly on their looks, and sea urchins and starfish, which didn't. There was a rain forest, where fog generated at upper levels dripped down the leaves of the tallest plants to coalesce into a warm rain at ground level. There was a marsh, a savanna, and a desert with real snakes, which I considered carrying the commitment to a balanced ecosystem entirely too far.

Everything was recycled. The carbon dioxide exhaled by the colonists was inhaled by the plants; they returned the favor by exhaling oxygen. Human waste fertilized crops and fed the fish. Five different kinds of termites ate their way through the city dump.

The agricultural diversity rivaled that of Terranova's original design; crops included figs, berries, beans, potatoes, peanuts, oats, tomatoes, peppers, spinach, bananas, papayas, oranges, and grapefruit. Those were rubber trees I'd spied in the forest, along with bamboo and coconut palms; they also grew plants for medicinal purposes, including agave and jojoba. A resident herbalist tended to these, and Sean ingratiated himself into her notice and picked her brain, as well as a few cuttings to further diversify his own agricultural inventory.

The livestock had been raised from test tubes and was thriving; goats, chickens, and pigs. There were sheep, too, and I made a mental note to find out if there was yarn on the premises. I hadn't knitted in years, since my last sweater had left this part of the galaxy on Elizabeth's back, but it might be fun to try my hand at it again.

Each unattached settler had his or her own apartment, each family the same. There was a large library filled with tapes and even a few real books, a gymnasium equipped with pool and track, and they had just completed a five-hundred-seat auditorium, buried beneath the west wall of the crater.

The entire habitat had its own respiratory system, with three lungs. The lungs were three huge oval diaphragms, hollow elastic mounds, sited equidistantly around the habitat and connected to it by three buried tunnels. As the air inside the habitat heated, it expanded. Instead of blowing out the various roofs, as it expanded it rushed through the tunnels into the lungs, whose elastic construction expanded with the heat of day and contracted with the cold of night. The twins got a kick out of standing at the mouths of one or the other of those tunnels at the beginning or end of the day, shouting down the howl of the wind.

Vernadsky even had a propellant factory, consisting of a single compressor to suck up Martian atmosphere and extract the carbon dioxide, which was then shipped off to a thermal converter which broke it down into its individual components. They were in the process of developing planetary probes, but I was surprised at the small size of Vernadsky's transportation department. There was one engineer and two overworked technicians, and the rocket factory was only a cramped little shop on the outskirts of the habitat, lacking adequate space and sufficient tools to complete a rover, let alone a satellite. As near as I could discover, Vernadsky had launched two vehicles thus far, one a land probe and the other a satellite. The first had blown up on the launch pad. The second, yet another victim of the Great Galactic Ghoul, had failed to achieve orbit, and it was probably just dumb luck the *Kayak* hadn't had a close encounter of the third kind with it on the way down. When I asked why they didn't initiate a flight test program with miniature boosters, the engineer looked at me blankly. "If it works, it works," Nick translated. "If it doesn't, we try again. There's no hurry."

In the meantime, they stayed close to home. They had plenty to keep them busy. They mined iron; made glass bricks from the soil residue left by Meekmakers after the microwaves had boiled off the hydrogen and helium; tapped into calcium carbonate deposits for lime; experimented with ceramics; mined sulfur for explosives, insecticides, and fungicides; manufactured acids, dyes, and detergents; and with the iron they mined, smelted steel. In their immediate surroundings, say within a hundred kilometers in every direction, or the distance their two go-carts could go and return in a day, they had discovered and mined small but adequate amounts of phosphorous, zinc, lead, and magnesium chloride. They were an industrious bunch, I'd grant them that, and yet . . .

In many respects life for the Vernadsky colonists was idyllic. There was no rain that was not planned and no sleet, no snow, no floods, no mud slides, no forest fires. Marsquakes were weak and rarely registered with anything except the seismometer. Dust storms were their only real problem, as every two years or so the entire population had to turn out, shovel in hand, and clear the solar receptors of sand. Everybody had enough to eat, a place to sleep, and clothes to wear. The temperature never got below 12.5 degrees Celsius.

Still, something about the place bothered me. The New Martians were well-fed, well-housed, and seemed content, but they had also cut themselves off from everything in the outside environment, everything that made Mars what it was. Except for sunlight, and even that was filtered and refined down to its most basic and nonthreatening essence. They'd mapped and spec'd the surrounding countryside, but only far enough to identify and flag essential mineral deposits. They were either so wrapped up in colony construction or so incurious or both, as to ignore what might unlock the mystery of Prometheus and provide answers to the beginning of human life. They had escaped the Terran cage and the geocentric viewpoint of people inextricably bound to the earth, what spacers contemptuously called flatlanders, only to construct another and even smaller cage on the first available planet.

I realized that I was describing myself when Helen had first offered me the *Kayak*. I'd been on Outpost for so long, had run the mining and A World of Your Own operations for so many years, that at the time she approached me I must have thought there was no other life. It was an unflattering realization, and I squirmed beneath it.

I was hiking in one of the biomes early one morning soon after this realization, climbing the steep path that led up the cliff face from the ocean below to the savanna plateau above. It was good to stretch my muscles without the necessity of first donning a goonsuit, good to sweat and have the breeze fan my cheeks. I stood at the edge of the cliff, breathing in the cool morning air. Sol was just raising his sleepy head, and through the habitat window I watched him yawn and stretch and begin the slow climb to his feet. The first rays touched the roof of the biome. The breeze slowed, and then stilled completely, like the slack between tides on Terra.

I heard a sound, a low, keening wail. At first I thought it was the beginning stir of the wind, coming back from the other direction. Then a movement caught my eye. There was someone, squatting or kneeling in a clump of rubber tree fronds, farther down the cliff and dangerously close to its edge.

It was a woman, her uncombed hair streaked with white. She sat with her legs crossed beneath her, her staring eyes fixed on some object only she could see. Her jumpsuit was worn and filthy, her arms cradled an invisible baby, and she rocked gently back and forth, all the while crooning that thin, wordless wailing sound that had first attracted my attention and, even now that I knew where it came from, froze me where I stood. *The mirror crack'd from side to side*, and I started forward to help, only to be brought up short by a firm hand on one shoulder.

"There are some in whom this planet inspires at first sight not love, but hate and fear," Nick said softly. "For a few it is too much." He stepped around me. "Anya." She made no reply. One large hand caressed her hair. She took no notice of him, or of me.

I was a fixer. I wanted to fix this. I wanted to fix her. I wanted to pick her up bodily, wash her, clothe her, jolt her out of her abstraction, make her see me, make her see herself, call her back from her waking nightmare.

The Lady of Shalott rocked back and forth, keening her macabre lullaby to a misbegotten child. Nick led me away.

During our first week at Vernadsky another dust storm hit, effectively obliterating any trace of Kwan's trail. The second week, Nick invited us to summer at Vernadsky, or stay at least until the worst of the dust storms had passed, whichever came first. After consultation with Sean and Paddy, we were pleased to accept. We still hadn't been able to raise Cydonia on the net or off the beacon on Phobos, so I updated our initial looped message to include recent history and present location and set it to transmit once a day. I included a description of Kwan's vehicle and advised the archaeologists to go armed at all times. Kwan and company would have gone to ground to wait out the storm season, same as us, or so I hoped, but I worried about the eggheads at Cydonia. From the personnel files in the *Kayak*'s computer, there wasn't one of them I'd trust to back me up in a playground fistfight.

"You've got us," Sean pointed out.

I looked at him, sitting next to his sister and regarding me with no little degree of cockiness. I supposed they were entitled to it. They had seen their first combat and proved themselves capable of performing in the clutch. With Kwan on the loose, Mars felt awfully small to me, and I feared their experience would have an opportunity to broaden all too soon. "So I do," I said, and left it at that.

Nick helped us move the *Kayak* to a sheltered tie-down closer to the habitat. I powered down the He-maker so there was just enough pressure inside the charliere to keep the envelopes off the ground and no more. That evening one of the New Martians' teenage daughters invited Paddy for a pajama party, and her mother seconded the motion. Sean had been invited to the herbalist's home, so I let them both off the leash for a weekend.

"So, Star," Nick said. "You will go back to your ship now, yes?"

"Yes."

"Or—" He paused delicately. "You could stay here."

I must have looked blank, because he huffed out an impatient sigh at my obtuseness. "With me. Tonight."

I still didn't get it. I think I thought that part of me died with Caleb.

Nick moved pretty fast for someone of his bulk. The next thing I knew I had that luxuriant beard and several chins and all three of his bellies pressing up against me and two tree-trunk-sized arms wrapped around me. The last time somebody had tried that, he'd wound up in traction. I kept very still within Nick's embrace.

His voice rumbled up out of his chest like a bass played strictly in G. "Your children tell me your husband is dead, yes?"

"Yes."

"For these twelve years and more, yes?"

"And more," I echoed.

"And you have not—?"

"No. I have not."

"This is a very long time," he observed.

A very long time.

Nick put one massive hand beneath my chin and kissed me. His beard tickled. He kissed me again and murmured a few sweet nothings in my ear. I always go a little weak at the knees at the sound of English spoken with an accent. I stayed. Nick was a kind and generous lover. It felt good to be held again.

The following Monday all hands were involved in routine maintenance on board the *Kayak*, and Paddy said, "What's that you're humming, Mom?"

"What?" I had to think, and when I realized, I think I may even have blushed a little. "Oh. 'Moscow Nights'."

"Pretty tune," she said solemnly. I gave her a sharp look but her expression was perfectly sober.

"I like it, too," Sean called down the curve.

"Yeah," I said, and I grinned at Paddy. "Me, too."

We stayed at Vernadsky for four months, waiting out the storm season. We worked side by side with the New Martians, tilling their fields, tending their animals, cleaning their air scrubbers, helping with the thousand and one chores that come with being a homeowner, especially a homeowner on Mars. We swam often in the ocean biome, spent an inordinate amount of time at the very top of the mountain biome letting the wind blow through our hair, and waded through the jungle biome hunting for a sighting of the bush babies. I saw the Lady of Shalott from time to time, always at a distance, always rocking, always crooning to her invisible baby.

At solstice there was a harvest festival, with feasting and dancing to a three-piece band, and I dusted off my guitar and brought it in. It was worth it to see the expressions on the twins' faces when I opened my mouth and a not half-bad soprano came out. I spelled the band with "The Hills of Connemara" and "The Green Hills of Earth," and taught the Martians every sea chanty I'd ever learned, starting with "Blow Ye Winds" and finishing up with "Rolling Down to Old Maui," which they all loved because of the verse featuring the cold Kamchatka Sea. When the balalaikas took over again I saw maidens with garlands of marigolds in their hair making merry with Sean. Paddy sat sipping punch surrounded by half the Martian male population. Both sightings would have alarmed me if I'd been given time to think about it. There was even vodka—no wonder the potato patch was so big—and I found myself matching shot for shot with Nick, who outweighed me by fifty kays, and awoke the next morning with a surprisingly clear head and a Russian the size of Dubuque taking enthusiastic advantage of me. Clearly there was nothing to do but cooperate.

When the skies cleared once again and we prepared to lift ship, Nick said, "You must go?"

I thought of Helen. "Yes."

"Why?"

I shrugged and spread my hands. "Got to see what's there."

He looked at me oddly. "What do you expect to find?"

"At Cydonia? I don't know. Maybe nothing. Maybe everything." I looked at him. "You could come with us. Always room for one more."

His refusal was probably the most graceful and painless rejection I'd ever received. "No, Starushka. The drillers have struck a pocket of sweet water, and soon we will be adding another cube to the ocean biome. No, you go." He snatched me up—I'd never felt petite before in my life until I met Nikolai Yevtushenko—and kissed me long and hard. "But come back. And make it soon."

I promised I would. A week later we lifted off and set course for 40 degrees 86 minutes north and 120 degrees east. It wasn't until we were three days out that I discovered the pair of golden-crowned sparrows in Paddy's room. "They're both male, right?" I said hopefully after the first shock passed. Paddy shook her head. "Both female?" Nope. Sean avoided my glance.

I could hear the rumble of Nick's laughter from a thousand kilometers distant. I only hoped the sparrows weren't horny, and if they were, that they were at least infertile.

—8—

Sermons in Stone

Can these bones live?   —**Ezekiel 37:3**

"We're not going to bypass Olympus Mons, are we, Mom?"

"Which way is the wind blowing?"

"South-southwest," Sean replied promptly.

"Then I don't see how we can miss it."

He whooped and charged down to Sciences to tell Paddy, leaving me to pop both jibs for a run before the wind.

The Tharsis uplift was an extra-large bulge of Martian crust that occurred at almost exactly the same latitude on Mars that the island of Hawaii did on Terra, that the Great Red Spot appeared on Jupiter, that Perry Austin's volcanoes erupted in on Io, that some of the major ring formations occurred on Saturn, and that the Great Dark Spot manifests on Neptune. This regular recurrence of interesting planetary phenomena had to do with the vorticular fluid dynamics in the formation of planets. Every planetary geologist I'd ever met was more than happy to instruct me in Platonic solids and tetrahedral geometry, so I usually ran when a planetologist made a move in my direction. I've never been all that interested in the way planets form. They are the gift of a benevolent universe. It's enough that they're there and I can get down on them and poke around.

There is of course no sea on Mars, so no sea level. Instead, the mean level of Martian topography rejoiced in the term "datum surface." Mars' datum surface was the altitude against which other topographical features were measured, and was what the zero meant on the *Kayak*'s altimeter. Mars is shaped like an egg with a soft shell that had been dropped once on the narrow end; most of the northern hemisphere is below datum surface, some of it to the tune of two and a half kilometers. Whereas most of the southern hemisphere rises higher than the datum surface, from two and a half to six-plus kilometers higher, as witness Vernadsky's altitude.

On the whole, I disapproved of the design. I'd never build a habitat that rudely shaped—just think of trying to get the gravity right when you put on spin. Ever try to throw a pot with all that wet clay even just a little off-center? No, thank you. Centrifugal force, unlike gravity (so far), was a force that could be generated, tamed, and made to serve, but if you're smart you don't ever get into its cage without whip and chair firmly in hand.

However much I disapproved, Olympus Mons was the crowning jewel in the Tharsis bulge, the largest volcano in the Solar System. The *Kayak* was incapable of making the summit, 27,450 meters, an altitude at which Mars' already tenuous grip on its atmosphere was at its feeblest. The twins bemoaned the fact that they wouldn't be able to look at the caldera (a mere 3,050 meters deep and a paltry 81 kilometers wide), but even they had to admit that there was plenty to see at the lower latitudes. Olympus Mons was the size of Arizona and, like its companion volcanoes at Tharsis, very like Mauna Loa in its gradual rise. It was so big and it weighed so much that the Martian crust couldn't hold it up; the surface of the planet itself sank beneath it, so that a kind of trough encircled the entire mountain like a drainage ditch. Martian gravity was stronger on Tharsis Montes than anywhere else on the Red Planet—big surprise.

The sky had faded from pink to a pinkish kind of azure, and the way the light slid around the gentle slope of the enormous volcano the curve of the terrain was so pronounced it was as if we were looking at Mars from orbit. A wisp of shadow caught my eye. "What's that? Down there, to your left."

"I don't know, Mom," Paddy said. "Doesn't really look like fog or haze, does it?"

"All the fog should be burned off by this time, anyway," Sean said, peering over my shoulder.

The hint of white tantalized me, but the sun was lowering inexorably into the west and we still hadn't found a place to drop the hook overnight. Get thee behind me, Satan. "Time to find us a parking space. Mark that spot. We'll take a closer look first thing in the morning. Paddy, man the jib controls just in case. Sean, stand by the altimeter."

"Jib controls, aye."

"Altimeter holding steady at twelve thousand meters," Sean reported.

"Eek. Nobody look down." I blew some more air, and the pockmarked, cratered surface of Olympus and its environs grew clearer in our windows.

"Looks like God used it for target practice," Sean commented.

Paddy agreed. "This whole planet is just lousy with craters, isn't it?"

"Not the northern hemisphere, though," Sean replied. "How come?"

"Good question. Let's drop a rock bug and take some pictures."

The rock bug, or roboprospector, was essentially a robot with a bag and a hammer designed to random-sample geologic specimens and then home in on the *Kayak*'s signal by liftoff the next day. We dropped the bug and shot spectra and pixels all the way down, mooring eventually inside a small splosh crater halfway down the volcano's eastern slope.

At sunup we played scissors-paper-stone and I lost, so I suited up again and went out to retrieve the rock bug. It was nuzzling up to the Number Three leg like the runt of the litter goes for Mama. Sean was standing by in Sciences and I set the database to fast forward. "Data received," Sean said over my headset, and I reset and restowed the rock bug.

It was almost anticlimactic to look up and see an automated probe trundle over the rim of the crater. I was startled, and for a moment disbelieving—Oh Helen, Helen, and you told me we'd be all alone on our Red Planet! There is no truth in you. It was a measure of how relaxed I was by then that I didn't immediately blast the probe to bits with my laser pistol, which was a good thing. When we— the twins suited up and joined me—went out for a closer look, it turned out to be an Agoot Gallivanter, the eighth in a series of planetary probes launched every two years by Maria Mitchell Observatory to whatever System destination Tori deemed worthy of study. It looked like a very large centipede, a segmented, tracked vehicle with a solar-paneled umbrella for power, cameras pointing in every direction including up, and waldoes busily stuffing anything they could grab into its spectrometrical maw. I toyed with the idea of interrupting its data transmission to send Tori a howdy, but I didn't want to mess with the equipment— didn't want to tempt the Great Galactic Ghoul.

The twins were not so restrained. That evening I discovered they had fed one of the waldoes a peanut butter sandwich; "just to see if Tori's paying attention," was how Paddy explained it, her eyes big and blue and oh-so-innocent. I stamped and snorted and made maternal noises of disapproval, and then I went to my room and smothered my laughter in a pillow. I would have killed to have been a fly on the wall at Maria Mitchell Observatory when that transmission came in.

"Why do you think life never developed on Mars?" Sean said at breakfast the next morning.

"That's easy," Paddy said, her mouth full of herbed eggs.

"No water. Not bad, Mom. These are almost edible."

"You overwhelm me, Paddy."

"But there was water once, or else what are all those dry river beds we've been charting?"

"Rivers are one thing. You need a stable body of water to develop life forms. Ponds of liquid water may never have existed long enough in any one place on Mars to allow living organisms to evolve. And then there's the ultraviolet. It does sort of sanitize the surface."

Sean's brow puckered. "Did the lack of atmosphere and the resulting flood of UV cause the water to boil off? Or did the water boil off and then the atmosphere, and then the UV got in?"

"Maybe there never was enough gravity on Mars to hold down an atmosphere," Paddy suggested, and snickered. "Remember the Mons."

Sean winced but persevered. "Perhaps there once were organisms—"

"You think we should be looking for fossils?" Paddy sounded skeptical.

Sean shrugged. "It's possible. We never did get really down and dirty in some of the deeper channels of the Valley. Maybe there is life here, just in long-term hibernation." He stared through the port, as if he looked hard enough he would find some sign.

"It'd be nice," Paddy agreed, "but hardly likely. They'd have found something at Vernadsky by now."

I sighed. "I don't need this."

"Need what?"

"Mother."

The twins looked mystified. "What about her?"

"If there is life on Mars, no matter how microbiotic, she'll say we should leave it alone. She'll probably say we should leave, period."

" 'Never underestimate the tenacity and stubbornness of life,' " Paddy quoted Helen.

" 'Don't sell life short,' " Sean counter-quoted. " 'It's more ingenious than we think.' Maybe Emaa's right."

"Still, you never know. Mars is the closest thing we've

got in the Solar System to a sterile planet. Who knows what kinds of skeletal mummies we're going to find in what kind of sedimentary tombs? Sermons in stones, books in the running brooks."

"Maybe Helen's right. Maybe at Cydonia we'll find out what happened to Prometheus."

"Sean, the Prometheans' existence is still only a theoretical possibility backed by a few alleged artifacts and a lot of guesswork."

"I bet the Librarians could tell us."

"They could if they were still speaking to us," I agreed, and sighed.

For a moment we sat, not speaking, staring out the port over the vast flat slope littered with boulders and pocked with craters. Busy old fool, unruly Sol was well up over the horizon, outlining the summit of Olympus Mons as we crouched adoringly at its feet. "What did happen here?" I wondered aloud. "From all indications, once there was several hundred feet of water on the surface of Mars. That volcano was active. At one time, planetary evolution was proceeding here much as it was on Terra. For its first billion years, the climate on Mars was nothing short of balmy. What made life begin on Terra, and a three-billion-year winter begin here?"

"Is winter the right word?"

I looked at my son. "What do you mean?"

"I don't know exactly," he said. "Winter implies spring will follow, I guess."

"Mars, planet-in-waiting?" Paddy suggested.

"Always the bridesmaid, never the bride," Sean said, nodding agreement. "Don't you get the feeling—"

"What?"

"I don't know," he said again. "Look at the planets in this system, the inner ones, anyway. Mercury and Venus too hot, Mars too cold, Terra just right."

"Kind of like someone groping for the right formula?" I suggested, interested in spite of myself.

"Exactly," Sean said, pleased with me, and I was proud I'd said a smart thing. "Like someone was running a test to define the limits of the proper thermal band around a star to develop and sustain life."

"I suppose, assuming life is as prolific and promiscuous in other star systems, the configuration of the Solar System at the very least gives us a rule of thumb."

"A guideline," Paddy said, nodding. "We know where to look."

Sean, very sober, said, "I wonder if Prometheus was too cold or too hot?"

"Or if it was too cold and they blew it up trying to warm it." Paddy said.

"Or tried to cool it down too quickly."

That hint of white shadow the previous evening had dissipated by the following morning and not replaced itself. I was disappointed, and it showed. "What did you want, Mom?" Paddy said, grinning.

"An eruption?" Sean suggested. "Steam? Ash? Lava?"

"Don't be silly," I said, without conviction. Our seismometer had not picked up any significant tremors during our stay, but that didn't mean anything. Earthquakes come when they will and if they will. I'd been born during the Great Alaskan Earthquake, 8.5 on the Richter scale. It was fifty years before another that size hit again, and by that time me and my family were well and truly off-planet for good. I've never considered earthquakes necessary. Made for a very unstable habitat. "Don't be silly," I repeated, with more conviction this time.

We spent the next two months mapping Tharsis, and could quite happily have spent much longer, if some of us had not been in the regrettable habit of responsibility and reminded the rest of us that we were there not to map Tharsis but to explore Cydonia. By then, Helen was bombarding us with bi-monthly bulletins, all of which began with the latitude and longitude of the Cydonia complex. I decided we'd better head in that direction before she hopped a ship for Mars and dragged us there by our short hairs.

Between World War III and the Great Galactic Ghoul there wasn't much record left of the Cydonia studies on

Terra. Maria Mitchell had been preoccupied with charting the Asteroid Belt for commercial exploitation, so for the most part Mars had been only an afterthought, especially after the United Eurasian Republic beat the American Alliance in establishing the first colony there. The feeling was something like, okay fine—disdainful sniff—you've got Mars, we'll take Luna and the Belt.

In the nearly forty years since its discovery, until Helen coerced Terranova into an expedition, no one had bothered to take a closer look, much less actually send someone out to poke around. Nowadays, backers of space projects never did anything without expecting a return, and the quicker and cheaper the better. I was pretty sure the only way Helen had managed financing for the Cydonia Archaeological Expedition was to make extravagant and wholly spurious promises about what would be found in the way of essential elements. I wouldn't have put it past her to convince them that the entire Iron Planet was really made of titanium.

Helen had always been interested in Cydonia. The first time I'd ever heard of the place was in our room at Stanford, more years ago now than I cared to remember. She'd had Hoagland's book, the JPL study, the NASA study, and blown-up reproductions of the Viking photos tacked up on the wall, all of them underlined and highlighted and annotated and circled in her neat handwriting. She held forth at length on the purposes of the various structures. At first I merely endured it. After a while I got interested and began to listen.

What first attracted Terran attention was the Face, a mound found in the northern desert of Mars in the shape of a head 1.6 kilometers in length. The Face looked vaguely like Tutankhamen's death mask crossed with a rhesus monkey, and alone, it could have been an anomaly, explained away as one of those natural erosional phenomena like Cochise's profile in the Chiricahua Mountains in Arizona and the Sleeping Lady in Alaska and a hundred other such formations on Terra.

What made people begin to take the Face seriously was its geographical context. To the right of the Face was a cliff on the edge of a splosh crater. To the left of the Face was the so-called City, four pyramidal structures with walls pretty straight for having been carved by wind and sand. The City, the Face, and the Cliff were arranged so that at summer solstice 500,000 years ago you could have stood in the center of the City and watched the sun rise over the exact center of the Cliff and Face. This jolted observers into taking a closer look, whereupon they discovered a pyramid with a ridgepole forked on both ends with the dimensions of da Vinci's *Man*.

The observers began to add things up, literally, and found some queer mathematical relationships, not only between the various structures at Cydonia but between Cydonia and the rest of Mars. For example, if one arbitrarily placed the Tharsis bulge at zero degrees longitude, Cydonia lined up on 120 degrees longitude. The vertices of tetrahedral geometry, the basis of vorticular fluid dynamics and the first step in Einstein's Unified Field Theory, occur precisely 120 degrees apart. The distance between the Pyramid and the Face was precisely 1/360th of the diameter of Mars. The Pyramid, in its mathematical proportions, repeated a set of fundamental constants, including pi. All the structures were located within 100 square kilometers, a parallelogram which formed other mathematical relationships with the enclosed structures and with the planet of Mars itself.

Somewhere along in here, someone pointed out that the Face bore a definite resemblance to Homo erectus, a Terran ancestor of the human race who was inventing fire at about the same time the summer solstice sun was rising over the Face, and the rest was madness. "Monkeys on Mars!" screamed the tabloids, but enough serious people were interested to equip the next probe to take a closer look. A month before Pyongyang, the Eurospace Probe Endeavor IV received a few fuzzy pictures that seemed to confirm the existence of artificial structures at Cydonia. World War III put further inquiry on hold.

Helen didn't talk much about Cydonia after that. It was a tactical decision, first things first. Her immediate goal had been to secure and consolidate our foothold in space, and to do that the venture had to be proven profitable to investors. The biggest investors were nations, and nations were notoriously citizen-driven, and citizens were notorious for demanding the biggest bang for the buck. Following the war, every buck not spent toward Never Again was fiercely challenged, which led a frustrated Helen and Frank to devise the Big Lie, which got Terrans back into space and, eventually, on the road once again to Cydonia.

For the first time, I wondered why Helen wasn't aboard the *Kayak*. I had been so absorbed in myself that I hadn't even thought to ask. I wondered, shamefully, if she had sacrificed the dream of a lifetime to give me a purpose, a direction, a time to heal.

We still hadn't been able to raise the Cydonia expedition on the commnet, and the longer we went without communication the more nervous I got. The landscape didn't help. When we left the Tharsis uplift behind us, the terrain changed dramatically. Most of the northern hemisphere of Mars was composed of vast quantities of flat. It made it a safe site for the Viking landers but there wasn't much to see once they set down, other than the ubiquitous splosh crater, formed by meteorites striking the surface millions of years before when the planet's crust was still liquid. Mars was just lousy with splosh craters.

The up side was that we made good time because there wasn't much to stop and look at and whatever there was we could see coming from a long way off, but we fought mental mañana every klick of the way. The features on the PlanetView crept by, the spectrometer seemed incapable of recognizing anything but iron, and the pixels came out flat and uninspiring. I was beginning to think we weren't going to see anything worth looking at until we got to the ice steppes of the North Polar Cap.

Which is why, when we saw it, we thought it was the rim of yet another splosh crater.

It wasn't.

It looked like a splosh crater, much the same as the one the New Martians had used to build Vernadsky, a round hole in the ground surrounded by a rim of debris thrown out on impact. Red sand had piled up around the rim, presenting a smooth front on all sides. Inside was a bowl-shaped depression, filled with more of the ubiquitous red sand.

Only not quite. I was sitting in CommNav, my feet crossed on the board, practicing the chord changes for "Early Morning Rain" (B seven's a bitch) when Sean called downship. "Mom?"

A minor was a snap by comparison, and I preferred the way it sounded, too. "What?"

"Could you come here a minute?"

Although E minor was my favorite, and no wonder, since it was what I sang in most of the time, whether the song called for it or not. "Why?"

"Mom!"

Muttering beneath my breath, I put aside the guitar. Paddy was in the galley, inventing an origami otter. She rolled her eyes as I passed. Sean was in Sciences, or Atlas and Igneous, as he had recently dubbed it. We were all pretty bored.

I stopped behind him. "What?"

"Look," he said, one finger pointing through the bubble port. By a miracle, Paddy had stowed her telescope the night before and the view was unobscured.

I looked in the direction of his finger. "So what? Another splosh crater? Big deal."

Wordlessly, he handed me the glasses. "Do I have to?" He frowned at me, and with a sigh I focused the lenses.

He waited.

"Wait a minute," I said. "What's that?"

"What's what?" Paddy said from behind me.

"In the bowl of that splosh crater ahead."

She squinted at the horizon. "I don't—Oh." She snatched the glasses from me. "Looks like a spire, or some kind of pedestal rock." She lowered the glasses. "But inside a crater?"

I didn't think so, either. Even from this distance the slim pillar was too smooth, too regular. We were cruising at a thousand meters, in front of a breeze making about eight kph. "How tall is it?"

It was before ten in the morning, so Paddy measured the pillar's shadow and added a few numbers. "About one hundred seventy meters."

It looked taller. As we came closer it looked as if it had barely survived a bad case of smallpox.

"Mom." Sean was leaning over the control board, his nose flattened against the graphplex of the port. "There's people down there."

There were people down there, half a dozen p-suited figures, standing in a half-circle, looking up. I popped both jibs and trimmed them to put us in irons, but made no move to descend. Their goonsuits looked Terranova SI, same as ours, but I kept the *Kayak* where she was, at a thousand feet, with one hand clenched on the He-maker switch. If there were anything other than mad scientist types down there, I was prepared to climb high and fast and rig for running back to Vernadsky, where the odds would be more in my favor.

"Mom, it's okay," Paddy said. "It's the gravediggers."

"Gravediggers" was the accurate though less than felicitous nickname Sean had given the Cydonia expedition. "How do you know?"

"Look."

I leaned forward, my forehead against the cool surface of the port, and stared down. The six figures had been joined by two more, evidently from the inside of the pillar. Five of the figures had extended their arms and formed themselves into a five-pointed star. The other three, also with extended arms, were arranged in something that looked like a dipper standing on its handle.

"It's a question mark, Mom," Sean said. "A star, followed by a question mark." He looked at me and grinned. " 'Is that you, Star?' "

I refused to relax my guard. "Kwan recognized me at Vernadsky. This could be a ruse to get us down on the ground." I went into CommNav and punched up Channel 9. "Cydonia Base, this is the *Kayak*, Star Svensdotter, commanding. You folks got your ears on?" I leaned my forehead against the port, looking down.

The star and the question mark melted into an agitated mass of waving arms. At the same time several excited voices erupted over the speaker. "Hello, *Kayak!*" "Is this really Star Svensdotter?" "About time you got here!" "Where have you been, we—"

"Cydonia Base!" Silence. "Could I talk to just one person at a time, please?"

There was a pause. As we watched, one of the figures below detached itself from the group and stood a little apart. "Of course, Ms. Svensdotter. I beg your pardon, but when the first new person we see in over a year is Star Svensdotter, one can hardly blame us for a little natural excitement." He gave a rich chuckle. I loathed people who chuckled richly.

"Well, thank you." I think. "Who am I speaking to?"

"I beg your pardon a second time, I'm sure. This is Maximilian Woolley."

"Mr. Woolley—"

"Dr. Woolley, please."

"Sorry, Dr. Woolley. Dr. Woolley, I've just come from Vernadsky, the Russian settlement down on the equator. Four months ago they were attacked by a group armed with laser weapons. No one was killed, but three months prior to that we landed in Vallis Marineris and found another, smaller colony destroyed and all its inhabitants killed, also by laser weapons. Have you had any trouble?"

For the second time, everyone tried to talk at once. Dr. Woolley prevailed. "Quiet, please, ladies and gentlemen. No, Ms. Svensdotter, I am delighted to report that we have not had any trouble of any kind. Since we landed, the only moving thing on this benighted landscape we have seen is yourself."

"Selves," I said. "My son and daughter are with me. Good. I'm glad things have been peaceful for you. But as a precautionary measure, are you armed?"

"I'm afraid so; Ms. Ricadonna insisted."

"I am delighted to hear it," I said. Paddy elbowed me and I said, "Where's your camp?"

"We have a temporary camp set up on the north rim." The white arm pointed.

Sean handed me the binoculars and I surveyed the site. "All right, we'll park on the crater floor below it." I let out a jib and caught a passing breeze, and an hour later we were down and anchored. It took another thirty minutes worth of housekeeping before I gave the okay for EVA. As we suited up, Sean said, "They weren't wearing any."

"Any what?"

"Pistols, rifles, fragmentation grenades, shoulder-fired rocket launchers, anything. They weren't armed."

I locked down his helmet. "I noticed. Probably left them back at camp."

Even through the visor, his snort was audible. I gave his helmet a light slap with my open palm. "Behave. These are scientists, not soldiers. There haven't been a lot of shots fired in anger over whether Crete was Plato's Atlantis. Make allowances."

He didn't snort this time, but from his skeptical expression he might as well have. Buy them guns, send them to battle, this is what you get.

On the ground we were surrounded, excited faces peering at us through visors that were pockmarked and scored, as if they'd spent a lot of time pressed up against a rough surface trying to peer inside.

"Excuse me, please. Excuse me, pardon me, thank you very much." I caught a glimpse of a luxuriant white handle-bar mustache as the stocky figure pushed his way forward. "Ms. Svensdotter. I'm Dr. Woolley." He paused. I wondered if he expected applause. "Welcome to Mars."

I smiled with all my teeth. "Thank you, Dr. Woolley, but we've been on Mars for over seven months."

Rich chuckle. "Of course you have, of course you have. Well, then, I may welcome you to Cydonia, may I not?" He waved a hand in a proprietary gesture which included most of the northern hemisphere of the planet.

"Certainly you may, and I thank you." I can be as pompous as the next guy when the occasion calls for it. "May I introduce my son and daughter. Patricia, Sean, this is Dr. Woolley."

"How do you do," Paddy said.

"How do you do," Sean echoed.

"And how do you do," Dr. Woolley said jovially. "Welcome to Cydonia, children. How nice it will be to have some little people about the place for a change."

Suddenly I felt like the mother of leprechauns, a neat trick since both twins stood just five centimeters short of my own one ninety-three. Sean, spine stiff with outrage at being called a child, a stage he considered to have left behind him a minimum of ten years before, was about to rip Dr. Woolley a new bodily orifice when I stepped between them. "Thank you, Dr. Woolley, how kind of you to say so. Where exactly in Cydonia are we?"

We turned in a body to regard the tall, slender structure standing alone and fragile in the center of the splosh crater. By now it was noon, and the structure cast very little shadow, so that if you weren't looking right at it, it barely registered on your peripheral vision. From the air at this time of day it might not have been visible at all.

"We are at the Tholus, dear lady," Dr. Woolley said.

"Yes, we know that, at the splosh crater at the lower right-hand corner of the Cydonia complex," Paddy said.

Woolley drew back, no doubt surprised my leprechaun could speak in complete sentences. "Why, yes."

"So what's that thing in the middle of it?"

Third rich chuckle. I was counting. "That, my dear, is what we were about to discover when you, ah, hove into view."

"Well?" Sean demanded. "What're we waiting for?" Without waiting for a reply, he set off, churning up red dust in a straight line for the structure. Paddy fell in behind him.

"Well, um, uh, yes, of course," Woolley said. "Children, please, slow down. Please, slow down! Don't touch anything when you get there, please!" He lit out after them, a short, stubby little figure in dogged pursuit.

If pressure suits can look amused, these did. A soft drawl came over my headset. "Howdo, Star Svensdotter. This here's Art Evans, photographer, speaking." One of the suits waggled the fingers of his gauntlet. "Also present is

Howard Carter, project artist, and Evie Carter, conservation expert." Two other figures raised their hands. "Over there's Claudia Sestieri, epigrapher extraordinaire, Irene Sukenik, surveyor of all she beholds, and Amedeo de Caro, geochronologist, have carbon, will time-travel. Not present and unaccounted for are Tom and Jeannie Champollion. They're the team leaders. Also the team's physicist and astronomer, respectively."

"I know, I've seen the crew roster. Why aren't they here?" I said bluntly. "There aren't enough of you to split up like this."

"Well, ma'am, we had us a dust storm the other day and they got stuck up at the Pyramid. We suspect they'll be back this evening sometime."

"Good, I look forward to meeting them." I gestured at the rapidly retreating figures between us and the structure. "Looks like you hit the jackpot."

"We've been pinned down by storms for the last four months," an unidentified voice said. "This was our first project, after the initial survey."

"Did you do a fly-by?" I said, starting out.

A figure fell in next to me and the rest brought up the rear. "Yeah, one. We're trying to conserve fuel."

"Why? I've read your mission specs. Your supplies were well above mission parameters to facilitate aerial recon and mapping. You should have had fuel to spare."

"We should have," Evans agreed, "and we would have, if we hadn't had to make three course corrections in the half hour before entering the atmosphere."

Without willing it, my voice sharpened. "You had problems with entry?"

"No shit we had problems with entry," a new voice said. "We near as damn wound up on a heading for the Oort Cloud. If Jeannie wasn't the pilot she is, we'd be on our way there now. As it was, she said it was the Great Galactic Ghoul messing with our minds. Why?"

I was saved a response by our approach to the structure in the center of the crater. "You've done a lot of work here."

"No shit we've done a lot of work here," the same voice said with feeling. "I should have majored in ditch-digging instead of epigraphy—I would have been better off."

"Quit bitching, Sestieri," Evans said good-naturedly. "At least we're in."

"In?"

Evans grinned at me. "Uh-huh. We'd just located what looks like a door when y'all popped up on the horizon."

I admit it, I was excited. "Then what are we waiting for? Let's see what there is to see."

"Sean was right, Mom!" Paddy yelled over the headset. "It is an air foil!"

"Yup," Evans said laconically. "We figure they measured the prevailing winds and built it to minimize drifting."

He didn't say who he thought 'they' were.

The piles of red sand to either side attested to the efficiency of the design. The marks on the side of the slender, rectangular pillar were tiles, 10-centimeter squares made of some hard substance that did not reflect light, as I discovered when I pressed my visor up against one, trying to peer inside. It was opaque, impervious.

"Somebody really did build this, Mom," Sean said.

"Somebody sure as hell did, Sean. The question is who, and when. Especially when. How old is this place, Art? Has your dating expert been able to run any tests?"

"Nope. We hope to get to it shortly. For now, would y'all like a look-see inside?"

My heart beating so hard and so high up in my throat I felt like I was going to choke, I allowed as how we might find that educational, and Evans led us around the base. On the fourth side we found an entrance, framed in freshly dug piles of red sand. It was a rectangle cut into the face of the pillar, and if we ever got it open, it was going to be a tight fit for me. I didn't see hinges, or more importantly, a knob. "It don't seem to want to open," Evans confirmed. "We've done everything but ring the doorbell. Would y'all like to take a shot at it?"

Woolley uttered an inarticulate protest, but Paddy and Sean didn't need to be asked twice. They were all over it, visors pressed to the crack, hands sliding over the surface, fighting to stand on each other's shoulders to examine the top of the frame; crouching on the ground on reddened hands and knees to scrutinize the sill. Before Sean remembered where he was, he nearly ripped off a gauntlet to see if he couldn't fit a fingernail in the crack where wall met door.

They were at it an hour before they gave up. We stood around in thoughtful silence for a few moments longer.

"I'm very much afraid we'll have to wait for the team leaders to return," Woolley said regretfully. There was a chorus of protest, not least from the leprechauns, and he said firmly, "I'm sorry, really I am, but we cannot simply break in."

"Why not?" someone demanded hotly, I hoped not Sean.

"Because," Woolley said, still firm, "we are not here to destroy, we are here to learn. There must be a method to our madness or we may inadvertently and irretrievably ruin something of value. We were extremely careful in our excavation," he explained in an aside to me, "not to impact the wall in any way."

Evans' crack about ringing the doorbell stuck in my mind. Maybe the doorbell wasn't working. What do you do in that case? I stepped up to the rectangle and gave three sharp raps with a clenched fist. "Yoo-hoo, anybody home?"

Somebody laughed. I didn't blame them.

Of course nothing happened.

Or nothing happened for ten of the longest seconds of my life.

"Look! Mom, look!" Paddy caught my arm as I was about to turn away.

The frame of the door lit up, the beam of light beginning with a single glow on the sill, splitting into two to crawl slowly and steadily across the sill, around the corners and up the edges of the door and around the corners again to meet at the precise center of the top of the frame. I expected a flash of light, a starburst, something. Instead, the completed line of light glowed brighter for an instant, and went out.

The rectangle of the door popped inwards.

As easy as that. It recessed into the structure and slid into the left wall. I braced myself but there was no corresponding expulsion of air, no sign the building had been holding its breath for this moment. The door opened and the entrance sat there, waiting. I'd never been propositioned so shamelessly or so irresistibly before in my life, not even by Caleb. Whoever had built the place had known a lot about human nature.

I saw a halogen torch hanging from someone's belt and appropriated it without asking permission. I shined the light inside the doorway and found a staircase leading up. It was a tight squeeze; I had to hunch over like Quasimodo to walk at all. Sean and Paddy tried to shove by me. "No. We stay together." They grumbled but obeyed.

I didn't feel anyone behind us, and managed to screw my neck around to see all seven archaeologists still standing outside. "Well? What are you waiting for?"

They didn't move. "How do we know what's in there? Or who?"

"What if the air is poison in there? Remember the pyramids at Giza."

And then the real reason: "What if the door closes and we can't get out again?"

"If there's somebody in here, they've been buried alive an awfully long time, you're breathing off tanks, and put a rock on the sill. Come on!"

My impatience galvanized them, and to his credit the short, stocky figure of Dr. Maximilian Woolley was first in, followed, more or less enthusiastically, by the rest of the team.

The staircase led directly to the top floor, no exits to the floors we must have been passing. During our ascent the light grew inside the stairwell. At first I thought it was my eyes adjusting to the available light; when we were halfway up I realized it had to be some kind of indirect lighting system kicking in as we climbed. I remembered the latch on the front door and wasn't surprised. I extinguished the halogen torch and went on.

There were no windows and no other way to determine

our rate of ascent or how far we'd climbed. After an eternity (five hundred steps, I counted), we emerged onto what turned out to be the top floor. It was a single room, as if the building had no cause to exist but for this purpose. The ceiling and walls were one enormous, transparent dome that looked as if it had been cast in one piece. It had much the same texture as the paneling on the exterior walls, and although we could see through it, I saw no reflection in it when I looked closer.

The view was stupendous, all pink sky and red earth as far as the eye could see. "Y'all look yonder," Evans said. "Ain't that there the Pyramid? Reckon we could see Tom and Jeannie to wave to?" They lined up along the window's north face and guessed at the identity of the various lumps and bumps on the horizon.

I went exploring, which didn't take long. The only thing in the room was a circular pit of some smooth dark material, a bowl ten meters across placed in the exact center of the room, looking like a recessed antenna dish. At the bottom of the bowl was a faceted bubble, five meters across, made of what looked like the same material as the tiles that covered the outside of the structure.

For the rest, the place was as bare as Mother Hubbard's cupboard. It was frustrating as hell. I wanted a sign, preferably in System English, saying, "Constructed in 499,937 B.C., by Alpha Centauri Contractors, Inc., press this button." Then when I pressed the button I wanted the entire history of the Cydonia project to scroll up the wall, starting with who built it and why, and was anything in it likely to hurt my kids.

"Hey, Mom, watch this."

Sean stuck his foot over the edge of the dish recessed into the floor, or tried to. It bounced back.

"Sean."

"No, it's okay. Watch." He raised a hand and tried to push his palm into the circle of air encompassed by the edge of the dish. He couldn't. I could hear him grunt with the effort over my headset. He flung up both arms, stood up on the toes of his goonsuit, and threw his body forward.

"Sean!" I shouted, starting around the circle.

He was laughing. "Look, Ma, no hands!" He wasn't exactly floating through the air with the greatest of ease, but something I couldn't see was holding him up, keeping him from falling face forward into the bowl. And off the bubble in the bowl.

"Hey, Mom, watch this." I looked up, and saw Paddy's attempt to vault over, feet first. Something nudged her feet aside. She tried again, same result. I tried it, pressing both hands out in front of me, and got nowhere. My palms tingled until I pulled back, but that could have been me, from the pressure I was exerting. I didn't think so.

By now we had an audience, as the archaeologists deserted the view outside for the conundrum inside. One by one they tried to pierce whatever it was surrounding the depression in the floor, and one by one they failed. Whatever it was would not let so much as a fingertip through to the other side.

I stood back, watching, thinking. Paddy came up to stand next to me. "Isn't this cool? Some kind of electrostatic force field, do you think?" She gave an excited laugh. "It's like it's a nucleus and we're the electrons. Except we can walk away. Mom?"

I turned and walked to the window. With my back to it, the domed ceiling was merely an echo of the bubble in the bowl at the center of the room.

And then I got it. It was so simple, it fit so well with the few known facts that I couldn't believe I hadn't figured it out sooner. I looked at the bubble in the bowl. Its range would be horizon to horizon, with a 360-degree radial reach. I wondered if there would be some way of extending that reach to encompass the entire planet. I'd bet my last dime there was probably one—no, two—other mechanisms just like this one, spaced equidistantly around the planet.

Sean, less excited and more observant, came over to stand next to me. "What is it, Mom?"

I raised the halogen torch I was carrying and threw it overhand, not as hard as I could, but on a trajectory that should have had it impacting on the bubble two seconds later.

What happened then supported my thesis and scared the hell out of everyone else. Halfway there, the torch was nudged to one side. Nudged, not knocked. Its original trajectory was altered just enough to make it land outside the circle. It bounced once and remained intact, a testament to Eveready durability and craftsmanship.

Nobody moved for a moment, and then everyone moved at once, hurling objects at the dish—three more torches, two whiskbrooms, and an oxygen tank. The dish never missed a catch, nudging them all out of the way with gentle deftness.

Into the second silence I said, "Art?"

Evans' voice was minus its usual cheerful drawl. "Yes, Star?"

"What was that you said about missing your first approach to Mars?"

There was a brief silence, and then he said, "We missed our first approach, and our second and third corrections were screwed practically before we entered them into the IMU. In the end, we got down with some real seat-of-the-pants stuff, basically just dead-reckoned our way in."

"What happened?"

"We don't know. All of a sudden in the middle of our orbit we were off course."

"Which orbit?"

"Our second."

Paddy moved suddenly on my right, but kept silent.

"Did you run a check?"

"We ran a dozen after we managed to get down. There wasn't anything wrong. The verniers weren't even firing; it was as if something was fending us off, like a bumper between a boat and a dock. . . ." His voice trailed off, and the entire group turned from us to stare at the dish in the center of the room.

"Do you think that's what it is, Mom?" Sean said. "A defense mechanism?"

"The Great Galactic Ghoul," Paddy murmured, marveling.

They were both right. "Paddy, do you remember how

many probes and ships have been lost in attempting to orbit or land on Mars?"

"Gosh, Mom, I don't know. A lot. The majority of them, that's for certain. What was it Crip was griping about on the way in? Something about only one in fourteen early UER probes making it down to the surface intact?"

"And that one only transmitted a couple of pixels," Sean confirmed.

I walked back to the dish and leaned against it. Again, my arm tingled from shoulder to wrist. "Did any of you feel anything when you tried this?"

"A kind of buzz?" someone suggested.

"A ripple, like a wave of some kind."

"Like a sonic rifle on low?"

"You're thinking maybe compressed sound waves?" Evans asked.

"Maybe." I turned my back to the dish. The tingle transferred from arm to spine. I crossed my arms over my chest and enjoyed the feeling of being propped up by nothing. "Supposing I was construction boss on a site located on the fourth—or fifth—planet out of the system of a main-sequence yellow star, surface temperature fifty-five hundred degrees Celsius."

I paused for a moment, thinking that over. Just the right temperature for a Librarian's ship to plug into and refuel. Main-sequence stars made up ninety percent of the stars in the known universe. Smart of the Librarians to build their ship around the most available fuel supply. Not like us Terrans, who propelled our best and fastest ships with nuclear propellant, the source of which we had exhausted on Terra and were rapidly depleting in the Belt. Maybe Brother Moses had the right idea after all. I thought of Simon's reaction to that and grinned involuntarily.

"Mom?" Sean's voice drew me back to the present.

"Okay," I said, "suppose further that my team had to leave that planet, and leave everything behind, and—"

"Why?"

I shrugged. "The project ran out of funds, I was called home after a change of administration, I'd accumulated all the data I needed from this particular project, I got a promotion—I'm just supposing, here. So suppose further that I'd done some of my best work here on Cydonia, and now I'd been ordered out, and I couldn't be sure when I'd get back, if ever. This is a solar system pretty far down the arm of a mediocre galaxy not exactly located in the center of the universe, remember." I waved a hand toward the window. "And look around. Mars is lousy with splosh craters. What causes splosh craters?"

"Meteors."

"Well, suppose after all my hard work I can't bear the thought of a stray meteor messing up my handiwork. What would I do, providing I had the technological know-how?"

Sean's voice was excited. "Of course! You'd build a defense mechanism!"

"Of course. And five hundred thousand years later the inhabitants of the *third* planet in the same system poke their heads up for a look and the Tholus goes into action, resulting in the loss or misdirection of probe after probe, and great anguish at various Terran Departments of Space."

"I'll bet the force generated is proportional to the mass that passes in front of it," Sean said, frowning at the dish. "It's not a killing machine. It exerts just enough effort to nudge whatever is approaching it out of the way."

"And that's all it takes," Paddy said, nodding furiously inside her helmet. "A little nudge at any approaching object, just enough to knock them a little bit off course. Remember that trip around the Belt with Mom and Dad? Remember that corkscrew approach we made to No Return? We almost missed it completely because of a misfire in the portside vernier that lasted less than a second."

"Remember the time Leif was missing for two days because he came too close to 19201Hi Ho and its mass moved him one-tenth of one centimeter off course?"

"It doesn't take much," I agreed.

"I like 'Great Galactic Ghoul' better than 'the Tholus,' though."

"So do I, Paddy," I said.

There was a cough and a harrumph over my headset. "A

most interesting speculation, Ms. Svensdotter, but I must remind everyone that it is only the sheerest of speculation." Dr. Woolley looked at me, leaning up against nothing, and harrumphed again. "It is, of course, one possible thesis."

Do you have another? I almost asked him, but forbore. He was quite right. The tingle running up my spine was proof enough for me, but it would not be for others, not until we took a ship out of the Martian atmosphere and made a series of test runs at insertion. I said mildly, "Dr. Woolley, did you count the steps up to this floor?"

"What? Why, no."

"There are five hundred of them."

"Fifty floors," someone said.

"Fifty floors between ground level and top floor." I looked back at Woolley. "What else do you think is in this building?"

Woolley sounded testy. "I don't know, what?"

"Did you notice the exterior?"

"Certainly I did."

"Did you take a close look at the paneling?"

"Of course."

"And?"

"And," Evans said, taking Woolley off the hook, "we reckoned it was some type of solar cells."

"I figure that, too. Why'd they build this place so tall?" I answered my own question: "To have the largest possible area for solar collection and energy generation. And they shaped the building like an air foil to avert for as long as possible its being buried and covering up those cells."

"Batteries?" Sean hazarded.

"There would have to be, wouldn't there? With the certain prospect of yearly dust storms that literally block out the sunlight for months on end, there would have to be a backup power supply built into the system. If you were going to go away and leave something for centuries, for millennia even, you'd want to have enough redundancies built into the systems to last. My best guess is, everything beneath this top floor is just one big solar generator, backed up about a thousand times."

"And they don't want us dimwits messing with it," Evans said. "That's why no exits off the stairs except this one."

Sean gave a long, blissful sigh. "I can't wait to tell Crip."

"Yeah," Paddy said. "He'll be relieved to know it wasn't him."

"Y'all—" Evans said, and paused. "I keep thinking about that door downstairs."

"What about it?"

"About how it was just the right size, and how the steps were just the right height for us to climb. This thing is awful user-friendly, don't y'all reckon?"

"You think they were expecting us?" Sean said slowly.

"Oh, please," Paddy said, "not again."

"I shore do," Evans said doggedly. "And once we got up this far, they protected the only thing of value in it from our ignorance."

— 9 —

Live Ruins on a Dead Planet

> Some circumstantial evidence is very strong, as when
> you find a trout in the milk.
> —**Henry David Thoreau**

A yellow light flashed inside my helmet. We'd been EVA
for more than six hours and my goonsuit was running on
empty. "Time to head back to the ship, boys and girls. Folks,
it'll be a tight fit, but you're welcome to come aboard the
Kayak for a light lunch."

Naturally they all wanted a gander at our balloon, so I
led a quick march down the stairs and back to the rim of
the crater, which was beginning to look more regular in
feature every time I looked at it. Inside, the gravediggers
oohed and ahed over the golden-crowned sparrows while
Sean got busy with lunch, herb omelettes with cheese sauce.
That sauce effectively wiped out our store of sharp cheddar
and put the FBE synthesizer on overtime for a week, but
the omelettes were superb and the crowd went wild. I got

more elbow in my face than lunch, but the talk was worth it. "They weren't expecting trouble from the surface," Claudia Sestieri said thoughtfully.

She was a slender brunette with a thin, sharp-featured face and a rare smile. Sitting cross-legged on the floor next to her, Irene Sukenik ran a finger around her plate and licked it clean. "Maybe Star was right and the Ghoul was built specifically to deflect meteorites. That it knocked our probes and our ships off course was just coincidence. They weren't expecting anyone to land and walk over."

"Then why the door and the stairs? And the Face?" Amedeo de Caro had the classic Latin features of a Michelangelo sculpture, broad brow, high cheekbones, and square, firm chin all clothed in flawless olive skin. His brown eyes were ardent and thickly lashed. His body looked as if it had been designed for competition in the decathlon. He was a beautiful young man, and Paddy was watching him with far too much interest for my peace of mind.

"Why the Face?" I echoed. "What do you mean?"

"The Face is what caused Terrans to take a closer look at Cydonia in the first place. Why build the Face to draw our attention to Cydonia, then build the Ghoul to keep us away?"

Howard Carter, a stocky man with dark blond hair that looked as if it had been cut with a pair of sheep shears, and wide blue eyes that never really focused on anyone except his wife, said, "Analyses of the proportions of the Face indicate a similarity between its features and the features of Homo erectus."

His wife, Evelyn, was a bouncy redhead whose words came in a rush punctuated by a quick, infectious grin. "Maybe they were watching us." She frowned. "But if that was the case, why did they leave?"

"Last night on the radio, Tom and Jeannie were telling us that the east and south faces of the Pyramid are really damaged, compared to the rest of the structure. Maybe they were attacked."

I shifted uneasily. "I have a hard time buying into a theory that requires a full-scale planetary invasion. It just isn't, I don't know, economical I guess is the right word. Think of the distances involved, the materiel required. My God, the *time*."

"Could have been an internal dispute," Sukenik said. "Wouldn't be the first time that happened on a dig."

Sestieri gave her a skeptical look. "We archaeologists don't generally blow up the structures we discover."

"Speaking of blowing things up, where is it?" I asked.

"Where's what?"

"The device." I looked around the galley. "Whatever it was you found that you told Helen Ricadonna about, the thing you thought might be a weapon and might be pointed at Prometheus."

All eyes turned to me in blank astonishment. After a brief silence, Art said carefully, "Star, the Tholus is the first structure we been inside since we got here. Basically, for the past year we just been mapping the area, getting a feel for the relationships of the structures. They're too big and most of them too crusted over to start excavation. The scale we're talking about here—we're too small a crew even to think of that. The only reason we started digging at the Tholus was because it had the base with the smallest circumference, so our chances of finding something were good relative to the time we'd spend. We just purely lucked out."

"There isn't any weapon?"

He shook his head.

"You haven't found anything that indicates whoever was here was taking an interest in Prometheus?"

He shook his head again. "In Terra, maybe, if Amedeo is right about the Face."

Paddy and Sean were sitting on grins, and I leaned back with a sigh. "Do you know Helen Ricadonna, Art?"

"Can't say I've had the pleasure."

"You don't know how lucky you are."

There was silence for a moment as we all became busy with our own thoughts. Sean broke it eventually, a frown creasing his forehead. "Mom?"

"What, Sean?"

"Remember all those evenings on Outpost when we used to sit around the galley and talk about Prometheus and if it really ever did exist and if so, what happened to it?"

"Yes," I said, and explained for the gravediggers' benefit, "Our favorite topic of after-dinner conversation on Outpost. Did the Belt grow or was it made? Was it once a planet or just a loose collection of cosmic dust flying in formation?"

"It was my understanding that some proof had been found of previous planetary presence," Woolley said.

"So far, it's pretty inconclusive." I told them of the few artifacts we'd found, and he stroked his mustache and nodded wisely.

"So who won the nightly arguments?" Evans said with a grin.

"Nobody. There were almost as many theories as there were asteroids, and the theoreticians outnumbered both." I turned to Sean, who sat waiting with an impatient expression, "So you were saying?"

"So, as I was about to say before I was so rudely interrupted, when a scientist starts a new culture in a lab, he doesn't start just one sample." Bright blue eyes met mine. "He starts a bunch, and tests them with different stimuli, and then he watches what happens, and takes notes on how each reacts to that stimuli."

"Here we go," Paddy said, rolling her eyes.

Sean looked at her, his jaw pushed out. He looked positively australopithecus. "Paddy, maybe Emaa and Maggie Lu are right. Maybe Terrans were planted. Like cultures. Maybe, just maybe"—he raised his voice when Paddy groaned—"the Prometheans were, too."

" 'Too hot, too cold, just right?' " I quoted his own words back at him.

Evans regarded Sean with a crooked smile. "Y'all reckon we've come home to Eden?"

Sean looked uncomfortable. "I don't know. Maybe. Maybe the scientist lived here, at Cydonia. When something went wrong on Prometheus—it doesn't matter what—the survivors fled to Terra. Maybe they were farther along than

Terra, and maybe they brought their knowledge with them but they didn't have room for anything else. Like—like maybe Democritus; we were just studying him in our history of science class, remember? Democritus' speculation on the existence of the atom was strictly philosophical, not practical. He couldn't physically prove the atom's existence. But he could plant the seed of its probability."

"And the seed sprouted twenty-three hundred years later with Dalton," Evelyn Carter said, looking at Sean with a dawning respect.

"Democritus was born a hundred and fifty years after Prometheus allegedly exploded," Paddy pointed out.

Sean shook his head. "Stop being so dogmatic, Paddy. What is it with you, you're so in love with Darwin you can't admit another possibility? I'm not pissing in the face of the theory of evolution, I'm just saying we may have stumbled over a corollary. It's one hypothesis that fits the facts available to us thus far." He paused, pleased with the way he'd put that, and added shrewdly, "You can't ignore facts just because you don't like them, Paddy. You have to recognize them, make them fit into some kind of framework."

"You still haven't told us what all this has to do with the Face," she said obstinately. She got her stubbornness from her father.

"Isn't it obvious?" he said impatiently. So did Sean. "If we were planted, cultured, whatever, maybe the scientist had an idea that sooner or later we'd start exploring." At her look of blatant disbelief he said hotly, "Who says we're the only Petri dish in his lab? I've got one pot for strawberries and another for tomatoes."

Paddy rolled her eyes again. "Great, so now we're tomatoes."

There was a titter of laughter and Sean flushed. "Compared to the scientist, maybe we are. Anyway, about the Face. If the scientist had a reasonable expectation—a close-up and personal look at Homo erectus, say?—that we would evolve to the point where we could build telescopes to look through and spaceships to travel in, maybe he'd put something here to draw our attention. Maybe it would be a face, shaped in the likeness of what we looked like back then. There's nothing like looking in a telescope and seeing yourself look back to pique the curiosity." He looked at me. "Maybe we're meant to be here, poking around. Maybe that's why the door to the Ghoul opened when Mom knocked on it, and maybe *that's* why the steps up fit our stride."

"But why the Ghoul?" Paddy said.

"Meteors!" he yelled. "If the scientist thought we were going to get smart enough to come look, he probably figured *we'd* figure out a way to get around the Ghoul. And Paddy"—he pointed a finger at her—"we *did*." He sat back, very erect, and dared her to contradict him. When she opened her mouth he beat her to it. "Okay, smarty, if Cydonia is none of these things, then *what is it?*"

She had no answer for him. Nor had I.

Into the silence Sestieri said, "Curiouser and curiouser." She ticked them off on her fingers: "Terra, Prometheus, now Mars. Has anybody else noticed how much weirder things get the farther out we move from the sun?"

We relaxed into a laugh, and Sukenik gave her an affectionate hug. "There's a lesson to be learned in that profound observation, I'm sure, but I'm damned if I know what it is."

Me, either.

That night I forswore sleep for staring at the ceiling.

Sean was right about one thing: Prometheus had nothing on Cydonia. The stairwell in the pillar had been too small for me, but I was 193 centimeters tall and weighed over 70 kays. I remembered the suits of armor in the Tower of London, the reconstruction of Homo erectus skeletons in the American Museum of Natural History. What if that stairwell had been constructed for the human race as it had been and not as it would be?

Had the pillar in the Tholus been built with the long-term goal of admitting us one day?

Had the Face been constructed solely for our benefit, to intrigue us enough to take a closer look?

If so, what else waited for us on this spot in the northern hemisphere of the Red Planet?

It took a while to resolve the various relationships of the Cydonia Expedition, and when I did I was more confused than before.

Thomas and Jeanne Champollion—team leaders, physicist and astronomer, respectively, unusual occupations for archaeologists, but then this wasn't your usual archaeological expedition and it was far from being the usual archaeological dig. Jeanne was also ship's captain. We had yet to meet them, as they called the Tholus base camp the evening we arrived and said they were staying on at the Pyramid for a few more days. They didn't say much more, according to Evans, who seemed a little aggrieved at their lack of excitement over the team's excavation and entry into the Ghoul. I didn't have the heart to suggest that they may have uncovered something even more exciting.

Maximilian and Agatha Woolley were the team leaders-in-waiting, and with every glance, every hint of a sneer, every disdainful sniff, indicated that they should have been in charge. A tubby, fussy little man, Dr. Woolley was an archaeologist's archaeologist, son and grandson of archaeologists before him, and so steeped in the lore of his craft that with little encouragement, and frequently no encouragement at all, he held forth for hours on the philosophical raison d'etre of excavation. He was determined to be the definitive voice on Cydonia (he had taken furious notes throughout the discussion following our entrance into the Ghoul), and was equally determined to fit the complex into historical perspective, complete with beginning, middle, and end. He thought in layers, or strata as archaeologists called them, one stratum at a time, and fussed over details. It had taken the team three days to get him to agree to removing the sand around the base of the pillar. His rationale? Excavation by its very nature was destructive. If the Cydonia Expedition was ever to be able to render with honesty an account of the lives of the creators of the Cydonia complex, it was required of the team not to be rash or foolhardy in their haste to strip bare the bones of this archaeological skeleton. He really talked like that.

Action was not Dr. Woolley's forte, which might have been the Champollions' reason for leaving him in charge. For nothing to happen until they returned might have been their primary goal; if so, the Woolleys fulfilled that goal admirably. But I might have been attributing Machiavellian purposes to an entirely innocent couple. Any scientific expedition financed by a multinational coalition was always an acutely political animal. I remembered some of the incompetents wished on me by Colony Control in the early days at Copernicus Base, and reserved judgment.

Dr. Woolley was short, so naturally Mrs. Woolley was shorter, and thin, and sour in expression and disposition. Agatha was a Cordon Bleu chef, as she reminded everyone at least once a day. So far as I could tell, that was the only skill she contributed to the expedition. It was quite enough. When she discovered Sean's herb garden, she geared down like International Harvester in Iowa in August. Sean caught up with her between the parsley and the basil, both hands full of incriminating sprigs, and for a moment I was afraid he would do her bodily harm. Roger Lindbergh would have been proud of him.

Howard and Evelyn Carter were the third couple. Howard was the team's artist, specializing in exact, delicate water-color illustrations of his immediate surroundings. From what I observed, the only time he looked at anything other than his wife was when he was drawing it to scale. Evelyn Carter was the team's conservation expert, and the one most responsible for soothing Dr. Woolley down to the point where he could bear to see a shovel bite into the soil surrounding the entrance to the pillar in the Tholus. She was everything her husband wasn't; bubbly, outgoing, even a little rambunctious from time to time. She made people laugh. She could also make them angry; her pugnacity in insisting on what should be done to preserve an artifact was as irritating as it was inflexible. Evans, who had advocated immediate excavation upon discovery of the pillar, and Woolley, who had held out staunchly against it, were neither of them speaking to her when we arrived.

For the rest of them . . . I've had people call me prudish because I don't see sex as a team sport. I don't mind; monogamy is a matter of personal preference and a lot of people find it limiting. The gravediggers at Cydonia certainly did. Sestieri, the epigrapher, and Sukenik, the surveyor, were gay and the fourth couple in the group; but de Caro, the dating expert, and Evans, the photographer, weren't and weren't the fifth. Twelve months' enforced celibacy could have led to some sexual tension (back on Luna and Ellfive I'd seen just twelve weeks of it result in unique, I might even say bizarre, mating dances between couples old enough to know better), and I admit I was curious to find out why there was none in the Tholus camp. From what I gathered in general conversation, the Champollions were an efficient and self-sufficient team. Bed-hopping would lead to the deterioration of their authority and the team's effectiveness, in that order, so they didn't. Max and Agatha considered the whole subject beneath their dignity.

That left Howard and Evelyn. Their attraction to and attachment for each other was evident in every look and gesture, but Tuesdays Evelyn slept in Art's room, Thursdays in Amedeo's, saving weekends for her husband. The first Tuesday evening I spent in their camp and saw this happen I was hard put to it to get my jaw up off the floor, but mine was not to reason why, and it worked, as witness the affection and esteem the four of them showed each other, and that was all that mattered.

Until Paddy and I showed up.

Under the pretext of reviewing the Martian data the *Kayak* had collected to date, both Art Evans and Amedeo de Caro spent a lot of time on board. We'd have had to have been blind and deaf not to notice they were as interested in Paddy and me as they were in the data, but they behaved themselves, so I let it slide. They looked a lot, yearningly, but they didn't touch. I maintained an air of cheerful friendliness and waited for our newness to wear off.

Then one day I walked in on Paddy and Amedeo in Atlas and Igneous. They were kissing, if you can call an activity that involved that much tongue and both sets of teeth and all four hands and an intense, steamy kind of concentration mere kissing. The temperature in the room went up five degrees in the four seconds I stood there, petrified. I had to clear my throat twice before I was heard. They pulled apart. Amedeo's face was flushed and he wouldn't meet my eyes, which was okay since I couldn't meet his. Paddy was pink-cheeked but perfectly composed.

"Amedeo, I think I hear Dr. Woolley calling you," I said.

Dr. Woolley was at the Ghoul some kilometers distant, but Amadeo gave an inarticulate murmur and brushed past me. Paddy met my eyes calmly. "Yes, Mom?"

This was going to be difficult. I took a deep breath and the plunge. "You're sixteen years old, Paddy."

"So I am," she agreed cordially. "So?"

"Don't get defensive."

"I'm not getting defensive. You said I was sixteen and I agreed. So?"

Very difficult. "All I meant was that you're sixteen, is all, and that sixteen is a little young for those kind of, er, shenanigans."

"Sex," she said helpfully. "You think I'm too young to have sex."

"Yes," I said, meeting her eyes bravely, "I do. You are too young, and I wish you'd wait." I spread my hands. "I know it's up to you; I can't watch you every minute."

"You could trust me," she suggested.

"I could," I agreed, "and I do. But you're at an impressionable age, and so are your hormones, and you're all going to have to realize that at this stage of your life Caspar Milquetoast is going to look like Lazarus Long simply because he's got something you want." With real feeling, I added, "And Amedeo certainly qualifies."

The twinkle lurking in the back of her eyes was there if you looked for it. "I heard that." She thought. "What about kissing?"

"Is even just a little kissing fair to Amedeo? No, Paddy; think about it for a minute. You know what the situation is with the expedition; sexually it's artificial, to say the least. Is it fair to tease Amedeo with what he can't have?"

"I suppose not," she said grudgingly.

"Okay, then. Hands off?"

"Hands off."

I put a hand on her shoulder and squeezed. "I know, there is no itch you want to scratch worse than this one. But you are only sixteen, and it isn't a decision to be taken lightly, or on impulse. You don't have to wait till you're married, or even in love, but if it's just propinquity . . ." I made a face. "Take your time, Paddy. Making love is the closest you'll ever get to another human being, and when the time and the guy are right, believe me, it's worth the wait. Okay?"

"Okay." She eyed me curiously. "How was it with you and Dad?"

"None of your business," I said in my primmest voice, but I made no effort to hold back the grin that spread across my face.

She laughed, and we hugged and kissed, and then I got out the first-aid kit and gave both her and Sean a contraceptive implant, something I should have done before turning them loose inside Vernadsky, where the opportunities for letting propinquity have its head had been far greater than at Cydonia. "What's going on?" Sean said plaintively. "Ouch!"

I swabbed his buttock with antiseptic. "There. You're set for five years. Paddy?"

"I sure wish somebody'd tell me what's been going on around here," Sean grumbled, and stalked out of the room, hauling up his jumpsuit. Paddy, rubbing her behind, followed, presumably to fulfill his wish. I suited up and ran Amedeo down in the campsite on the rim. "She's only sixteen, Amedeo," I said. Why change a winning opening line? "She's tall for her age, and more mature, but she's still just a kid."

Looking like he'd just robbed a bank and been caught cash in hand, he muttered, "I know. It's just that she was there and so was I, and she was curious." He caught my expression. "All right, and so was I. It won't happen again, Star, I give you my word." He paused. "I do like her, you know. I like them both. They're good kids. I do want them as friends. Both of them."

"Hold that thought. It's not fair to tease friends, Amedeo, especially given our situation here."

"I know; believe me I know. I am sorry."

Magnanimous in victory, I bestowed my gracious forgiveness and went outside to lean up against the nearest bulkhead and take the first real breath of air I'd had in three hours.

Art, on the other hand, wasn't Paddy's problem; he was mine. The Cydonia team photographer, as well as ship's co-pilot, he made Sean his closest and most personal friend and was underfoot from dawn to dusk. He was a good photographer and was sincerely interested in Sean's work, so it took a while for the twins to catch on. When they did, they naturally found it all too hilarious, and delighted in finding excuses, the more idiotic the better, to leave us alone together.

I was tempted. He was the original long, tall Texan, a slow-walking, slow-talking man with knowing gray eyes and a lazy grin, and if there'd been anything remotely resembling privacy within a hundred square kilometers, I might have taken him up on the promise in that grin. There wasn't. I didn't.

The archaeologists' campsite was made of aerogel cells; prefab, pressurized foam structures that, released from their containers, inhaled and expanded into cubicles placed side by side. Known across the Solar System as "Camp in a Can," they snuggled together in a hollow on the rim of the crater. Sticky on assembly, they accumulated local color at a geometric rate, and shortly looked as if they'd been there as long as the Tholus. Inside, the walls were the original color of the aerogel mixture, a kind of hospital green. "Tacky," Paddy said under her breath. "I bet we could—" I looked at her and she shut up. Furnishings leaned toward the utilitarian; nearly every item, including chairs and beds, were inflated. They'd knocked out the walls of four cubicles placed in a square to create a large common room in which they ate and played; another four cubes was the work area and there was a Lilliputian cubicle for each of the couples and singles.

I took one look at Stalag 17 and issued a nightly invitation to dinner to each expedition member on a rotational basis, with the proviso that weekends were reserved for the twins and me to recuperate. The Cydonia Expedition was well-stocked in essential foodstuffs and no one ever came not bearing gifts, so it wasn't a strain on our pantry.

Our second day in the hole with the Ghoul we broke out our wings, climbed up to the rim of the crater, and launched toward the pillar. In retrospect, it probably wasn't the smartest thing I've ever done, since the Ghoul could have nudged me into plowing a furrow with my nose. But it didn't, supporting the argument that it wasn't meant to discourage an interest demonstrated inside planetary atmosphere. The three of us spent a day sectioning and quartering the floor of the splosh crater that housed the pillar. We relayed what we saw from the air to Sukenik, the surveyor, on the ground.

The longer I looked at the crater, the more convinced I became that it wasn't a naturally occurring geographical phenomenon. The walls were too equal in height, the slant from base to rim too even, the centering of the pillar too exact on a crater floor that, beneath the cloaking effect of centuries of sand drift, was still entirely too flat. "Although," Sestieri said over my headset, "it could have been constructed from a previously existing crater. From what we've seen so far, it would be in character for whoever built this place to take advantage of whatever topography was handy. There's the Cliff on the edge of that impact crater, for example. And we're pretty sure the Face was carved out of a pre-existing mound. These guys never wasted a move if they could avoid it."

"True," I admitted. "I can't fault them for that; I'm a charter member of the Keep-It-Simple Department myself."

"Why don't you make a circuit of the exterior rim? While you're up?"

From the corner of one eye I saw one of the twins falter a little. "Tomorrow. We've been up long enough for one day."

"Oh. Well, okay." She sounded a little disgruntled, and I didn't blame her. I would have killed for my view, too, and I've always disliked getting my data second hand. The Cydonia Expedition had not included wings in its mission inventory, and lacked the skill or the equipment to fabricate individual pairs from our design, although Howard and Art had hopes of jury-rigging an observation balloon from an aerogel, with the help of our He-maker.

That evening, after dinner guest Agatha had departed to the general relief of all hands, Paddy said over a game of cutthroat pinochle, "That Ghoul sure is a nice piece of engineering."

"Uh-huh." I concentrated on the deal.

She sorted her cards. Paddy was always very methodical in sorting her cards, by suit and numerically, diamonds, spades, hearts, clubs. The diamonds began on her left with the highest card in the suit and ended on the right with the lowest club. She'd been sorting her cards this way for ten years, and still couldn't figure out why she always went out the back door.

Sean gathered his cards together in an untidy fan, didn't bother to sort them by suit or by strength, and left them that way.

Paddy adjusted what I was pretty sure was a spade, so that each card was neatly spaced between its neighbors. "Mom?"

I compromised; I sorted, but only by suit, not by value, and never put my suits in the same order from hand to hand. "What?"

"I've been thinking." The tone of her voice made me look up. "If the Cydonians, if whoever it was who built this place could build a Ghoul to protect its structures from falling meteors . . ." She hesitated, her expression troubled.

I laid down my hand, which had nothing but nines in it anyway. "If they did?"

She took a deep breath and looked at me, serious, a little stern. "If they could build a Ghoul strong enough to do that, could they build a—" She hesitated again. "I don't know, a weapon of some kind?" She saw my expression. "I know, I heard Art say they hadn't found anything. But they haven't looked, either."

Sean and I were silent. It wasn't as if we hadn't conjured up that Boojum out of the dark reaches of the night ourselves.

"Maybe a weapon strong enough to destroy a planet?" Her face lost color beneath its dark skin as she spoke her worst fear out loud. "Could Helen be right? Could the Cydonians have blown up Prometheus?"

"I don't know, Paddy," I said gently. "That's one of the things we're here to find out."

"I don't know if I want to know that," Sean muttered.

"Oh, sweetheart." I reached across the table and took one of his hands in mine. With my other I reached for Paddy's. "Is this the young man who only last week preached the moral imperative of establishing the facts, no matter where we find them or what uncomfortable things they tell us?"

Her head down, Paddy said, "What's the use? If Sean's right and we were planted, what's the use of any of it?" Suddenly angry, her head came up, eyes blazing. "Somebody plants us here like bacteria on a wet sponge, and then maybe they decide they don't like the fact that we evolved with binocular vision and so they swat us out of the sky and we don't have anything to say about it. Is that right? Is that fair?"

"What's really bothering you, Paddy?" Sean asked wryly. "Spit it out."

"I don't know." Frustrated, she pounded her free fist on the table. "I don't know! All I know is I'm going to hate it if we were put here, instead of grew here on our own. What does that say about the universe? Every new star I find, has it been put there, too? Every new planet I identify orbiting around that star, has it been incubated and colonized by somebody bigger and smarter and stronger, who can end the experiment on a whim? Or maybe not even a whim, maybe he just accidentally knocks the Petri dish off the counter with his elbow."

"Cydonia's giving you an inferiority complex," Sean said. He held up his hand and said quickly, "No, I'm sorry, I didn't mean it like that, Paddy."

Her shoulders slumped. "I know. You're probably right, anyway." She looked at him, her smile rueful. "Be careful what you wish for, little boy, you might just get it."

He matched her smile with his own. " 'All experience is an arch wherethrough gleams that untrodden world.' "

It was time for me to step in and from the wellspring of superior age and experience draw forth words of authority and comfort and encouragement, to buck up my little band of merry men, to reassure them that because we were right and virtuous and showered once a day, in the end we would prevail over the Sheriff of Nottingham, no matter how many evil King Johns backed him up or how great his strength of arms. Our strength was as the strength of ten because our hearts were pure.

I understood their feelings all too well. Like Paddy, I'd never taken kindly to being limp in the hands of Fate. Like Sean, I'd never turned my back on the truth, no matter how unpalatable. There were no easy answers. There never were, or at least none to the questions that mattered.

Today's great thought. Star Svensdotter, resident philosopher. I was glad I hadn't said it out loud.

I picked up my hand. I just knew there was a jack of clubs in the kitty; I felt it in my bones. "I'll open."

"Sixteen," Paddy said.

"Twenty," Sean said.

I threw in my hand. Paddy ran up the bid and got it, then went in the hole when Sean shot the moon. I only hoped his luck ran as well in real life.

—10—

The Hard Way

Does the road wind uphill all the way?
Yes, to the very end.
                    —**Christina Rossetti**

A week after we arrived, the gravediggers got a message from the Champollions to break camp and move the forty-plus kilometers east to the Pyramid. I was all for it; we'd pretty much exhausted the possibilities of the Ghoul. After three days in the air, the area had been mapped down to the smallest pebble. We took a series of core samples, over Woolley's strenuous objections—we might do irreparable damage to something below the surface, he didn't say what; we should wait for infrared satellite reconnaissance and spectrographic study, in spite of that the fact that there were no satellites orbiting Mars at the moment and none scheduled to do so any time soon. I was beginning to think Helen was smarter than she knew when she sent me on this trip; I overbore Woolley with my air of female dominance and told Sestieri to get on with it. He harrumphed and stamped off in a rage, and she sent me a look of burning gratitude and got on with it.

Analysis of the core samples proved there was no vast underground apparatus beneath the Tholus. Whatever made the Ghoul go resided inside its impenetrable walls. So far as we could tell, the Tholus had been designed (or, as Sestieri increasingly believed, redesigned from its pre-existing splosh crater) for a single purpose, the support of the pillar in its center. I had a sneaking suspicion that once the millennia of debris was cleared from around the pillar, the crater would form a dish whose natural shape had been enhanced to aid the Ghoul in amplification and accuracy of its aim. I made a mental note to look for others on the Martian surface the first chance I got. "There might be something on the PlanetView already," Sean suggested. "When we get time we should review it." I agreed.

Woolley was still reluctant to embrace my thesis—after all, I lacked a doctorate in exoarchaeology and, horrors, I hadn't even been published in the subject—and it would remain unproven until we were able to run a series of test insertions. That would require a ship, which we didn't have and wouldn't have for another thirteen months, when Crip was due back to pick us up. I bounced a message to Helen, summarizing our discoveries thus far, secure in the knowledge that five minutes after she received it she'd be concocting an elaborate scheme to hijack a vehicle appropriate to the task. What's more, I wouldn't have bet an Alliance dime against her riding in on it like the United States Cavalry.

The camp was closed up and sealed against drifting sand, and we loaded the team's gear into the crawler, an aerogel cube cab mounted on a pair of tracks. Life support in the cab was solar-powered from cells on the roof of the cab. The tracks were fueled by carbon dioxide distilled from the soil of the crater's rim during their stay at the Tholus, and refined into oxygen and carbon monoxide with the help of a thermal decomposer mounted behind. It was a nifty little gadget; I read its specs into the gondola's computer for future reference.

Four of them climbed in and took off due east. I'd offered the other four—Sestieri, Sukenik, Evans, and de Caro—a lift on the *Kayak*, which they accepted with alacrity. When I saw the aptly named crawler's top speed, I understood why. Till then, I hadn't thought anything could go slower than an aircar on Terranova.

It was a slow trip for the *Kayak*, too. We were heading directly into the prevailing winds and the *Kayak* wasn't exactly a Silverado Schooner. It was a close reach all the way; port tack, starboard tack, port tack, starboard tack. As Sean observed, we were on course only when crossing it. It took us all day to make forty kilometers, and it was with a sense of relief that I recognized the proportions of da Vinci's *Man* loom up in front of us. I ducked in as close as I could get to the east face for shelter from the wind, and called out to the galley, "Okay, folks, we is arrived."

Sukenik appeared in the doorway. "Can we raise the boss on the horn?"

"We can try. I'd like to know where they are so we can set the *Kayak* down next to their camp." I flipped on the transmitter. "*Kayak* to Pyramid, *Kayak* to Pyramid, come in please."

We waited. No one responded. "They've got headsets in their helmets, same as everybody, right?" Sukenik nodded. "*Kayak* to Pyramid, Svensdotter to Champollion, come in please."

Still nothing. Sestieri pushed past Sukenik. "Let me try." She slipped into my vacated seat and triggered the transmitter. "*Kayak* to Pyramid, *Kayak* to Pyramid, Tom, Jeannie, this is Claudia, you got your ears on?"

Still no answer. Sestieri looked at me and shrugged. "I don't get it. We talked to them this morning before we took off. They were expecting us."

A hand grabbed my shoulder. "Mom! Look!"

I followed the pointing finger. Around the left foot of the Pyramid trundled a rover, a platform made of a jumble of different geometric solids suspended between and dwarfed by four enormous wheels made of inflated, triangular bags.

"Paddy, hit the He-maker! Sean, seal the deflation port! Sestieri, Sukenik, get back to the galley! Move, move, move!" I did everything but blow into the inner envelope to get us up off the ground and out of range before the rover got close enough to shoot. For a long, sickening moment, we hung suspended in midair, and then we began to climb. When we came out from behind the shelter of the Pyramid, I rigged both jibs to act as a makeshift sea anchor, and slowed our rapid drift in the face of the wind.

Paddy, shaken, said, "It's Kwan, isn't it?"

Tight-lipped, I said, "Yes."

Sean couldn't resist. "I told you we should have gone after them and finished them off when we had the chance."

"Kwan?" Evans demanded. "The hijacker from the Belt? The guy who killed the Tallshippers and attacked Vernadsky?" De Caro, Sukenik, and Sestieri had crowded into the CommNav behind the twins. "If that's Kwan down there, you've got this bucket headed in the wrong goddam direction! Jeannie and Tom are down there, too! You—"

"Shut up!" I accessed the transmitter. "Svensdotter to Woolley, Svensdotter to Woolley, do you read?"

The doctor took entirely too long to answer and I was ready to lay a curse on him the equal of King Tut's when the transmitter crackled into life. "Woolley to Svensdotter, I read you, over."

"Where are you?" I interrupted myself. "No! Don't say where you are over the net!"

In the stiff voice he reserved for quelling presumptuous peasants, Woolley said, "I beg your pardon?"

"Do you remember the problem I told you about at Vernadsky?"

There was a long silence. "Yes."

"Well, we've got that same problem at the Pyramid. Find some cover and go to ground. I'll get back to you when there's more news."

His voice sharpened. "Now, just a moment, Ms. Svensdotter. I'm afraid I can't just set up camp out here in the middle of nowhere. I have my orders from the team leaders to proceed to the Pyramid. Unless one of them—"

I hit the override button. "Woolley, shut up! The problem doesn't need to know how many people there are at the Pyramid!"

"How can they—Oh."

Hallelujah, the light dawned. "Exactly. We're not the only ones with transmitters on Mars. Try to keep that in mind before you broadcast everything everybody wants to know about us but was afraid to ask." There was a nervous titter behind me. I phrased my next question carefully. "Have you spoken to our people at the Pyramid?"

His voice subdued, Woolley said, "Not since this morning, no."

"All right. When I end this transmission, maintain net silence until you hear from me." And then I added, "I'll contact our people at the Face and the Cliff on the other net and have them meet us here." There was a stir in the background as I thought rapidly. "You remember what my kids nicknamed the device in the Tholus?"

"Certainly I do."

"The next time I call, I'll begin by saying it twice. Don't answer me unless you hear those words. When you've found a hidey-hole, think of a way to describe the site to me that won't give your location away to anyone else. Svensdotter out."

I shut down the He-maker at a thousand meters, floating even with the peak of the Pyramid; high enough to be out of range but low enough to keep an eye on developments. We continued to rise for another fifty meters before slowing to a stop. The sun was setting and, naturally, the wind had died just as soon as we stopped fighting it. Our drift was imperceptible, and I judged it safe to hover while I thought up what to do next.

Below, the rover trundled around the left foot of the Pyramid and continued up the east side. It hadn't paused in its journey, no one had emerged to take a shot at us—as far as we knew, we might have lifted unnoticed. I wasn't about to bet the balloon on it. I swiveled my chair around, or tried to. "There isn't enough room in here to inhale. Let's move into the galley."

Everybody did except Evans, who remained militantly in place, arms folded, face stubborn, his drawl a distant memory. "If Tom and Jeannie are in trouble, we should land now."

"We're going to," I said sharply, "but not blind." He would have said more; I beat him to it. "We are not charging out there like the Texas Rangers. First we take a look around."

"What if there's no time? What if Tom and Jeannie—"

I went nose to nose with him. "We go charging in without some kind of plan, there'll be no time for any of us. I've seen what Kwan can do, not once, not twice, not three but four times, four, and I've heard enough horror stories about his other activities to keep me awake all night every night for the rest of my life. Do you want me to elaborate?" He didn't. "All right. First we take a look around." I pushed past him into the galley. "All right. Who has first-aid training?"

"We all do," de Caro said, "and I'm a physician's assistant."

"Good. Any of you rated in weapons?" No answer. "Any kind of weapons?" Nothing. "Dammit, I thought Woolley said the expedition was armed?"

"He is," de Caro said.

My jaw dropped. "You mean to tell me all your weapons are on the crawler with him?" I demanded, and he nodded. "Jesus! You people heard me tell Woolley about Kwan! You got some kind of death wish?" I mastered my anger with difficulty. "Paddy, break out the armory. Give them the sonic rifles and show them how to use them. Unloaded!"

"You didn't have to tell me that," she said, brushing past me.

"Here's my pistol. Check the clip, and yours and Sean's, too. Charge up the paks and the spares. Sean, show Amedeo where the medical supplies are and make up packs for everyone."

"What're you going to do?" Evans demanded.

"I'm going to circle the Pyramid and see what there is to see, and I'd better do it before the sun sets completely and we run totally out of wind." I headed for CommNav. The rest of them followed Sean and Paddy.

During our conversation the *Kayak* had drifted a little to the south, so when I looked up I could see around the left foot and across the base to the right one. The rover was still in sight, crawling north along the east face of the structure. It was also the most damaged face, and the rover found it slow going. Good, anything to keep their minds off us. I tried to remember how many figures I'd seen, first on Ceres, then at Vernadsky. One had been killed at Vernadsky. The person I'd shot in the arm had made it back to the rover. That meant at least six.

Any other time I would have admired the view. The red, faceted Pyramid was on a scale with some of the mountains I'd grown up around in Kachemak Bay, and the thought that it had been built before my family had been heard or thought of was enough to set the most geocentric person back on her heels, but if I didn't want to slide too far south too fast, I had to trim the portside jib and to hell with the view. Like an actor with an ego, the *Kayak* was slow to take direction. I insisted, and she began edging reluctantly west. We reached the Pyramid's right foot without incident. When I slacked off on the port jib and let out the starboard, I saw it. "Evans!"

He was behind me in an instant, sonic rifle, chamber empty, in his right hand. "What?"

"Is that the Champollions' crawler?"

A two-man version of Woolley's larger crawler was sitting, abandoned, halfway up the side of the west wall. "Yes." Evans sounded grim.

"You say you haven't been inside yet?"

"No. We couldn't find a way in, and it was so big we left it until we had the inventory done on the whole complex."

"Then what's that?"

He leaned over me to peer down. "Son of a bitch. It looks like an entrance. Is there—there is! It's just like the door to the Ghoul!"

"That wasn't there before?" He shook his head. "Maybe the wind blew it clear during the storm, or enough of it that the Champollions spotted it and went in."

"Or Kwan."

"Or Kwan," I agreed. "Sean, Paddy, how you coming?"

"The packs are ready," Sean called.

Paddy said, "At least now they all know the difference between the safety and the trigger."

"Okay, one of you come up here and stand by the jibs."

They both came, and I grasped the deflation port control. "Reel in the jibs; we're going down."

I accessed the control and we sank like a stone, the smoothest descent we'd ever made. "Paddy, drop the hook."

"Dropping the hook, aye. How far?"

"Let it out all the way."

"Letting it out all the way, aye."

I raised my voice. "The rest of you, listen up. Here's what we're going to do. We'll let the anchor scrape along until it catches on something. When it does, we winch it in until the gondola touches down, and we go out the hatch." I looked at the twins. Now came the hard part. "You know the drill. One goes to the party, one stays home to babysit." I saw both heads turn toward the four archaeologists, and I said, "Come on, you know better. It has to be someone who's familiar with the *Kayak*."

Sean jerked his head at the listening scientists. "I don't trust them to back you up," he said bluntly.

"I'm not staying behind, not this time," Paddy snapped.

"Not this time," I agreed. "Sean?"

His mouth tightened but discipline held. "Aye, aye, Mom."

"We maintain radio silence unless you see something I ought to know about, like if Genghis Khan is about to march up my ass, or I give the All Clear. If you don't hear from me within the hour, climb to a thousand meters and wait until morning. If you don't hear anything by then, bounce a message off Phobos, telling Simon everything we know up to this point, pick up Woolley, and make for Vernadsky. Got it?"

He lost color but his voice was sturdy. "Got it."

The west face of the Pyramid loomed nearer through the port. "Come to think of it, start recording that message for Phobos now, and load it ready for transmission. If somehow you're boarded, the last thing you do is trip the transmitter. Got it?"

"Got it," he repeated.

I held his shoulders in a tight grip. "Keep your pistol next to you every minute. If one of those assholes actually does make it on board, you start shooting and you don't stop until you run every ammopak left on this ship down to zero charge. Got it?"

"Got it."

I gave him a fierce hug. "All right. Bring us down. The rest of you listen up. So far as we know, we got six bad guys down there, and two friendlies. We don't know that one group has encountered the other, but we go in on the assumption they have, and that the good guys are prisoners. Remember that before you pull the trigger. All right? Okay, suit up. Sean, you keep your pistol. Paddy, where's the spare?"

"Here." She shoved it at me. "It's charged. Here's an extra pak."

"Okay." I hauled everything out to the corridor and started climbing into my suit. As I was about to lock down my helmet, the *Kayak* gave a sudden jar and I almost lost my balance.

"We're on the hook, Mom!"

"Okay." A moment later there was another jar. "Are we fast?"

"No. Yes! Yes, we are!"

"Start the winch."

My helmet sealed into the neck ring and his voice came tinnily over the headset. "Starting winch, aye."

"Okay, everybody got their headsets on?" De Caro didn't but he switched it on quick enough when I smacked his helmet with an open gauntlet. "Everyone switch over to Channel One. It's an in-house frequency we use for maintenance; it doesn't work farther than ten meters, so even if

Kwan's got it, he won't hear us until we're in his lap." I switched back to Channel 9 and told Sean. "You monitor both channels, in case Woolley or the Champollions have something to say."

"Roger that." We all felt the nudge of the gondola as it sidled up to the Pyramid. "We're down."

"All right, one at a time through the lock. Paddy, you first, me last. Sean?"

"I hear. Paddy, watch Mom's back."

"I will." She rotated into the lock, the light went red, then green, and the Fab Four followed. I would have sacrificed a goat if just one of them had been Caleb.

When I emerged on the Pyramid's surface, the sun was split in two by the horizon but there was daylight to spare for the view that had been wished on me. The gondola hovered over our heads. The surface of the Pyramid was caked with red dirt set like cement. Sestieri, I saw for the first time, had a length of line coiled around her torso with a jury-rigged grappling hook at one end. She dug it into the surface and tossed out the coil of line. Leaning all her weight on it, she tugged hard. It held, and she offered it to me with a flourish.

I looked at the grappling hook, made of half a sample canister with the edge made jagged, and said dubiously, "You sure that thing'll hold?"

"I'm an alpinist," she said. "It's one of the reasons I'm on this trip."

Considering the general height of the structures at Cydonia, it was the first thing that made sense all day. She showed me how to loop the line through my legs and over one shoulder. "Sean? One hour from my mark. Mark."

"Mark, fifty-nine minutes, fifty-nine seconds, and counting."

He'd never sounded so forlorn, and before the last words were out of his mouth I was on my way down the side of the structure, taking it the way I had taken ladders on the *Kaia* out in the Mother of Storms, sideways and fast. In spite of the angle, I was able to dig in with my boots, although the slant of the building was severe enough that I could see all the way down to ground level between them. The *Kayak* had done her usual sturdy job of putting us right in the gold; in the waning light I could clearly see the crawler and the black rectangle in the wall beside it.

Five minutes later I slid to a halt next to the entrance. I belayed my end of the line while the rest of them scrambled down. "Art, check the crawler, the rest of you—" With the exception of Paddy, the rest of them had yet to unsling their weapons. I'd had my pistol in my hand from the instant my feet touched down. "Man those rifles, dammit, and train them on the entrance! No, Sukinek, that means point them at the door, not at my daughter. Art, check the crawler." Paddy had already flattened herself against the door frame. "Do you see anything, Paddy?"

"I think there are stairs, like the G—like the other structure. And light, same thing, but it's up a ways."

"Anything moving?"

"No."

"Art?"

He came panting up behind me. "It's our crawler. It's empty, and it looks like it's been looted."

"Sounds like Kwan, all right. Paddy, ignite a flare and toss it inside."

"Something else, Star," Art said. "Those tracks we saw the rover making? They're all over the place."

"Maybe they're all still on board," de Caro quavered. "Maybe only Tom and Jeannie will be inside."

That was so silly I didn't bother answering it. Paddy twisted the top of the flare and heaved it inside the open door. A moment later, the interior lit up. Nobody shot at the flare, and as Paddy had said, there was a flight of stairs leading back up in the direction of the top of the Pyramid. I groaned to myself. "I'll take the point, Paddy; you bring up the rear. Shoot anything that moves behind you. You people got your safeties on?"

"Yes." "Yes." "Yes." "I think so."

"Who said that?" I fairly screamed.

One p-suited figure held out his rifle. "Uh, me."

"The red button, Art—depress the red button; depress the green button only when you mean to fire. You think you can keep that straight?"

"Yes."

"See that you do. I'm in front. You stumble one time and that thing goes off, then *you'll* be in front. Okay, Paddy?"

"Okay, Mom."

"Okay. I'm going in." I took a deep breath and ducked inside, knees bent, pistol swinging to cover the stairs. There was no one on them. "All clear. Come on."

As in the pillar in the Tholus, the stairs went up forever, and then they went up forever some more. I stopped counting after I reached a thousand. Sweat was running down the inside of my suit, and my life support systems were operating in the max. At this rate my waste receptacle would be full before it could recycle enough to make room for more. Even as the thought passed through my mind, a red light flashed inside my helmet. "Damn. Hold it. Everybody check your johns."

"I'm almost full, Mom."

"Me, too. Okay, everybody take five and empty them out."

"What about dehydration?" somebody said. "Shouldn't we wait for the fluid to recycle?"

"There's no time—just do it, dammit!" I bent over to fumble at my leg. I could feel the liquid inside sloshing around, and groped for the manual drain. It popped and I watched the fluid pour out to puddle on the step. It took a second to hit me.

"Mom!"

"I see, I see." I felt around my utility belt. "I can't reach my sniffer."

She shoved past the four scientists. "Here. I've got it."

"Turn it on."

She turned it on, and we hunched over the several digital readouts on the face of the instrument. "See?"

"See what?" de Caro said. "What's going on?"

I looked up and pointed at the liquid draining from his honey bucket. "This is Mars, right? That should be boiling away into the atmosphere the instant it hits air."

"It's oh-two, Mom, and nitrogen, and even a little hydrogen!" Paddy's voice announced excitedly. "And there's pressure, almost a thousand millibars!" She looked up at me. "I don't believe it!"

"Me, either," I said. The last drop of water drained from my waste collector. I twisted the manual drain closed. When I straightened, I realized that, as in the pillar in the Tholus, the stairs were lighting before us. I switched off my torch.

"Do you mean we can breathe without helmets?" de Caro said.

"That's what the sniffer says, but it could be wrong. Don't—"

Too late. De Caro already had his helmet unlocked. I was in front of him in two leaps and I slammed his helmet back down over his head so hard his knees bowed beneath the pressure. "Don't do that!"

He sounded aggrieved. "Why not? The air smelled fine, if maybe a little stale."

"It might get you maybe a little dead if you're not a little more careful. We haven't come through any locks. Until we do, keep your suits sealed."

We climbed again. The only communication over the headsets was heavy breathing. I called another halt, made sure everyone drank water and took a salt tablet from their helmet dispenser. Overheating was something the human race had down to a fine art. Not even the best pressure suit could entirely compensate for it.

After a while it seemed I'd never done anything before in my life except climb stairs. My knees felt like spaghetti. Every ten steps I called a halt just to inhale. Hadn't these frigging Cydonians ever heard of elevators?

I stumbled into the room before I was aware it was there.

There were people there before us.

There was something odd about them; for a moment I couldn't figure out what. I sucked air into my lungs and blinked my eyes, squinting.

They weren't wearing suits.

For a second I just stood there and gaped.

They were alive, they were breathing, and they weren't wearing suits. Most of them weren't wearing anything at all.

A piece of wall shattered next to my helmet.

They were also shooting.

Acting on a sudden flood of adrenalin, I yelled, "Stay back!" and dove for the floor, coming down arm extended and locked. Through the sight I saw a body sprawled in one corner, naked, with another rutting over it, and without conscious thought I fired. The laser burned through his side with such force that it knocked him off her. His body rolled twice before crashing into the far wall. There was a flurry of shots in our direction and a confused scurry through a doorway on the far wall.

"All right—the rest of you, come on in!" I scrambled to my feet and ran to the woman. She was unconscious, bruised, and bleeding from every bodily orifice. "De Caro! Over here!"

He thudded up next to me. "Oh, Jesus, Jeannie!"

"You're with her, the rest of you follow me!"

"Mom, wait up!"

I charged out the door, exhaustion forgotten, running on rage. There was another flight of stairs and I took them three at a time without waiting to see if anyone was following me. It was a short flight and one of Kwan's men was waiting for me at the top with a weapon he'd forgotten to cock. Before he remembered I whipped my pistol across his cheek and with my other hand caught the back of his head and flung him down the stairs.

Someone screamed over my headset. "Oh God, oh Jesus, oh God, oh Jesus," someone else chanted. "Mom, wait up! Mom, dammit, wait up!"

My last leap took me over the threshold of a room the twin of the top floor of the Tholus, only about five times as big and crusted over with 500,000 years of sand and debris. A line of light ran around the perimeter of the room where the floor met the dome wall. It was empty but for three men, one struggling into a pressure suit, a second banging frantically at a section of the dome with the butt of a rifle, and a third covering me, and this one was ready. But I was pure of heart and mad as hell—and faster. A small red light burned its way into his chest and through his pressure suit, blood flowed out, and he fell, face forward. The first man, suit halfway up his legs, turned to blunder toward the second. It was the last move he ever made. The second man saw him fall, turned and saw us, and started to raise his rifle. "Drop it or I'll shoot!" The rifle continued to rise, and I burned him down where he stood. Some people never learn.

"Mom?"

Paddy's voice was high and afraid and I whipped around, only to freeze in place. "Paddy? Baby?"

"Mom?"

The muzzle of a laser pistol was pressed against my daughter's helmet. He had both bare legs wrapped around her waist, a bare arm around the neck of her suit. He rode her back in a parody of a child playing piggy-back. His face was so contorted with rage that it looked simian, whatever intelligence there was eclipsed by the berserker in all of us. I looked deep into those mad eyes and saw myself looking back. Not again, please, no, not again. Through her visor Paddy's frightened eyes begged me for help. "No!" I chinned the helmet's speaker. "Kwan! Let her go!"

"Drop your weapon, bitch, or I'll kill her!"

I dropped it. It bounced twice and landed a meter away from where Paddy had dropped hers, both of them well out of reach. I held up both hands, palms out. "I've dropped it, it's down. You can do anything you want to me, Kwan, just let her go. Let her go!"

He laughed, a guttural, satisfied sound I remembered all too well, and tightened his hold. Paddy stumbled back a pace. "Kwan! Let her go!"

"Not a chance, darling Star. You know I'll always love you best, but let's face it. Your daughter's younger. She'll last longer."

He laughed again, and then suddenly he cried out like a dog whose toe has been stepped on, a high-pitched, indignant yawp. He looked astounded, and in an involuntary movement turned to look behind him. In his moment of distraction Paddy flung off his legs and arm and staggered forward toward me. I shoved her down to the floor and hurtled over her, clawing at the back of my suit for the spare pistol. When I got it out and up, over the sights I saw Kwan fire and a figure fall through the doorway. I squeezed the trigger, and a rose-red flower blossomed between Kwan's shoulder blades. It spun him around, and he looked down at me with an incredulous expression. Sweating, straining, his trembling hand began once more to bring his pistol up. I shot again, and another flower bloomed on his chest.

His face seemed to collapse in upon itself. He fell, body twitching, pistol dropping, to lie on his back, staring up at the opaque dome curving gently overhead, hands opening and closing as if they were still reaching, clawing for us.

Paddy's shaken voice broke the silence. "Mom?"

She started to her feet and I pulled her up the rest of the way. "Don't look," I said. I holstered my pistol and drew her into my arms, clumsy in my pressure suit. "Don't look."

She pulled free. "No. I want to look. I want to know that he's really and truly dead."

She walked steadily to the body and looked down.

I walked over to the figure that had pulled itself up to lean against the door frame. It was Evans. I knelt next to him. He had his helmet off and was fashioning a makeshift tourniquet above his right knee. The leg of his jumpsuit was soaked red. His face was white and drawn, his eyes clear and alert. "It's not as bad as it looks. Second-degree burn, I'd say." He shifted. "Hurts like hell, though."

I found the button on his chest panel for vital signs. His pulse was strong but rapid, his blood pressure low but not dangerously so. "You sure you aren't a Texas Ranger after all?"

He gave an imitation of a snort. "Not hardly."

"Art." I met his eyes. "You saved our lives. I don't know how I'll ever be able to thank you."

He smiled, a pale imitation of the lazy grin. "Do I get to choose?"

I had to laugh. "You might."

"Hold that thought."

I looked around. "Where are Sestieri and Sukenik?"

"They found Tom."

"And?"

"He's alive, barely."

I gave a weary nod. "Good." I tried to think what to do next.

"Mom?" Paddy had come to stand next to us. "Shouldn't we call Sean?"

"Oh. Right." I'd set my wrist chronometer with Sean's mark. Time left before Sean began to lift: 33 seconds. I chinned over to Channel 1. "*Kayak*, this is the Pyramid. Sean, this is Mom. Do you read?"

The headset crackled instantly into life. "I sure do, Mom," Sean's relieved voice said. "Are you okay? Is Paddy?"

"Not a scratch on either of us," Paddy said with a forced cheerfulness. "We've taken casualties, though. Evans has a leg wound. And we've found the Champollions. They're both alive, but they're both hurt."

"What about Kwan?"

Paddy's young voice sounded subdued. "He's dead. And four others."

Sean's young voice sounded grimly pleased. That was the difference between doing the shooting yourself and someone else having done it for you. "Good."

"Is there any sign of that rover?"

"No."

"Have you run a scan on the infrared?"

"Yes. He hasn't come around the head yet."

"Okay. Do you think you can bring the *Kayak* up to the top of the Pyramid?"

He was wounded. "Of course."

"Do it. We're going to kick a hole through the dome and get out that way. Look for a flare."

"On my way."

In the end, we had to burn a hole through the dome with our pistols, using up most of the rest of the charges in two of them. Sean was waiting. I retained just enough energy to follow the three wounded and the four walking up through the hole and the ladder and through the lock. Paddy doffed her suit and helped me with mine. "Sean, call Woolley. Tell him to stay put, that we've still got at least one bad guy on the loose, that we'll call him tomorrow."

"Okay."

"Don't forget the password. De Caro?"

He looked up from Evans' leg. "What?"

"They going to make it?"

His lips set in a thin line. "Art's okay; it was just a flesh wound. Lots of blood and there'll be a chunk missing from his thigh, but it'll heal all right."

"And the others?"

He shook his head. "I don't know. Tom's in and out, Jeannie's completely nonresponsive. They've both been raped and beaten, and they've both lost a lot of blood."

"The twins and I are universal donors."

His face lightened. "Good. That'll help."

—11—

future Imperfect

We think our civilization near its meridian, but we are
yet only at the cock-crowing and the morning star.
—**Emerson**

We picked up the guy on the rover first thing the next day. It
turned out he'd never seen our first touchdown the evening
before, and he was totally unnerved when we dropped out
of the sky to land literally on top of the cab of his vehicle, a
nice bit of piloting if I says it who shouldn't. Sean shinnied
down the rope ladder, forced an entry, and brandished a
laser pistol before the guy's terrified eyes. He folded without a peep. He wasn't quite up to the Kwan standard of
predator.

I had a difficult time restraining the Fab Four from stuffing him out the airlock sans pressure suit then and there,
but I had questions I wanted answered and he bought his
life with them. It turned out he was more than willing to
talk. Miffed that he'd been landed with sentry duty while

the fun and games went on without him, he actually had
the temerity to say so. After that, I was ready to stuff him
out the airlock myself. When he became aware of that fact,
he couldn't get the words out fast enough.

The Kwans of this world always seem to ferret out the
kind of information that will do the most harm to the most
people, and this was no exception. Helen must have been
planning my trip to Mars well in advance. Like the Big Lie
thirty-odd years before, her quote, exaggeration, unquote,
about the expedition to Cydonia and its quote, discoveries,
unquote, had filtered down to the spacer's equivalent of
the bush telegraph. Down far enough for Kwan to come
into possession of it. The entire trail of bloodshed that led
from the landing field on Ceres to the destruction of the
Tallshippers' habitat to the attack on Vernadsky to Kwan's
presence at Cydonia—all of it had been predicated on the
existence of a possible weapon at Cydonia. Kwan wanted
to be Master of the Universe, and he surrounded himself
with a group of like-minded mental midgets who thought
that was a nifty idea.

It wasn't that I minded Helen's Big Lies so much; it was
that they so often led to my escaping death by mere centimeters. I resolved to tell her so the next time I saw her.

I called Woolley in from the cold, and that afternoon
the crawler trundled up. I appropriated one of the cube
canisters and carried it up to the top of the Pyramid, Kwan's
sole remaining henchman under heavy and unfriendly guard
bringing up the rear. At the top floor I popped the canister
in a corner. When the cube solidified I stuffed the prisoner
inside and welded the door shut behind him. Paddy climbed
up on top, and with her pistol cut a small hole in the cube's
roof; that would serve to toss him food and water and bring
up a waste bucket now and then. I should have executed
him, but truth to tell, I didn't have the stomach for it. If
either of the Champollions died, the feeling of the expedition team was such that the decision would be taken out of
my hands, and for the moment I was willing to leave it
at that. He wouldn't suffocate, as the atmosphere inside
the Pyramid was so close to being Terran standard as to

make no never mind. Over the vociferous objections of the twins, I'd brought the sparrows inside and left them there with no visible means of life support. At the end of a week both were still alive and singing, even with the door open at the bottom of the stairs and the hole burned into the roof. "Some kind of containment field?" Paddy suggested.

"A version of the one that protects the Ghoul," Sean said, nodding. "Or a scaled-down version of the Ghoul itself."

Paddy nodded. "Has to be."

It didn't have to, but once I was convinced the atmosphere wasn't going anywhere, I gave the okay to assemble the cell and a camp on the Pyramid's top floor. There was plenty of room; the prisoner's cubicle, tucked into one corner, was barely within shouting distance, and the ambient temperature stabilized at 15 degrees Celsius. Someone 500,000 years before had gone to an awful lot of trouble to make things comfortable for us. I kept my eyes peeled for a water faucet.

We began to chip away at the crust on the dome and, as we expected, uncovered panel after panel of solar cells. We started on the south face, hoping for the impossible, and were not disappointed. After millennia of idleness those cells spit on their hands and started in to work with a will. First the dust of the centuries began to disappear from the stairs, then from the Penthouse (Sean's nickname for the domed room at the top of the Pyramid). An elevator appeared next to the stairwell, thanks a lot, that went straight from the front door to the Penthouse in five seconds flat. I made Sestieri stand by in the Penthouse, while on the ground floor I put a goonsuit on the platform and sent it up and had her send it back before I tried it myself. I survived, and our thigh muscles groaned their relief when we began using the elevator on a regular basis.

We uncovered another bank of solar cells, and the exterior of the dome began to clean itself, literally right out from under our feet. Another bank of cells shed its skin of solar-fired clay and the elevator began making a second stop, at another enormous room about halfway up the Pyramid, this one filled with rows and rows of towering, rectangular boxes

that vaguely resembled card frames. Although I'd not seen
the inside of the Librarian's ship, for some reason those
stacks made me think of it. Perhaps because everything
in the Pyramid seemed to be powered by optics, and perhaps also because the stacks reminded me of the computer
banks at O'Neill Central on Terranova, or battery storage
on Luna, or both. It drove Sestieri, the epigrapher, mad. She
hungered for a hieroglyphic, a rune, a cuneiform, anything
to make a start in deciphering the history of Cydonia. But
there was nothing, or nothing she recognized, as written
language.

It reminded me of Archy patiently explaining to me back
on Ellfive seventeen years before that I would have to wait
for the information I wanted from what the Librarians had
left behind, that they had no written language, and that he
was transcribing light waves into System English as fast as
he could. I wondered what the fastest and the smartest and
the only sentient (so far) computer in the System would
make of the Pyramid. I thought we should both have a
chance to find out, and I said as much to Simon on the
bounce.

Paddy and Sean were prowling through the stack room
on their own one evening when they saw some kind of
screen flare into life on the side of one of the stacks, and
from it a face stare out at them. It seemed to be speaking,
but there was no audio. Broken, distorted, it flickered for
fifteen or so seconds, and faded. "What did the face look
like?" I said. They exchanged a glance. "Well?"

Paddy hesitated. "Young, dark hair and eyes." She fumbled for words, and looked to Sean for help.

"She looked like that picture of Elizabeth on Auntie Charlie's desk," he said bluntly.

I sat up, startled. "Are you sure?"

"No. It was only on for a few seconds. But that's who it
reminded us of."

I cross-examined them. They stuck to their story.

Well? Why not? At Cydonia I was forced to believe
six impossible things before breakfast every day. Why not
Elizabeth, too?

The screen had yet to relight, and the stacks resisted every attempt at admission. I didn't force it. Once we cleared enough solar cells, I might get my "Press this button" sign yet.

A month after we took back the Pyramid, Tom recovered enough to care for Jeannie, who had achieved consciousness of a kind, although that was about all. We buried Kwan and his buddies in a common grave a klick off the Pyramid's right foot and didn't bother to mark it. It had been bad timing all around for the Champollions to stumble across the Pyramid's uncovered door just before Kwan & Company rolled up in Johnny Ozone's rover. Woolley, his ego subdued when faced with their injuries, took over as team leader with a previously undemonstrated tact and diplomacy, and the work went on. He orchestrated the inventory and the dating of the complex while deferring the running of the expedition to me. No matter what I did, people still kept coming to me for all the answers. You are what you are.

We used the *Kayak* to make a foray north to the City, a quadrangle of four smaller pyramids placed around a central core, another northeast to watch the sun rise over the Face at winter solstice. We were going to have to take a closer look at the Cliff, too, and sooner or later we were going to have to figure out a way to test my theory about the Tholus, although by now even Woolley was convinced I was right. We were going to need ships, and supplies, and about 100,000 pairs of willing and expert hands, and I told Helen so. Her response had been an ominous silence, so I was expecting her arrival any day, trusting her to be first in line on the Red Planet run.

During my leisure time I'd been paging through the works of some of my favorite poets, as fiction now seemed too pedestrian, and history was being rewritten before my eyes. Some of the poems I found were eerie in their prescience, like Frost's *Star-Splitter*, Paddy's favorite poem, probably because Frost's backyard stargazer burned down his house and he used the insurance money to buy his telescope. Paddy could relate. Sean liked Frost, too, especially anything that happened down on the farm—apple-picking,

fence-mending, wood-splitting—but his favorite poet was
Housman. There was something about rose-lipt maidens
and lightfoot lads that never failed to move him. Sean
was the unreconstructed romantic of the family. Kipling's
The Sons of Martha reminded me of Maggie Lu and of
every other engineer I'd ever met—"It is their care that
the gear engages; it is their care that the switches lock."
And Eliot's closing lines from *Little Gidding* were always
stirring; hell, as Crip said, they were the oath you had
to take before they let you into the Aerospace Pilots
Association.

I scrolled down and came to Shelley's *Ozymandias*, and
felt the chill all the way down to my bones. *Sic transit
gloria mundi.*

I took off the headset and looked out the port. From the
Kayak's galley I watched the sun set, turning the western
surface of the Pyramid a deep, reddish-gold. If I squinted
toward the southeast, I imagined I could see the tip of the
Tholus, poking up out of its splosh crater, on eternal guard
against the careless whim of the cosmos.

At Cydonia, we had uncovered not the decay of a colossal
wreck but the partly working remnants of a cosmological
Camp in a Can. I had no difficulty in superimposing Kwan's
maddened, berserker image over the shattered visage of
Shelley's poem, and realized that the poet's warning might
not have been of the indifferent passage of time that cast
the statue down, but against the building of the statue in the
first place. If Kwan had won, he would have built just such
a statue, and in a hundred years or a thousand years it, too,
would have been cast down.

We had won. What would we leave? A legacy that was
built to last, like Cydonia, or . . . what? The Prometheans
might have provided the human race with one catalyst long
ago. Twenty-six hundred years later, Cydonia was giving
us another nudge, refocusing our attention. The danger was
clear. The last time we let ourselves be suckered and side-
tracked away from cold hard truth, 1,600 years were lost
to the Great Interruption. This time, did we go the way of
Vernadsky and complacency, or Kwan and chaos?

Kwan was the barbarian at the gate, the berserker in all of us, and make no mistake, he was there, waiting, hoping, ready to spring out at the first opportunity. He was with de Gama at Bombay, with Cortez at Tenochtitlan, in Spain during the Inquisition, with Soloviev in Unalaska, with the Japanese in China, with the S.S. at Auschwitz, with the Serbs in Bosnia, with the Chinese in Korea twice. He was energetic, amoral, and ruthless. He stopped at nothing, not even death.

Vernadsky was the other side of the coin. The beast of complacency lurked within each of us, side by side with the berserker, like him just waiting to be let off the chain. He abided with the Indians of Bombay, who gave in to de Gama; he was boon companion to Montezuma, who knelt to Cortez as God; he lived next door to every German who ever said, "We did not know." He was the ultimate cosmopolitan, tolerant, smug, and self-satisfied. He was the end product of two thousand years of civilization. The berserker would kill us quick. The beast would kill us slow, and make us enjoy it.

Throughout the history of mankind, one of the preeminent questions of our condition has been: Are we alone? We created a pantheon of gods to prove that we were not, and spilled enough blood to float an armada convincing others to believe it, too. Then the age of mysticism gave way to the age of reason; the world became less mysterious and more predictable and the physical sciences rushed in where angels feared to tread, proving with biological calculation, astronomical observation, and mathematical probability that life in the universe is as infinite as the universe itself, that it would be the height of conceit for us to imagine we were the only living creatures in it. Berserker and beast, Librarian and Cydonian, we coexisted on the cosmic ocean of which my father had once taught me from the bridge of his boat. But who were the Cydonians? Were they gods or men? Were we nothing more than peas in some far off Mendel's garden, marks on a social scientist's bell curve a thousand thousand light-years distant? And when would the experiment end, and who got to say it was over?

For myself, if I was nothing more than the rat in some-one's maze, I was going to be the smartest, quickest, stron-gest rat there was. Our end might be our beginning, but we now had the advantage of knowing it for the first time, and with knowledge comes wisdom, and the shedding of fantasies and myths of the past, all the baggage that drags you down and holds you back.

I wandered into Atlas and Igneous and found Paddy in her usual position, genuflecting before her telescope, eye glued to the ocular, attention fixed fifty light-years in the past. She turned at my entry. "Hi, Mom."

"Hi. Good seeing this evening?"

"And how; the Red Spot's hot enough to warm my hands by. Want to take a look? There's a storm brewing down around the Tropic of Capricorn; it's real pretty."

"Sure."

Sean joined us, and so we whiled away the night, watch-ing Io and Ganymede and Europa transit Jupiter's broad face, admiring the hazy glory of the Orion Nebula, calling down the stars in the Big Dipper one at a time—Alcaid, Alcor and its binary sibling Mizar, Alioth, Megrez, Phecda, and Pointer Sisters Merak and Dubhe—in a naming ceremony worthy of the storyknife, still snugged safely into the small of my back. I reached around to touch it, just to be sure. If I knew Mother, she'd be riding shotgun on the same ship that brought Helen, and I would be able to return the storyknife to her, with my love and my thanks.

The lucent spark of Deimos paced slowly across the sky. The pale, misshapen orb of Phobos faded into the first blush of dawn. Slowly, obstinately, Sol heaved up over the hori-zon, the quintessential cockeyed optimist, hoping against hope that this time, at long last, we might get it right.

We just might.

Like the man said, the best thing we're put here for's to see.